A Song in the Dark

S.D. Reeves

RIVERSONG
BOOKS

An Imprint of Sulis International Press
Los Angeles | Dallas | London

ISBN (print): 978-1-958139-26-4
ISBN (eBook): 978-1-958139-27-1

Published by Riversong Books
An Imprint of Sulis International
Los Angeles | Dallas | London

www.sulisinternational.com

Contents

Prologue 1

Chapter 1 5

Chapter 2 13

Chapter 3 19

Chapter 4 27

Chapter 5 31

Chapter 6 41

Chapter 7 53

Chapter 8 63

Chapter 9 69

Chapter 10 77

Chapter 11 91

Chapter 12 99

Chapter 13 105

Chapter 14 111

Chapter 15 119

Chapter 16 129

Chapter 17 141

Chapter 18 149

Chapter 19 161

Chapter 20 179

Chapter 21 189

Chapter 22 201

Chapter 23 211

Chapter 24 225

Chapter 25 233

Chapter 26 241

Chapter 27 247
Chapter 28 253
Chapter 29 265
Chapter 30 273
Chapter 31 291
Chapter 32 299
Chapter 33 309

Prologue

The heavens are restless. Clouds sneak under the sun. Gales threaten their descent. It is midday —midday, and the two travelers have not moved in hours. The trek that led them here was long, and even magic cannot ease all weariness. What little respite has been granted to Niena?

Titania's thoughts race. *At least one of us can.*

The fairy shields her face from the wind. Above their ledge is a peak, marking both land and memory. In her younger days, she would visit the tribes of men who wandered into the pass to graze their livestock. That time has passed like the summer heat on the roof of the world.

"As Sofie, I at least had attendants," she says.

Titania's feet shift in snow smelling of forgotten lands. Below, her granddaughter snores on a wool blanket.

"Step-granddaughter."

The Evercharm rests nearby, the lyre's silver arms capped in black lacquer and obscured by the dull light shining from its pantomime faces. Titania crosses her arms, tilting her chin down at the steam rising from Niena's breath. "Bloody hell. The moment she uses the lyre…"

Between this fear and another, the Teamor reach out and touch her mind.

You are thinking of the Artisan.

She shivers, feeling their presence crawl up her spine. "He's dangerous," whispering. "He's an Inspector of the Princeps Inspectorem, and very clever. Even if he acts the buffoon."

There is wisdom in fear. For, look, the hunters close in!

A gust scatters the snow, lifts it high and, as she watches, higher still. Where the flakes fall, an image reveals itself. Three hunters. One, an elf with dark hair and darker glances, his face seeming stolen from an old statue. Then there is a barrel of a man who could only be Higgins, the Inspector's apprentice. Curly hair hides his eyes, and his mustache threatens to turn into a beard. Last, of course, is Rein. The tall, almost gangly gentleman of years past, with his own facial hair somehow neatly trimmed and only a short mustache framing an oft-broken nose. Titania also recognizes the spot where they rest.

"We were nearly a week ahead," she cries.

The girl sleeps soundly upon the wool. Titania hesitates. If true, they could be less than two days behind. The news rankles. She draws power from the wilderness, and the light from her action creates a distorted shadow against the meltwater trickling down the wall.

"I will not go down easily..." She stops, then smiles. "Oh, Rein should know I play the best games."

Remember your bargain. You must bring the girl to Cuiven's Lee, back to the place where it all began.

"Yes, yes."

Titania's shadow shrinks. Vanishes. The winds from the north howl and batter at her face and limbs. Darkness follows, clutching, clawing. Titania is taken by a sudden pain in every joint, as if a great hand has reached in and twisted her from inside out.

The knots that bind and separate the worlds must be undone if we are to enter.

Her eyes shift to Niena. "We will be there," in a wheeze. "I will teach her the song."

Go.

The darkness relents as Titania gasps for air. She clambers to her feet, a spell of concealing upon her lips.

In the forest dale, in caverns unknown,
Where black things hide and mountains groan,
I lay a bell upon my door,
And whisper not,
And listen more.

The hasty spell heightens her inner awareness, and she uses it to probe every corner of her mind for the Teamor's influence. It is a strong work. Titania is a mighty queen.

Niena stirs at her feet, and the fairy woman kneels, placing her hand upon the girl's forehead.

"I will teach her other songs too."

Chapter 1

Two hunters take turns grumbling as they navigate a sheltered wood. Sethlan, an elf, guides them. Behind him, Christaan De Rein, of the Princeps Inspectorem, alternates between counting shadows and insulting the cut of Higgins's frock.

"Two," Rein says. "Weren't you a tailor?"

Their trespass echoes in the heart of the arboreal forest. The hunters' boots crush nut and stick, snapping in cadence. However, the fault of the noise mostly lies between Inspector Rein and his apprentice Higgins.

"One, "Higgins says, ignoring the implied insult.

A month has passed since they set out to find Niena, the holder of the Evercharm. At first, the tracks were easy enough to follow, but this has changed. Autumn works to delay through foul weather. Gone are also the easier-to-tread terrain, the fields and farms. Now the land is wilder, and food is scarce.

We've passed her, I know we have, I —Movement in the corner of Rein's eye causes him to smack his shoulder into a tree. He curses and brushes off his sleeve. "I still say two..." A flutter in a bush pulls his interest. "No, wait, see those shadows. Three."

"They are more than just shadows. The Udur track us," the elf says. "At least four of them."

The Inspector, Christaan De Rein, thrusts up his hand in victory. "Aha, I was closest, so I win…Er, we must strike to disperse the rabble then," he says.

"No." Higgins, weakly. "Do you not remember what happened before?"

"Of course, we were victorious.

"Those were only ghouls and thralls."

"Yet attack we must," Rein snaps. "What use are we to the girl otherwise?"

Higgins reaches out and lays a shaking hand upon his master's chest. "Sir, the danger the Udur show you is a deceit; it is not always what they are, but what they bring with them."

Away from them, the elf dips his head as if listening to birds chirp at one another. Rein shrugs at Sethlan's brooding, dusting off Higgins's hand in the process. "What else do they bring, cabbages?"

"The Udur have many powers, stirring the dead is one of them."

Rein harrumphs and clears his throat, readying for another volley at Higgins's fascination with blue overcoats. But the elf's raised hand forestalls it, and for the first time this day a breath passes between the men in silence. Within this, a queer sound finds them, carried on an eastern breeze.

"Just the wind filling a hollow," Rein says.

Higgins shakes his head. "Sethlan, didn't you spot a stream earlier?"

"At the foot of the mountain range. Beyond a field of scree," he answers, craning his head. "West by southwest. Not far…"

The buzz of insects burrows into leaf and petal. The life of the forest holds its breath in watchful concern. "There is more here," he adds. Sethlan's hands sweep the top of a weed patch as he brings one finger to his lips.

A wail cuts the air. Higgins blanches and Rein fumbles in his pockets. *"A tginbo selladh neochionta,"* he yells, throwing the wrong contents into the air. Nothing happens.

"No," Sethlan growls. The elf snatches the corner of Rein's sleeve and pulls him forward, stirring Higgins along in the process.

Rein gasps at the offense, but Sethlan's eyes are already turned, alighting upon hidden paths even as his first foot lands. The two men's pace is not nearly so graceful, and their feet drum against roots or slide in muddy grips. Above, the canopy thickens. Branches tear at Rein and Higgins's faces, or burrs catch upon a cloak, slowing them. All while the Inspector's stride is long, threatening the heels of the elf. And if it weren't for a branch here needing to be held for his friend, or a patch of brier there requiring the whole of his coat to pass, he might have equaled it.

"What is this new devilry?" Rein grumbles.

A bird darts between two trees and Rein swats at a fly delving into his nose. Behind and around them, the wails intensify. Their stride hastens to the terrible baying of their monstrous pursuers. Rein's and Higgins's mouths open in wordless screams.

Along the bed of a dry creek, the screeches unnerve Sethlan and his right leg slides into a trunk, jamming it between the ground and the wood. "Higgins, help his leg," Rein cries, dashing below to lift the elf's boot. As Sethlan squirms, a large blob drops from the blackened canopy. Rein grimaces. The view through the trees is terrible, and one of terror. "Get him moving, do not look back."

The way forward is bathed in red as the light from the west strains through the reddening leaves. The Udur gain, even as the elf returns to his former stride. Writhing shapes lurch alongside. Branches, appearing as hands and outstretched arms, grasp from the graying mud, or from the trunks of trees lying close. Sethlan steers them as far from these as possible, guiding them over two hills and into a hollow beyond.

"What new devilry is this?" Rein repeats.

It is Sethlan who answers finally. "Not new. The Udur stir the dead of men."

"We need that stream. Running water, guarded by a mountain as old as creation," Higgins says. "They will be hesitant to pass."

Has the veil thinned so, that the Teamor can personally direct their hounds? Rein stops and scans the forest left until Higgins shoves him. *"Klere..."* To his side, Higgins barrels forward. *They are chanting. But I...I killed Chancy.*

"Sir," Higgins says over his shoulder. "Do the old spells work here the same as back home?"

Rein grabs a hand offered by Higgins mid-climb and between the bough of a low oak and another tree. "Yes. Curatorium derivative of Gaelic, though. I would not suggest French."

"I wouldn't ever try French anything."

"The stream is just beyond the next thicket," Sethlan says, coming between the two. "Your research can wait!"

Rein grabs at his friend, turning him. A wild light dances between Higgin's watery eyes. *Just as he was resurrected*; a desperate, clutching visage. Full of madness. Rein slides a foot back, then another, until Higgins growls: "We shall make a fighting retreat, but quickly now," jabbing his way with the makeshift wand.

Higgins's gestures are precise. *Deft, and mesmerizing, for such a stocky man.* Rein's disbelief slowly turns into admiration.

"Suad na mair." Higgins draws out the last word, the Mort of the enchantment.

A chill wind touches Rein's arms. The spell is uncouth, eldritch, and his thoughts roll over Higgins's strange pronunciation —but what frightens the Inspector more is the fading of the land around. As if the vegetation had been washed and beaten against a rock, and so drained of all life.

The striking smell of rotting leaves wafts in. Then the first Udur appear.

"There," Rein says. "Two, three—"

Four. Five. Ten. They emerge out of the backdrop of trees. Long appendages bend and twist at painful angles. And in the middle where their torso should be, strange beaks move, framed by tears in the flesh that burn bright as coals.

"Ahh, *Kak.*"

"*Suad eao na mair,*" Higgins shouts, casting the spell over his shoulder.

"What have you done?" Rein cries. Around them, distinct shapes seethe.

"I have reversed a spell. It was made by the dead, to touch the living."

"Good God. You mean then the living can now touch the dead?"

Their gazes lock briefly.

"Run, you fools," Sethlan screams.

Twigs break in rapid staccato under Rein's boots. Saplings. Great oaks — fuzzy, blurred — seem imaginary as he grips them for purchase. Up and over. Yet, the Udur are real through glances at them stolen here and there. Encircling. Their cries wrench through the canopy. And there is worse: Rein can make out the words now of the ever-present chant. Spells of binding. Spells of terror.

"They have us," Rein yells. "They have us."

Pale things wiggle out of the ground. Left. Right. Ahead. Rein stomps one with the heel of his boot, realizing just as the sickening crack hits his ears that they are arms. Everywhere at once, and as if in response, there is a piercing cry. Gaining with each heartbeat. Even so, they run. Through broken trees and roots covered in loose stone. Down, past a fire-thinned band of trees. Over a log. The whispers now feel so close as to disturb the hair on Rein's neck. And he, unable to muster himself, swings around at the summit of a boulder. He rears to make a desperate fight.

"*Giath sporad,*" Rein barks. The shield spell explodes from his outstretched hands, then shudders with the weight of an Udur. The Inspector smiles, but briefly, just as a blade appears from behind and strikes away one of the clutching hands, then plunges deep into one of the attacking Udur. Sethlan has come.

"Keep going," Higgins yells.

The elf twists his dagger free, spinning left with the momentum. Dagger and tentacle rush past Rein's eyes. Shrieks erupt left and right of him as his blades strike tendril and appendage alike in an encircling throng.

We can hurt them? Rein scans the tangle of roots and weeds near his feet. "Crecy's Volley Higgins, Crecy's Volley!"

A nearby branch proves usable, and as Rein raises it for his own spell, the requested incantation thunders from Higgins to his left, and the result falls like rain, blanketing the field in arrows. Howls wash over them, and as Higgins lets loose another barrage, they are joined by the curses of the elf.

Rein rushes forward, bringing Sethlan into the arc of his shield. A summoned arrow had slashed the elf's arm, and the severed end of a tentacle wraps around his leg. Sethlan's eyes lance Rein as he helps him to his feet.

"We can't kill them," Higgins says, entering the protective arc. "But this is going to make them bloody determined to kill us."

On word, the barrier shudders under another press by the writhing mass. The same Udur the elf had struck down is among those rushing it. And as Rein tries to see past the shimmering edges of his spell, he notices, one by one, the feathered shafts from the summoning disappear.

"Listen," Sethlan says. "Can you not hear it?"

"Yes, they are screaming like banshees," Higgin says. "Rein? I think they are singing one of your Dutch lullabies."

"No, fool," the elf hisses. "The stream is close."

"Backup, backup," Rein says. "I can't see a—" The Inspector smacks away a decayed hand. Dark mud squelches around his feet while he backpedals up the foothill. *"Krijg de tering, you bloody Optyfussen!"*

Another crash against the shield staggers Rein. Both elf and Higgins close around him, protectively. Together they press, Sethlan leading again. Every attack causes Rein to wince as more of the dead underfoot drag themselves from their beds. Until some, even inside, have pulled their torso clear from the ground.

And the power of Higgins's own spell begins to fade. At first, it is the sounds, the crunch of grass and weed underfoot no longer dulled. Then the smells. Of grime, or the odor of rotting leaves returning. Then too does the Inspector's spell-shield break.

Rein's foot is caught then, and he stumbles — losing touch, losing the ability to affect the horde. Higgins is immediately at his side, but all he can do is help the Inspector to crawl on. So he does. One hand. One foot at a time. The smell of river muck and damp stone hits him. Rein licks his lips and struggles to his feet.

"Are they retreating?" he whispers.

Sethlan's feet crash into the water. "Not yet, look they come again."

A surge against the rear sends Rein sprawling into the stream. And like a crack in the dam breaking away, the Udur's hiss rumbles into a roar. The cries of his partners follow, with the sound of blades slicing air and the casting of spells.

Rein's hands tremble as he tries to keep from drowning in the flow of ankle-deep water. He crawls another foot. The clash of battle dies away.

"Solna nea, Oran cruchaid, an beath an tene," Higgins chants three times.

"Hellfire and damnation," Rein coughs, spitting up water. Higgins's altered light spell sears away the whispers of the Udur behind him, leaving a terrible, terrible heat in its wake. The pain from this would send him back into the brackish waters, but something grasps him by the collar of his frock coat and drags him forward.

The shouts of Higgins and Sethlan dissolve as the sun sets.

Chapter 2

"Heathen barbarian," Rein cries, his fingers clawing into Chancy's chin and mouth, pushing the back of the man's head to the ground.

But the spell continues till the end. Somewhere to the left, Higgins stands and then yells as he is thrown by the shifting earth. Chancy, fighting for his life, claws at the Inspector's eyes as Rein's hands find their way to his throat.

"Dare call me a murderer," Rein growls. "I'll kill you."

A crevice breaks near Chancy's head. "What do you know about justice?" The shaking intensifies as he speaks. "We are made of dreams, and we dream our making."

The Inspector's nostrils flare in rage, and he presses hard, and harder into the former Artisan's throat. Behind, and drifting with each second, is the elf's voice. Chancy, the Speaker of the Teamor, smiles, as he can see the fire in the town grow, casting a hellish background around Rein.

"May the devil take you."

"Mannelig," Sethlan says.

But Christaan De Rein, Inspector of the Princeps Inspectorem, plays at still being asleep. The swish of the elf's breath and the pop of a nearby fire play in the backdrop. Until the elf moves away.

Chancy. Rein's thoughts still on the dream. *Chancy and the Teamor. Good God, what a nightmare. As for the elf, why can't I ever hear that bastard move?*

Though bastard may be a bit harsh, considering the elf obviously pulled him to safety. Rein allows one of his eyes to open. The night is mostly overcast, and if it weren't for the occasional appearance of the moon, the shadow of the nearby mountain would exist as only a figure of speech.

"Give me a moment and I will wake him." The voice of Higgins is hoarse, dry. *No wonder,* Rein thinks to himself. *He's been casting most of the spells lately.*

"Every such moment we wait is a risk," Sethlan says. "If we climb this mountain as you plan, I will have lost all track of the girl."

So, between the water and the balefire, they were saved. Though, I suspect the river won't hold them for long. That must be the elf's fear.

"From what I guess, that is lost anyways," Higgin says. "We are going to need the Inspector to find her again."

"Why?"

Rein moves his head slightly, angling to hear more, yet the only sound between them is the incessant pop of what he guesses to be birchwood. Higgins was never much of a woodsman.

"Why wait?" the elf continues. "You can work the drycraft of men."

Higgins's laugh is cheerless. "I have come to know some secrets. But Rein...he has a special talent: he can sense something he calls music, some type of old, strange heathen magic. It's how we got here in the first place."

I would have preferred him not to reveal that.

"He can sense the chords?" The lift in the elf's voice is unmistakable. "Then this is how he tracked my brother and—"

Rein coughs, and stirs, causing an explosion of movement by Higgins. He then makes a dramatic scan of his surroundings, taking the time to nod appreciatively at this or that —especially at his placement so close to the rock wall. The others, though, currently dare the edge, drawing towards the fire with his awakening. Higgins is a mess of nerves, while the elf remains composed, expectant. The gentle crackle of the fire contrasts with Sethlan's intense face.

"Do we have anything for dinner? No, I swore something was cooking." Rein hums, then tucks his nose into his waistcoat's collar. "Musky. That's not it."

"Mannelig, tell me," Sethlan says. "Can you track the Evercharm?"

Rein tilts his head and makes a long stretch of his fingers towards the fire. He squints as the fire ruins his sight. *Look at the state of us.* His friend's clothes appear tattered in a way that must make the former tailor cringe, and the right side of his hat is singed. *It should indeed make him cringe, though he is without shame, I think. Tatty. Dreadful.*

"First, elf, tell me where we are?"

"We are in the foothills just beyond a stream," Sethlan says. "Now answer my question."

The rest of the camp is in better order. Rein smacks his lips, noticing the spit over the fire. "I can chase her to the ends of the…earth. Hearth, now. Assuming she doesn't learn some way to block me."

"Can you do so this moment?"

"No," Rein says. "That is to say, I will need to perform a ritual. And the word ritual should tell you enough. It is tedious, and it will take time. Lots of it. Though I suppose if we are going to suffer the mountain"—Higgins's face blanches—"then we may find your time."

15

Sparks from the fire cast a strange sheen over half Higgins' face. He turns the spit, and Sethlan leans in hungrily, a rare sign of emotion on the man. *Elf. Elf man.*

"Christaan, sir," Higgins says. "I am not sure this will be to your liking. You might want to conjure up yourself a Gaelic-flavored chicken…"

"Chicken? You know full well I can't conjure something that might have had a brain." Rein opens his mouth, then sighs. "Englishmen on the—"

"It was a joke." Higgins sighs.

"Your jokes are terrible," Rein says, then to Sethlan: "As you get to know him, you'll appreciate his bad timing. If he's telling jokes, then there's something that is eating at his little mind." The Inspector squints, looking at Higgins. "So, out with it, then."

"We cannot stay, sir."

"Why not? There is a bracing wind, and we have been through a rough patch. Plus, our stocks of wine are far in arrears. Mythical, at this point, I'd say. 'Course, it is for the better. I don't even know what goes with rat. Or whatever that happens to be."

"Because the Udur are already gathering," Sethan says. "Look."

Three heads, six eyes follow his gesture to find the river and the void beyond. There, nothing stirs. But as Rein surveys the edge, where a thin line of trees should be, the Inspector can't help but feel threatened. As if menace itself seethes. The Inspector shudders.

"I don't see anything," Rein says. "Except trees, and more damn trees that haven't had the good fortune of being Christianized by the saw."

"What of your ritual can be done on the run?" Sethlan says, edging closer to the fire.

Rein grumbles, turning away from both the edge and the elf's piercing gaze. "Little." He cocks his head and stares at Higgins from the corner of his eye. "Though some of the materials can be gathered along the way. We shall have to combine efforts and make do."

"Which means…" Higgins balks, then shows his already calloused fingers.

"You will be doing all the manual labor, naturally."

"And I will prepare our path," Sethlan says.

"Then it is settled," Rein says. "Now, Higgins, if you don't mind, pass me that rat."

Chapter 3

Moonlight descends over the mountaintop. There, with a northern wind at their back and snow under their feet, Niena and Titania plot the way down.

"You wanted an adventure," Titania says, smiling. She extends a hand to her granddaughter, who can't avoid looking past it; an earlier fog has receded, and the sky is clearing. Green and white. Forest, snow, and lingering mist cling to the opposite side of a V-shaped valley.

"I wanted something with less climbing and more meals," Niena says. "I thought south would be warmer."

"Someone told you a fairy tale...or something else has its hold." Titania nods at the Evercharm on the girl's back knowingly. "Come, sit by me."

Her grandmother's hand is warm, almost hot, and the chill that was settling into Niena's body flees from it. With Titania's help, she climbs down onto a smooth boulder. In a following sweep, the fairy queen pats a spot nearby, but Niena refuses it. Her bluecoat dances in the same breeze that scours the mountain top.

"It is the ten and fourth in the month of Aranman," Niena says. "Yet it feels like we are in the depths of winter."

"Yes, well, look at your attire under that coat and where we are. We are going to need to find you something more practical to wear than a light dress," Titania says. "Maybe something with pockets."

Niena steals a sideways glance at her supposed grandmother, finding her features thin and clouded — pale as the moon. She turns back to the land below.

"It's so huge."

"This is the Isfall mountain range," Titania says. "If we were to follow this line south, and west, we would touch the Hakaal Mountains and link up with the imperial wastes. I am surprised anything can live here. Still, this southernly direction will provide us certain opportunities." She tilts her head and looks over her shoulder at Niena, and conspicuously once more at the lyre strapped to her back.

"What is there for me?"

"Maro Unsterbberiz."

Niena cocks head. "Did you just sneeze?"

Titania sits down on the same rock and repeats the motion for Niena to join. "A city, and an old story; one I will tell you later. These mountains however..." She flinches, and a rare wrinkle appears above her eyebrows. "...have changed. Still, south is where it all began."

"I have a feeling you don't mean just this unfortunate series of events," Niena says quietly.

"In a way." Titania smiles.

Hakaal Mountains. The trees surrounding them are thin pines, far different from the oaks, beeches, and maples of the rolling fields they left. *That means we have left the Almar High Valley. We've also left the Midlands?* Niena isn't so certain of the geography. Two weeks of hard climbing, even assisted by Titania's spells, muddles the brain.

"What is it like, living so long?" The girl's question teases another smirk from Titania. "I...just called you old, didn't I?"

Titania laughs quietly. "At least you didn't say I was boring." She touches a finger to her lips. "I'm better company than that elf would ever be."

"Oh, that is true," Niena whispers. "The look on his face always gave me the shivers."

"Mmhmm," Titania says. "Elves are dull — terribly logical, and logical in their terror." She bounces her head left and right, then, as if weighing something. "That also makes them rather easy to toss on their backside."

As the two trade yawns, night snuggles up to the valley. Niena covers her nose for a sneeze and regards her grandmother through tented fingers.

"What are we doing out here?"

"We are sitting on a rock," Titania says slowly.

"You know what I mean."

Niena watches the fairy contemplate the horizon, then slump, resting her chin between knobby knees. Green eyes stare off, unblinking, and the girl wonders at what Titania is thinking. Niena withdraws into her coat, the one thing she has left of her paternal grandfather Marny. *He would not trust her.*

And then the fairy speaks: "Do you see the other side of this valley?"

"I don't think much is out there."

"Did you not notice those lights?" Titania indicates a line far off in the distance with a chop of her hand. "They are hunting camps."

She can't see it. The fires are little more than dull-orange smudges to her eyes.

"This is the frontier of the Empire of Naroth. Beyond is the Kronarum, what touches the old Almar Valley, and the capital. Or did; it is the dragon's wasteland now. Foul, and rotten. Yet not all is gone. There are seas beyond the wastes, seas that glint with silver and gold from winter lights, like a thief's catch tossed upon black velvet."

And as the fairy speaks, Niena's mind drifts like a bird over many vistas. She can see them. The glittering waters breaking against a sharp shoreline. Of lands dotted with farms, which in turn sprawl across toppled ruins. Swamps. Moors pocking otherwise unremarkable fields. Wild savannahs. Roads, that start and disappear into the memory of fallen cities.

She sees people too. Toiling, laughing, crying. Dying. Battles fought over hovels. Skirmishes, castle sieges. The clash of metal against metal and the reeking stench of iron and blood. These descriptions then tumble over places where little grows — visions of vast stretches of sand ruled over by the sun, where, amid one such, there is a city. And in that city are many strange and wondrous machines. All humming. All purring.

A corner of Titania's eyes sparkles, and Niena snaps out of the daydream. "I shall tell you stories. I will teach you songs. And as to where I shall take you? To the next hill, and the one after that, until your fear of the horizon fades to a daydream of springs to come."

Niena stands too quickly but grasps Titania's hand at the last moment. "I now know a thing or two about real storytelling." Then, hand in hand, she adds: "Tell me one about a roaring fireplace, and a nice cup of tea."

"A friend of mine used to always say this: Sofie, first you need to know what cards you are holding, before you start talking. Still, I can do you a little better than a cup of tea." Titania waves her hand over the rocks, and the scattered trees clinging to the mountain below.

"Once, long ago, a little songbird was planning a tea party."

And everything before which Titania waves her hand disappears. The fires. The trees. They all fade away, and the sky is plunged further and further into darkness. Until, as the fairy spreads her fingers, a glow conquers the horizon.

"The problem was the list; it was too long," Titania continues. "I must invite Mrs. Summer, the little bird chirped. And there is no way I can forget the sunshine on the meadows, or morning dew. Oh, and the bees, the bees! They would cause such a fuss. It carried on, and on like this."

Titania stands, dragging Niena up by her elbow. The ground, the rocks, disappear, leaving a featureless plane.

"She must find a way to whittle the list down. After all, there is only so much a little bird can carry on her wings, or grip with her beak."

Splashes of blue, of white explode across Niena's vision. Dashes of green and red mix. The sky flows, flows, washing away the bleakness. Titania leads the girl on, and they walk for what seems like hours before she speaks again.

"And then she realizes: I don't want to throw such a big party. It will be too much of a mess."

Niena staggers and throws up her arm to protect against the sudden flash. She is only half successful. As she blinks away the blur, shapes begin to coalesce.

"In the end, she took her tea alone," Titania says. "Instead of the grand event, it was only… a little lark."

They now stand upon a white field. Niena spins, gawking at the forest surrounding. "We were just…chords."

On a rock, in the middle of a clearing, there is a small picnic. Of breads, and within a crude wooden bowl, clear liquid. "Stories are among the oldest of the known uses of magic," Titania says, reaching out to touch Niena's face. "You weave them like songs, but investing more into each word, plucking the same chords of creation."

"Are they easier?"

"Easier, I am not so sure. The song-spells you have used may seem that way in comparison, but only because of the Ever-charm." Titania makes a waving gesture. "Also, with exceptions, sung spells don't normally persist long after the music stops."

The fairy queen brushes a strand of hair back. "Fairies like their songs. Elves prefer stories." She beckons Neina to follow while walking backwards. "Humans are where things get weird. Their collective belief in a thing reinforces their casting, and don't even get me started on the Curatorium's Construct."

"Oberon told me that human magic is quicker," Niena says. "He tried to teach me, but I wasn't any good at it."

The lines around Titania's eyes smooth out, revealing the twinkle beneath. "You are the melody of three, child. You have the blood of all races. I think it was more his failure than yours."

"Human, fairy," Niena says. "And elf?"

"Since gnomes don't exist, and centaurs have no souls, that sort of narrows it down, doesn't it?" Titania says.

"I mean…."

"Oberon didn't tell you? Of course, he would not, unless it suited his purposes."

Niena's chest puffs, then deflates, collapsing into the ground before the table. "No." She shakes her head.

"Gentle eyes and a kind voice can hide a devious mind, especially from the trusting heart of a little girl," Titania says. "Enough on him; what matters is this: because you have the blood of all three races, you can play the Evercharm while others cannot."

Blowing leaves, lifting their skirts to a red and brown dance, interrupt the girl's wonder. One of the gusts even threatens the dishes, forcing Titania to hover protectively over them. Her hair flows with the wind. West, then east. And Niena follows the silken lines, tilting her head to the clear view of autumn touching the land everywhere.

A bowl tips and rattles off the table and onto stone, but a quick foot from Niena stops the nuts inside from spilling. She leans over and retrieves it, thumbing the acorns. "Right now, food is all I want to think about."

"Good. So…" Titania smiles. "What type of honey would you like?"

After a pause, Niena leans forward. "Chords," she whispers, then looks past Titania's own gaze. Magic is nothing new to Niena, and by now her mind has become open to many possibilities. But her stomach remains grounded, quickly drawing her back to the improbability that lies upon a makeshift table. "The type that comes from bees?"

Titania's laugh is loud and cheerful. "We have forest honey. We have heather honey. There are no cheeses or meat. Anything that comes from large animals — anything bigger than, say, a bee — can be too complicated."

"It's all so—"

"Magical?"

The girl moves back to the bread. The light created from the story-spell begins to fade, settling to night. "How did we get down here so fast? Did you summon us here, or was that an illusion?"

"A bit of both," Titania says. "It is too complicated for me to explain over…dinner? Supper? More like a late tea."

"Can you just do this again, then, and take us to that place with the sands? It seemed warm."

"This I cannot do," Titania says. "Or I would have. And if I had the strength, we would not have climbed those mountains. Fairies need new stories to survive. There have been few of these, and I am cut off from the Fairhome."

Niena hugs herself, surveying the mountain behind her one last time. Ahead are the whisp-like lights of civilization they saw before. Only, more substantial. And threatening. Before them, though, and long till they reach them, are the sloping foothills and their snow-dusted fields. Then a river as blue and cold as Titania's face at rest.

"We will make for the hills early," Titania says. "Morning will come soon; we benefit from a clear night sky. It will not last, so we must quickly find suitable shelter."

"I thought I saw a cave earlier, though it could have just been a shadow," Niena says. "It shouldn't be far."

"I think I know the one you are talking about. We will look for it, but first, eat your honey bread."

Chapter 4

Coils of black stir Titania from her meditation, then disappear. But while her eyes adjust to the low light of the cave, the presence behind the coils remains. Embers of their earlier campfire still spark, sending trails to the corners of the cavern like angry villagers with torches. Niena, her young step-granddaughter, sleeps noisily nearer the entrance. Three hours have passed; in another two, they must again depart or risk discovery.

We are here. Low and high. Male and female. The voices of the Teamor shove open a mental door, eliciting a shocked gasp from Titania. *Explain your failure to us.*

"Failure? We have just entered the bloody valley," Titania whispers. "They haven't found us yet."

Yet, you waste your remaining power on the girl. Power we have loaned you.

Titania can't help but rub her hands, feeling the echo of their last conversation. "She is exhausted from travel."

Exhausted? Or pampered? A warning, Titania: the grandson of the Matriarch leads the hunt.

"I know, it's all the trees whisper about," she says, forcing the words out harshly so as to hide the tremble in her voice. "He will track me down, and fast."

Titania fidgets, and her arm strikes the back wall of the cave. One deep breath follows another. That the elven Matriarch's spawn would work with a representative of the Curators in any fashion is almost inconceivable.

"They have no love for my kind," she says. As she speaks, her voice rattles, and she stares straight ahead into the darkness. "The time of wild hunt is over. We only need to delay Rein until we can get to Cuiven's Lee, then there's nothing he can do."

The Artisan is not as big of a fool as you think.

"I will get her to Cuiven's Lee. Niena, of her own free will, shall sing the song of unbinding."

And then she quiets, expending all breath. She silences her thoughts, too, while not directly shielding them from the Teamor. To give the impression of her statement ending in a period instead of the comma she truly means.

We do not believe the girl should be allowed the freedom to choose.

"She must be able to feel the music, to want it," the fairy says. "There is nothing you can hold over her, except her own life."

Perhaps. Perhaps not.

Near Titania's feet, the girl stirs. Raven hair covers Niena's mouth. The girl's high cheekbones narrow a face that is pretty and thin —perhaps too much of the latter, thanks to their travels. The fairy queen inches away. Unto the cracks and crevices where the darkness hides. "Take Rein out of the equation and the rest will fall. Stall him, delay him with the Udur."

You are unimaginative. Death is a door, and ambition is the hand that opens it.

"But…" Titania's voice trembles. "What do you mean by that?"

Bring the girl to the point of binding, bring back to the beginning. That is your task. Do not fail us, fairy.

The last word echoes in Titania's head like a door slammed in an empty hall.

"I will not fail." To herself.

This could have gone better. Titania clears her throat. The presence from earlier recedes with the tide of light, and the fairy lets her shoulders slump. The moment of tension during her conversation with the Teamor translates into what feels like hours of aches for her poor muscles. She stretches, then reaches back to massage the knot on her neck.

I feel like a bloody fox caught in its bloody den. Promises of fresh air seethe in from an errant breeze. *Well, a huge fox, relishing in the freedom.* And that freedom — the loss of the oppressive presence of the Teamor — is enough to loosen clenched fists.

These last few days have tired her. And now, new complications: *Rein...* Her hands seemingly melt into the stone when she caresses it. She frowns. *I will set the trap myself then; to hell with them if it messes with their plans.*

Intent — sheer, brutal intent — is the knife that carves the spell. She weaves the chords into the music, catching it inside the story itself. Whatever magic is used will turn against them. Next, she will need to craft the line and the reel.

"Another object," she whispers. "Something with its own power." Titania knows just the place, if it still exists. The fairy queen lifts her head to the wind and closes her eyes. "Yes, I hear its song. It sings of the rush of water, and the long fingers of the river weeds."

This piece in the cave is the calling stone, and she seals her work at the last with a small measure of her own blood. Titania shakes, forcing herself to remain upright. The act will make something from her forever linger here. She quickly moves past, not wanting to think of the cost.

One step brings her to the threshold, with a foot near Niena's outstretched hand. Titania stares out into the early morning. Trees block most of the view south and west, but straight on from the cave, the moon peers back with a wide grin.

"A waste of the power they've given me? What, that trickle, I should just be rid of..." she whispers, turning away from the tree line and back to the cavern where Niena rests. "I can't...I mustn't. I still need it, even this little."

The world spins, and she clutches her head. "Damn you, Oberon! You've made me little more than a dream and left me alone in this nightmare."

She trembles, walking out into the air alone. Dead leaves rake against the cavern entrance, caught in the wind and shoved away into this dank hole by nature itself.

Chapter 5

Higgins' dirty hand reaches towards the sun, occasionally brushing past roots and weeds that cling to the mountainside. His hand stops. Wind from the south may be warm, but the ground remains cool. Above, the elf grimaces.

"You are slow," Sethlan says.

Higgins smirks as he grasps the elf's hand. "But not the slowest."

Below them, Christaan De Rein struggles. Higgins leans over the side, searching for a way to help his master, until a jostle from the elf stops him. The apprentice follows a sinewy forearm and from there meets Sethlan's face. With a quick flick of his eyes, the elf puts Higgins back on the path.

One grip at a time. The sun beats directly on Higgins's head and sweat rolls down. He blinks and tries to shield his eyes, therein catching a glimpse of their goal: a cleft forty meters up.

And if we make that, what then? he thinks, frowning. A bird of prey cries in the sky behind. Higgins pauses, expecting Sethlan to say something, but the elf's head disappears in the brush. Leaving this, the apprentice lets his gaze drift downward.

"To live is not to breathe, but to act. It is to make use of our organs, our senses, our faculties..." Higgins lets his weight sink into his right side. There is no answer from below, nor above. "What would Rousseau say about this view?"

A liquor of green-blue sky settles below a froth of while clouds, punctuated only by a burst of sunshine in the middle. As if God has decided his absinth needed a lemon wedge. Higgins laughs. "Maybe if he were here on this mountain, he'd ask what the hell we were thinking."

Cracking, grunting and moaning signal Rein's approach from below. The daydream then breaks on a line of pines. Higgin watches in slow motion as Rein finally decides to grasp the next hold, the Inspector's fingernails plowing the muck around a rock. Yet something is wrong. *A small thing like that can't possibly be anchored—*

Unable to hold Rein's weight, the stone gives way almost as soon as Rein places his hand on it.

"Rein!"

Branches crack as feet fight for purchase, and the sound of falling rock echoes. Rein's arms shake from the effort to keep himself upright. As Higgins scrambles, he sees the Inspector bite his lips, digging into more mustache than flesh.

"Stay right there. I am coming to help you," Higgins says, testing his own way down.

The Inspector's mustache twitches, and with a chorus of grunting, Rein answers, lunging at another promising bit of rock with his right arm. The pass misses, and he ends up snatching at grass and weeds. Roots tear, fingers dig, and trousers rip for the effort.

"Stop it," Higgins growls. "I'm coming, I'm coming."

"I'd bloody rather become geography."

There is a low rumble from the horizon. Higgins squints, catching a crash of lighting in a line of clouds hiding around the peaks. To his left, he can see the elf stopping while Rein dangles below.

"I will surmount this craig my bloody self," his master says.

The apprentice turns back. "Pride goeth before a fall."

"Abi in malam crucem!"

Higgins rubs the bridge of his nose. *Go to the cross. He's telling me to hang myself. Right, then.* "I stand by my statement, sir. Any breakfast without eggs is neither a break nor a fast. It is an abomination, sir."

"Abomination?" Rein yells. "Abomination!" He froths. "I've eaten the same thing every morning since I was a boy in Holland."

"Well, there's the first problem, you Dutch—"

Lightning crashes in the background of their conversation, distracting Higgins as the elf climbs down.

"Enough," Sethlan says. "Take my hand."

Thunder rocks. Finally, a twitch of Rein's mustache signals surrender. And as the elf extends his hand towards the Inspector, the first droplets of the oncoming storm arrive.

"We must keep moving." Sethlan blinks as sleet hits his cheek. *"Regna."*

The storm swells past the obscuring peaks and dominates the sky. Thunder rumbles on the mountainside. With one swift motion, the elf pulls Rein to a more solid footing, and as they all look on, the mountain is thrown into a strobe of alternating light and dark. Each instance at first barely lasts two heartbeats. Yet the passing of light slows — slows, until the mountain is cast into gloom, and the rain's patter echoes off their dirty clothes.

Sethlan mutters a curse, and the three return to the mountain face. Rein, wrapping his tattered cloak around his waist, offers a weary gesture to the brush they must cross. Thorny trees and saplings cling everywhere below the cleft. But it is Higgins that first breaks the path for the men. A difficult attempt, as he cannot take the same path as the elf — so loosened by effort, and not suitable for stocky men. There is more of an angle to the mountain here. Less rock, and more dirt. And what solid stone they find is slickened by sleet, slowing them, even as the loss of light spurs their need for hurry. An hour is stolen, torn between the two needs: speed and caution.

The rest of the way continues so, until the quiet between them rouses Higgins to the point where he forces himself to stop. Stop, even with the precariousness of their holds growing with each droplet.

"Maybe you were right, sir," Higgins says. When no answer comes, he cups his hands around his mouth and calls down to his master again.

Below, Rein's painful climb halts, and the circle of his top hat tips backward. The Inspector jerks his head up, revealing a soggy face. "Of course I was right. Wait. What the bloody hell are you on about?"

"Early you said civilized men should not be clinging to a mountainside in autumn. If say I am now inclined to consider those arguments, what spells can we use to get us closer?"

Rein grunts and adjusts his top hat, followed by the sounds of grass, rain, and dirt falling as he climbs a little higher.

"Oresme's stigan?" He says between coughs.

"That could work," Higgins says. "But isn't it Latin-based. What has worked here — German, Mandarin. French?"

"Yes, true. Gaelic, mostly, but even the sorcerer's dialect of Gaelic is not entirely stable. I will need time to adapt it and test the Étincelle and Mort."

"Sethlan wants us to hurry it up, I think," Higgins says.

For, all this time, the methodical climbing motion of the elf had played in the background, just under the storm. No more. Sethlan's angular features remain poised on an outcrop of rock, four meters above. Even with the unsteady light, the unspoken message tugging at the corners of his mouth is evident: *Shut up and climb.*

"That elf is getting uppity," Rein says.

Higgins cannot disagree, but a fast mouthful of whatever had been clamming up his hair keeps him from commenting. He spits and waves off his friend.

"Don't use the stone. Take the weeds on the left, they will hold," Higgins says. "I felt that rock move as I was coming up."

Rein grudgingly follows, and one foot at a time from there they try to meet the elf's pace. Crawling, sometimes scraping along. The rain takes the days' grime and washes it into all sorts of uncomfortable places. And bogs down their pant legs. Not for the first time, Higgins considers removing his shoes. Even before the rain started, he felt like they were dragging half the mountain up in the soles, and now — *Now I feel like the bottom of the Thames.*

"Why don't you use my shoulder to get that one around the crook?" the Inspector adds.

"You think you've got a good enough hold there?"

Higgins spits out a lock of his hair. Then another. Then the same one from before. Rein now has almost matched him, the Inspector's hat close enough for him to put his foot upon. Or wash his feet in the water sloshing around its rim. A rock, precariously wedged in mud and held by roots, blocks his view of the elf.

Rein smirks back. "Like Napoleon at Austerlitz, I do think."

"Bloody French," Higgins growls, then grabs at a sapling.

Rein joins him on his left. The two are now between another scrappy pine and loose shale. Sethlan has traversed around the latter, but he's ignored in the conversation. The rough bark pains Higgins's hands, yet it won't slip. He squints, guessing at the next move.

"We are going to have to shimmy around a bit," Higgins says.

"Mrmm. You know Rousseau, whom you are always quoting, is French? Or do you know many Jacques are faffing around England?"

"He's from Geneva," Higgins says through a groan, stretching over Rein. The cleft earlier teases them just above.

"Last I checked, that's nowhere near Horseguard."

For several more meters, it went like this, while a song built there in the west, where wind caressing the grass is the harmony to the storm's budding melody. So do the men also move, finding rhythm in their disharmony. Sethlan's feet disappear first over the rise, then their turn comes.

"One more hand to go, old man," Higgins says, extending his own. With one quick pull, the Inspector mounts the ridge and rolls onto his back, his face flush and his clothes ragged. The elf rests on the opposite end. Poised. Tense. As if ready to leap back into action.

Sethlan's eyes burn, full of fire and dangerous oaths. "How your kind ever imprisoned mine is beyond comprehension."

Rain had been building over the last hour. It comes now, sideways. Harder than the sprinkles of sleet that washed the elf's face earlier. Lighter than what Higgins feels the storm could be. Soon water trickles down splits in the stone at their back. Moments pass as they glare at each other in silence. Trickles become tiny rivulets.

"We are on the western face of the mountain," Sethlan continues. "This ridge will lead us north, and then east, before it must turn again south."

The Inspector's head lowers, letting his top hat obscure his eyes. Higgins knows his master is studying the elf, and a short bob in the rim of the hat a signal.

"We are not going to find drier," the elf says. His hands reach out and tap the stone of the hollow behind them. Sethlan's lips barely move as he speaks in a hiss. "The girl must have come south, but south covers a large area. Our chance upon her tracks earlier was luck, and she must have some woodcraft, for I have seen little since. How does she move so quickly?"

Rein sinks into his coat. "What's to stop her from going north? Or east?"

"Wisdom," Sethlan says. "Or good eyes, for those mountains are taller."

"What about the—"

"Do not speak to me of west, I would have seen."

"Rein," Higgins interjects. "Maybe now is the time to find the girl…your way."

"Fine," Rein says. "Better now, I suppose, than before we climb all the way up a bloody mountain." He then grimaces and squints at the elf. "Bugger off towards the edge, both of you."

"Because your spell requires it?" the elf says, eyes narrowing.

"Because I don't like being bloody wet!"

"Well," Higgins says, sneaking a look at Sethlan. "Someone hasn't had his tea."

Rain obscures the return gesture they receive. Thunder, whatever curse Rein was mouthing. The lip of the hollow is not much further, or dryer, than where the Inspector sits, and when Higgins and the elf move, they barely take more than a couple of steps.

"Sethlan," Higgins says. "Perhaps we should talk."

"Goats," the elf says.

"Goats?"

The far ground has Sethlan in this moment. He crouches low, and mutters to himself. The visage makes the apprentice feel as if he were watching a man turn savage. Finally, after some time, the elf picks up a thorn, now soggy amid weeds that lie crumpled on the ground, and returns to the wall.

"Goats," he repeats.

Rambling from the Inspector causes Higgins to move closer to Sethlan. He speaks, keeping one eye on his master. "What is it you plan to do, once we find the girl?"

A bemused stare from Sethlan is diverted as Rein's humming turns into a song that sounds more like a bawdy tavern ballad than a spell. Higgins takes the opportunity to come even closer, risking a dangerous look from the elf.

"Oh, I know what you said about freeing your queen or whatever billy-bolly," Higgins whispers. "I mean, how do you plan to use the Evercharm?"

"The girl will sing," he says.

"All right. I suppose that is needed for it to work, then? But what if she says no? She can do that," the apprentice continues. "And this Evercharm thing. You know I am no betting man, but I wager anything that can be used to break a prison of the Curators, can break a lot more than that."

A gust rustles the tops of the tree line and the pines sway west. There is the smell of salt in the air that briefly scrapes by Higgins's nose.

Sethlan does not blink as he stares through the apprentice. "In Cuiven's Lee, dreams can be made, and unmade. The girl will sing. She will play the Evercharm. Pray to your god that it is we who are by her side then."

"Can't one of us play the blasted thing instead?"

"Found her," Rein shouts, immediately gaining the attention of the others. "Even with your mangling of the reagents, Higgins. Or at least I should say, I found where she is not."

In the Inspector's hands is a button. Not some leftover from a device, or piece of an artifact — but a plain, linen-covered button — and Higgins notices there is now one missing from the man's overcoat. What he has done to it, though, is to take a needle and pierce the threading so that the metal sticks out on both ends evenly. Where were the sap, moss, and the berries that Higgins gathered?

"You two come closer," the Inspector hisses. "I'll need your backs to protect against the wind."

A quick tug on Higgins's sleeve brings him to position. There, huddled as close to the rock wall as possible, the Artisan works. Rein raises his right hand, and lets the talisman drop. Twine tied to the back pinch halts the plummet. "Observe," he says, letting his device dangle as he cups it protectively with his left.

Blue sparks spread across the needle's length. Faint, and dwindling, even as the point of the needle slows its spinning and rests on a direction: south.

"It's not the most elegant of solutions," Rein says. "Normally, I would interact with the chords on a…different level. Yet, for the sake of our hunt, this will work."

Higgins hunches his shoulders and stares at the needle with one eye closed. "South. So, we are on the right path at least. But wait…that would also mean—"

The needle-in-a-button twists in the wind. South by southeast. As thunder roars in the distance, Sethlan spins violently in the direction the needle points, his arms bobbing with his heaving breath.

Flashes of lightning expose a ridge following the peaks of a vast range. The trees below are sparse. The rock face to the right hides most of the features east. Higgins clamors next to the elf and looks down upon the western slope of the next mountain.

"I've done this sort of thing before, but with a different target," Rein says gently. "It's hard to estimate distance, though I think the girl would not be that close."

At once, Sethlan leans over the edge, then arches back as his head tilts up. His face is intent. Hunting. Higgins tries to follow his eyes.

"There is a path some ways, further up," the elf says. "It must lead around to follow the ridge line south."

"How could she have passed us?" Higgins asks.

The elf's nostrils flare. Then his breathing settles. "She could not. Not without help."

"Could be, or you…" Rein coughs and folds his hands over his chest, thinking better. "Maybe she did have help."

In this brief time, a few clouds southwest pull back, revealing the dusk behind the storm. Higgins sweeps his head west, then south at the white capped peaks. South, where a ribbon of moonlight flails at the edges of the western sky. He squints.

"So…" Higgins coughs. "What shall we do for supper?"

Chapter 6

Evening is heralded by smoke from the party's campfire. The storm continues to rage, or more appropriately, stomp around like a child not getting its way. But night is the adult in the room. There will be no further climbing. Higgins has returned from a brief forage, and Rein was able to work out the rudimentary magic to form clay pots. It is enough for this night. Even if any had the will for it, it might be best to throw a lid over everything and hope the pounding ceases.

Each of the party contemplates the fire differently. The elf has retreated within himself. Higgins and Rein argue as they usually do. And every so often, a drop of rainwater hits the flames, letting loose a quiet hiss. Sethlan shifts his shoulders each time it happens.

"Unless your magic is wrong, Mannelig, the girl had help," Sethlan whispers suddenly. "Powerful help."

"It's no fault of my magic," Rein says. As Higgins looks over him, he sees the old master hesitate. "Science, my lad. Intuition is far less reliable. Maybe you have merely underestimated the girl's capabilities?"

"The child is strong, but not that strong. She has little skill," Sethlan says.

"Yet she is carrying a divine instrument," Rein says, then quickly adds: "What about her woodcraft? If it could fool your eyes—"

The elf slaps the comment away. "She is no bird."

The fire pops loudly as Higgins pushes ashes around with a stick, watching the flame blacken the tip. The wood they found won't last, even with Rein enchanting it. He takes a deep breath.

"I think I may know who is helping her." Higgins lifts his eyes then. "A creature named Oberon—"

"Oberon?" Rein stutters. "Did I hear that right — Oberon, the fairy king himself? And we aren't talking about a bad bit of squirrel?"

"No," Higgins protests.

"What about the potato? Did we even have any potato?"

"No, and no."

"I must be careful around you, Mister Higgins," Rein says. "You are excitable, and prone to silliness. It would fit that you'd have a long, nonsensical dream about Shakespeare."

Higgins opens his mouth, then reconsiders. "It was not a dream," he grumbles. "We spoke, at length; or well, sort of spoke. The manner was queer."

"He contacted you in your head, then?" Rein says, slowly.

The three fidget awkwardly. Sethlan, looking down his nose at the Inspector. While he, Rein, appears more preoccupied with pulling summoned tufts of wool and testing them in the fire. Higgins rolls his shoulders as if to shake off their nonexistent glares.

"Indeed"—he shifts his feet—"it all happened while on the trail. Not long after Chancy's death. Oberon mentioned a woman," Higgins continues. "Titania, whom he feared would complicate things for us."

Rein leans forward. "Speak plainly."

"She'd run off with the girl." Higgins attempts to clarify. "Take. Coerce. Influence?" He dismisses the last with a shake of his head, then adds, "Kidnap — I am afraid I do not have a thesaurus with me for any other possible synonyms. The point is, he could be aiding this Niena, or Titania might already have her."

"And you tell us this just now." Rein says. "I am not the only one here that sees the problem, am I?"

"I thought I was going mad," Higgins says.

The tufts of wool twixt Rein's fingers flutter away as their gazes meet, and deep in the recesses of the Inspector's hood, blue eyes gleam.

"You are my apprentice. This is mutiny. Or does mutiny require a ship? Well, it is certainly insubordination. This is not done, sir." The last said in a testy explosion. He glowers at Higgins. "And here I was, thinking you were getting past the worst of your childish inclinations. Withholding information — what, for…for dramatic effect? Who does this?"

"What would you have me do then?"

"Report it to me," Rein says. "And endure my ridicule as is proper and befitting a gentleman of your status."

"Titania has not been heard from in an age," Sethlan says. "My people believed her to have shared the fate of most of the fairy folk. Oberon and Titania. Fairy king, and queen. This would complicate our hunt."

"*Kak,*" Rein says. "That's an understatement."

"Mm," Sethlan says. The elf shifts his weight, and waves off Higgins's budding question. "You will likely think it gets queerer from this point on. Their kind has also a unique relationship with time, existing on all points from their birth to their death."

He cranes his neck then, as if trying to push away a nasty thought. "They also grow madder, depending on where and when they are. If either he or Titania were to bring the girl to Cuiven's Lee at the right moment, in the right age, much mischief can be done. Much could be undone, even."

Rein pales. "This is not good, gentlemen. This is not good at all."

"And what do the Teamor and their deviants play at?" Sethlan stares at the sky.

"Not good," Higgins repeats. "Hold…" He then raises his hands and shakes a finger towards Rein. "How did you know that Oberon would contact me through my mind? "

"I am an esteemed Artisan and Inspector of the Princeps inspectorem," Rein says, puffing out his chest. "Fairies, elves and their methods"—he tips his hat to Sethlan—"these are all my purvey. You know this."

"In our long history, we've never directly encountered either. There is scant literature on the fey folk in the Curatorum," Higgins says.

Rein's eyes smolder. "Scant that they would entrust my sect with, but there is information to find, if you know where to look." But the Inspector can't hold his stare, and he looks away with a sigh. "Yet, you are right. No, I was getting to that," Rein says, returning to whispers. "I may have also encountered…"

Mumbles, coughs, and a string of Dutch curses muddle his next words. Whatever Higgins's master was about to say, a growl from a southeasterly wind spoils his answer, and thunder buries it.

But not Sethlan's, as he says: "Oberon has been involved from the beginning. It is just another obstacle we must plan around. Like a sleeping dragon. How will it play out, and will it burn us all in the end?"

"Dragons?" Rein says. "Who said anything about dragons?"

"It was an analogy, I think, sir," Higgins says.

"Language! Need I remind you of who we represent, Higgins?"

"There could be a way around all of this." Higgins rubs his hands. "Magic versus magic. How close can you bring us to Niena, like you've done before? But discreetly."

"Thinking of swooping in and rescuing the damsel in distress?" Rein laughs.

"If we get close enough, why not?" Higgins says. "Or we could just pace her for now, keep the girl from getting out of sight."

"The front door is always a terrible idea. In my experience, the dragon usually eats the knight."

But Rein cannot joke away the attention from both, and the longer the silence, the more hunched the Inspector gets. Until he suddenly spins on his heels and throws up his hands in a stream of curses. Nothing is safe from him. Not the sky, the storm, or everything chittering in the background. Most of all, not Higgins.

"It is delicate, what you ask." Rein points a finger at his apprentice mid-rant. "Getting us to Hearth was easy by comparison. I just knew the key phrase and was sitting pretty on an old leyline. The mystical equivalent of jiggling the key in the door until it turns. I have no idea of the lay of the terrain between her and us. Generally, it is better to first travel to a place, leave a calling stone, then—"

"Enough," Sethlan says. "Can you, or can you not?"

"Yes, I can," Rein says, then quickly: "Or, maybe. I am not sure how safe it would be, but I could try to skip some of the distance between her and us. With some scouting. It would be quite like a giant playing a game of scotch-hopper."

"Safely and discreetly," Higgins reiterates. "Let's not stir these cast-offs from *A Midsummer Night's Dream*. That's just

45

as important as not throwing us face-first into a mountain, or the business end of some pine trees."

"I could be your eyes," Sethlan says.

The back of Rein's head dips. "I don't think I have the fortitude for more than one per day, and definitely not tonight."

"Tomorrow, then," Sethlan says. "At first light."

"She likely isn't far," Rein says. "There is another matter to consider: once we make that jump, it will be like lighting a beacon for every malfeasance that exists in the other."

"The Udur may come," Sethlan says.

"And fast."

"But not tonight." At first, Higgins speaks in a whisper, until night falls from his lips, and then his voice returns to a darker timbre. "Gentlemen, elf, I think we should make plans."

"Sethlan and I will deal with the fairy," Rein says as the elf nods. "You should consider how we can protect ourselves from the Udur, since you know more about them than we."

"I could work out something," Higgins says. He looks at his master, then the elf, and watches their eyes flash as if sharing something otherwise unseen.

"When the time comes, I will tell a story," Sethlan says through his teeth.

Higgins blinks. "What, and then make some cookies before tucking them into bed?"

"Elven magic," Rein says.

The clouds southwest relent as if a hole were cut from the heavens, revealing the dusk sky. East, west, and south, white-capped mountains pierce the gray as the elf grumbles. South, where a ribbon of red and yellow frays at the edges of the sun in the western sky.

"I would do anything for a bit of tea right now," Higgins says. "Or to be back home in my chair, reading a book. Far away from this sort of talk."

"What book would you prefer?" Rein says, leaning in to sit beside his friend as he slumps.

"Any book," Higgins says. "Even one from your library."

"Ahh, you say that now…" Rein turns his head to the fire. "It's always these times, these types of places that make you appreciate the horribleness of home, and the measly comforts."

"Well…I don't think you could get me to read Radcliffe, even so."

Master and student — two friends — share a laugh. The passing of the storm lessens the tension between them. Saps the energy from the air. With exception: the elf's features grow more tense if it were possible. During their brief conversation, Sethlan retreated further towards the fire, and a rare twinge of disgust chases anger across his face.

Higgins breathes deeply. This earns him a raised eyebrow from the elf.

"Sethlan," Higgins says. "What is your home like. Do you think much about it?"

"The Elfsea?" For a moment, his questioning gaze seems to reach into the fire. "It is a light for men that swallows up lights," he says with a quick look, causing Higgins to jump. "And wolves seek ever to win it."

"That is a very weird description," Rein says. "I'd wager you don't have problems with the tourists, though."

Higgins then moves, and all the stones and rocks reintroduce themselves to his flank. He blinks, a memory from his days in the Curatorium's dungeons surfacing. "A riddle." To himself, then louder: "Sethlan has presented us with an old riddle. Which makes more sense if you read the Hervarer Saga."

Sethlan shrugs. "If it is easy enough, then answer."

"Yes," Higgins says. "The answer is the sun. It lights all the world and shines on all men; but there are two wolves, Skalli and Hatti; one goes before, and the other follows."

"The Elfsea is devoid of order, and rhythm," Sethlan answers with a curt nod. "Flowers that bloom in spring one season may wait to winter the next."

"Well, that doesn't sound so bad," Rein says.

"Or a pebble loosed from your hand may fall up, instead of down," the elf continues. "Here…" His eyes lighten. "It is different."

"But that does," Higgins says. "Can you imagine one day, outside doing your business in God's country, only to have it fly up and join the heavens?"

Rein leans forward, his mustache twitching in the light like some rodent trying to escape his nose. "I would just use the opportunity to turn the tables on some pigeons."

"How do you get around in that mess?" Higgins asks over his master's laughter.

Sethlan runs his hands over his face, and when the fingers pass, the mask changes back into the statuesque. "We tell stories."

The chill in the elf's voice oppresses Higgins's thoughts. As if he were suddenly plunged into a cave. "*Vires acquirit eundo.*"

Rein flinches away from the light while Higgins holds it aloft, looking south, then east and west. Their trail, somewhere in that darkness, lies upon the western sides before it splits, a pair of peaks jutting out from the surrounding countryside. The hole in the clouds widens, letting the moonlight flood.

"I was a tailor's apprentice, you know," he says jollily then. "I am sure you've heard Rein call me that before. Since we are talking about stories, should I tell you how we two met?"

If the elf's reactions were mercurial, in this rare case they would pale against Rein's. The Inspector's blue eyes, unwavering in their assault on his apprentice, digs through the space between them. In comparison, the slight twitch, the minor lessening or tension in Sethlan's shoulder is thunderous.

"It was a dreary afternoon."

"All afternoons are dreary in London, you loon," Rein says.

"As you wish," Higgins says, then angles the summoned light to cast his profile in deep shadow. "It was a dark and stormy night."

Rein's sigh is almost as loud as the hiss of rain hitting the fire. Sethlan crosses his arms and tilts down his head.

"I had just returned from placing an order for several meters of muslin when the most wretched, vile man pushed his way into the master's parlor," Higgins says, then makes the sign of the cross. "He was hardly even human, this one. Screamed like a banshee—"

"I wasn't screaming," Rein protests. "I hardly—"

"About dark wizards this, evil witches that," Higgins says, raising his voice. "The old master, Bixby, took one look at the filthy, rank, foul smelling"—with a wink in Rein's direction—"woefully attired vagrant of a man, and he bolted out the back."

By now, the Inspector has settled back onto the rock wall. Sethlan, though, for once, holds a look other than apathy or contempt on his face. "You may continue," he says, his eyes sliding back and forth between the fire and Rein.

"I thought it was gibberish," Higgin says. "Until I peered over his shoulder and saw four robed figures out in the street." His voice drops to almost a whisper, barely audible over the rain. "Where they had come from, I do not know. They moved almost as one. Slowly. Step by step, to the shop door."

Night approaches under the cover of the remains of the storm, not that any can tell. The wind shifts. Rain threatens to entreat closer.

The apprentice spreads his hands over the weakening flame. "You must understand the next few moments from my perspective. There were these figures surrounding the façade. And the colors, the air around — even my own heartbeat — felt somehow muted. I thought I was having a heart attack or going mad."

"Here it comes," Rein says.

"So, you must understand that this is why I put my hands on Rein and threw him back towards the door." Higgins wipes his brow and makes a sweeping gesture at his master.

Rein shakes his head. "The result for the cultists were the same: one lost his nerve on the mark, the others attacked."

"The rain came then, but it did not stop what was about to happen, I…" Higgins then nods, giving way when he sees Rein wants to speak again.

"And through the chaos, and through the fire that inevitably took the tailor's store and home — because fire magic is what all cultists fall back to — the man who is now my apprentice found his courage, fought off the remaining cultists, and saved my life."

The wind takes some of the ash and spins it around the ledge. The patter of rain rushes forward, then relents. Sethlan smiles and moves past the two men to look out over the mountain side. He says nothing. The silence is again taken by another growl of thunder.

"Fate has a way of bringing magicians together," Rein continues. "Through that contact, I found him. As it was, in a similarly destined though less chaotic way, I had found my own master."

"It is an interesting story," Sethlan says. He shifts his shoulders and turns back to the two men. "I believe we should find peace for tonight, and perhaps again try dinner."

Higgins crosses his arms. "You do not have a story you might share?"

"Not tonight," Sethlan says, his smile fading.

Rein slips back into his little crevasse where it is still dry, while Higgins turns his attention to the last of the coals in the fire. *It is going to be cold tonight.* He looks past the fire to the elf. *It will be cold tomorrow.*

"When this is all over," Higgins says, "maybe you will tell a story about us." He leans over the fire as Rein grumbles, then picks up one of the faggots at the edge and pokes at the mush of nuts and wild onions. "Food is done, I think."

The campfire they share is unnaturally quiet. Higgins looks away from his master, whose lazy-eyed stare is as thick as the mosquitoes this night. A shadow passes over his face, and he fiddles with his fingers, looking to the night for some sort of solace. A night whose air is cool, but warmer than the headlands they came from.

Each takes from the pot in turns. Sharing the meal, and little more. And each soon attempts sleep. The fire is allowed to dwindle, fading away along with the first watch, which is upon Higgins. He uses the time to mend a hole in his coat, ensuring to avoid too much noise. Even so, Rein stirs, interrupting the apprentice's mending with small talk every twenty minutes.

"I best clean up," Higgins says, his big, calloused hands wrapping his bowl. With one thumb, he rubs the smeared mutton grease out and then on his own tunic. "How do you all think this will end?"

Rein tosses a stick into the fire and at the same time looks at Higgins — who responds by alternating between staring into the fire and trying to poke a hole into his shoes.

In the end, his master says one word: "Badly."

"Morning will not be kind to us," the elf adds with a grunt.

The apprentice coughs, not realizing that he had woken. "Do you always speak like that?"

Sethlan pulls his cloak from his face. "Yes." He sits up then, shakes his hair free of a loose bind, and with a quick jut of the chin turns his attention to the dying fire.

Four deep breaths. Twenty seconds of reflection. *Gods, these two.*

The fire consumes the preceding silence, crackling as shadows flit between him and his companions. Laughter cracks Higgins's dirt-caked face. Sheer, powerful, belly-shaking laughter. Sethlan looks from him to Rein, seemingly horrified — then joins in.

Chapter 7

"What's below us?" Niena asks between breaths. "What were you looking at earlier?"

"Men. I sense an encampment of them not too far from us now. Beyond this, a river, touching the sea," Titania says. "Also, before the waters mingle with the eastward ley, there is a large promontory spanning the river. Their fires are no longer kindled during the day, but I believe they are the same as we saw before."

"A town?"

"How should I know?" Titania says. "Everything is different. Whatever they are, we must meet them with power."

"Aye, so we must bring forth the elder song, to tie the moon to our bodice," Niena says with a smirk and rolls over on her side. "And make the mountains quiver with our lace."

Titania guffaws. "I forget how easy it is to slip into that non-sense." She also shifts onto her side. "Don't let anyone tell you people ever really spoke like that."

"What I want to know is why we are risking going through them," Niena says. "Oberon taught me how to enter the Fairhome. If you know something of the Southlands, we could just go in and come out."

"I do not trust the Fairhome as you do," Titania says, looking at their chosen path and the dense bushes that lay in between. "Especially now."

The fairy then sets her feet against a shrub and tests the way forward. "I am assuming, since you want to be a bard, you've told a tale or two before?"

"About unicorns, and fairies?" Niena's tone lilts, betraying her usual sarcasm.

"No."

"About battles and great heroes?"

"No," Titania says, dragging the syllable. "*Nul ne doit craindre ce qu'il peut fuir.* When something would threaten you, it is better to not be found at all."

"Maybe, but there are times when you can't run," Niena asks.

"Physical violence is for fools, and they who have been fooled," Titania says. "I will teach you how to glamour those who matter, and to know who they might be. It is not always as clear as new fallen snow."

"Unless you are a little girl, cornered in an ally in Shenan," Niena says.

Titania reaches out and helps Niena along. "Listen to me: It is better to avoid attention in those times and travel unseen when you must. Lyre or no. Or set traps. As now, so we can turn back those hunters on your tail."

"Like Rein?" The look she sees on Titania's face confuses Niena, pain warring with something else. Admiration? Niena shakes the folds of her dress. "How are they tracking me? Us..."

Titania blinks. "The same way the elf did so before. The same way Rein found you. You have played the Evercharm. Every step you take. Every breath you exhale, the chords vibrate around you. And if they did not, our style of magic picks at the same chords, but to a lesser extent."

She rubs the bridge of her nose, then adds: "Magical creatures of all stripes are drawn as well. You will never trick them for long. Nor can you hide anywhere in the world from someone like Rein."

Niena lowers her head and edges closer, whispering: "What does he want?"

"The same as everyone else. You. The Evercharm," Titania answers. "He is a servant to the Curators, a group of stuffy old men who like to order reality to their designs on Monday and sleep the rest of the week. The elf's reasons you likely know, and your defeat of him will only make him more cautious. Ruthless. They are all coming for you both. For one without the other will do them no good."

Niena's gaze slips from her grandmother to an opposite tree, where the so-named lyre, rests. She sighs heavily. "And what do you want with it, with me?"

A brief smile is scared away by something darker on the fairy's face. She looks down, then up, and regards Niena with a thin smile. "I want you to enjoy this life free of expectations," Titania says. "But, for the moment, I would have one request."

The girl's eyes speak the question better than her lips, but still, she says, "And that is?"

"To get off this bloody mountain. Now, come on."

♫

Daylight blooms in the afternoon, and a white curtain of snow hides Niena. Titania returns from beyond the tree line after scouting. She walks — seems to float — towards the girl's hiding spot and away from the encampment they saw earlier.

"Where have you been?" Niena whispers.

Titania puts a finger to her lips. "There are many men in the hills below, and an outpost that blocks our path," she says. "I have set a trap for a patrol. It will keep them occupied."

"What did you do?"

There is another gust, and Titania's hair flutters over Niena's shoulder. The smell of roses follows, and the warmth fills her limbs once more.

"I didn't hurt them." Titania's says. "They will not see my work as anything more than nature being nature. It should give us a chance to slip away." She extends her fingers over Niena's hand. "You spoke of your spells before. You've used the Evercharm's power to hide, turn yourself invisible?"

Niena nods, already reaching behind her to take the lyre. The song she used to hide herself in Shenan and Sunford comes freely to her lips. The smell of magic fills the air with the empowerment, and the bitterness of iron touches her tongue. Once done, granddaughter and grandmother take to the wilds once more.

Ice cracks under their feet. Wood snaps while they traverse between clutches of trees, all to get within sight of a Watchtower. To the right, posts mark the buried lines of a fence, appearing like the remains of some ancient Arctic forest — barren, and broken. Beyond them lie more ruined walls. And further below, a hut cuddles up to a broken stone wall.

What are they guarding? It is clear this was once a large fort. *Maybe there once was a road through the mountains.* Knowing where they came from doesn't help — Titania has made a point of avoiding any large trails, something Marny would have been happy about.

Or maybe it was meant to guard against the weather. She looks back to trace the battlements. *We could go around it, though.* Even as she thinks this, Niena knows it is not her grandmother's intention.

Footprints mar the snow everywhere. Even now, the sound of tribesmen floats in on errant breezes, and from the corner of her eye, Niena can see the faint trace of movement. Thankfully, this proves to be only a hare, and she breathes a silent prayer, hoping that the lyre's spell will hold. It had never failed her before, but there is always a first time.

Near the watchtower, doors open from what she had thought to be solid ground, and Niena's eyes leap as Titania squeezes her shoulder. Features of what must have been buried outbuildings to the fort are hidden under earth and snow. Across the stretch of some trees is a gate.

Already, Niena's grandmother moves in that direction.

"Do not drop your spell, and stay with me, child," she says.

Snow trails, clinging to Titania's limbs. Yet it is Niena who is her tail, and with their passing the world is stirred — even if the girl remains unseen. Steam rises from numerous spots, twisting in warm undulation. The clouds break soon after, allowing the sun to play upon the white, and Niena to study the tower.

Along the way, a loose stone forces her to look down. *Maybe I was right, there is a path. That gate looks like it's for sheep.* White merges into blue as snowflakes melt on her coat. She stretches then, straining the song but pushing away the dredges of too little sleep.

And now, as the sound of a returning party turns a corner, Titania begins to sing.

Fear pulls Niena's lips tight while the fairy's song rises, soaring past the confused men. There are four of them, wearing wolfskins and other hides, and each holds a long spear between mittened hands. *Trained soldiers?* That seems like a stretch. Despite this, Niena misses a chord as the men widen their search.

Come. Titania beckons with a finger. The song lifts the snow and twists it around them, creating a vortex and concealing their passing. The fear leaves Niena in soft tremors at each step. First from the edge of her lower jaw, then traveling down into her shoulder. Until the entire girl is trembling with raw emotion.

The men scatter before them. The way forward is unblocked, save by the rage of the spell. Needles of ice howl around their little bubble — a bubble that extends and contracts with the two.

"Chords," Niena gasps. Ahead, the queen waits but does not turn. Neina lurches after her but finds herself stuck. One of her feet has been taken by the melting and now freezing snow.

Then, a thought touches her tongue. This she takes, and infuses each word with feeling, purpose. And power.

"I stand alone, near an aspen in the wood. I am not the fir, my branches stripped of their joy. Yet both of their sorrow covers the snow."

She wiggles her toes, just a touch, but Niena can already feel the ice loosening. Joy mixed with excitement nearly ruins the work, and the power of the spell dries her throat.

Niena concentrates. "For a tree in autumn must lose its leaves; the branches mourn in winter. I walk on these tears unnumbered, above the blanket laid down."

With a quick jerk, her foot is wrested free. Then, tentatively, she sets the same foot down. This time, the snow holds her weight as rigidly as a river of ice. Niena shuffles forward, throwing her arms out as if tightrope-walking. Beyond, the statue of the waiting queen exudes impatience.

No, Titania's attention is locked forward, drilling into the doors even as the last words of her song reverberate off wood and ice. Flakes drift around the fairy queen, and more — if it weren't for Titania's spell of warmth earlier, Niena would

freeze upon approach like her feet did before. As it is, the girl
barely feels anything when she joins Titania's side.

"It doesn't look like there's much wedging them, but your
spell has probably thrown ice against the doors," Niena says.
"'Course, we could just hop over them."

Titania sniffs, and the line of her chin lowers. She looks im-
perious. Ancient. *And cold.* Niena shivers, and this brings one
eye to bear upon the girl.

"No one but me can see you, child," Titania says. "Still, it is
no excuse for you not to keep your composure."

Now she turns to her granddaughter, and Niena can see
through Titania's posture — and the range of emotions that
must be bubbling under the surface, hinted at only by the
smooth, but too smooth, effort of breathing.

"Think of this as if you were about to take your first step into
the greater world," Titania says.

Niena laughs. "When I think of adventure, it isn't following
in the footsteps of sheep."

"It's a symbol."

"Tell me when we take our first step into a room with a fireplace," Niena says. "With pottage waiting for us."

"We are far removed from any ideas on the rights of hospital-
ity, or regular bathing. Still, I think you will find something of
value in this journey. In the end."

In the gaps of swirling clouds there is such a show that the
sun retreats every so often behind the veil of nimbi — as if it
knows better. The fairy queen's eyes flash against this veil.
Vivid purples, striking greens, and pale white gleam as she narrows her focus to the door. She lifts her palms to the sky.

Around the fairy queen's shoulders, the faux night flows and
mixes with the white, as if shedding mock-starlight. Niena
clutches her dress tightly to her thighs. The wood of the double

doors is hoary, burdened with the weight of time, and yel-
lowed.

Her grandmother flicks a wrist, and the doors open outwards
with a shriek. The sound dredges up memories of the dragon in
Shenan's courtyard, and Niena flinches. Yet, when the doors
open, there is no monster behind them.

Titania looks down at Niena, and smiles. "It's just a door."

From there, the women sweep through the forest. Deer,
hares, and other fauna note their passing just as a farmer might
the change of season. For the wild creatures can tell more read-
ily than man the significance of the fairy folk returning. But
that is a thought for another day. The wheel turns. The afternoon becomes late, and exhaustion slows their pace. Despite
Titania's conviction earlier, a weight seems to drag the fairy
down.

"While we dawdle, there is something I must teach you," Titania says.

She then leans closer, and sings softly:
"In Cuivananlee, the fairy bud,
The spring may bring the rain,
The tits may twitter, the waters flood,
The flowers bloom again,
Cloudless nights may shew the jewel,
Crowning the travelers' stars,
That lyre of old, the heavenly tool,
That strummed creation's bars
To lands where old men lie,
To the hollows of elven dance,
Where in barrows buried deep,
The roots of life do chance,
Above all, fair is home,
And clear like fairy bells,
Where dreams true children dare to roam,

Until they bid farewell. "

"Cuiven's Lee…" Suspicion ices Niena's tone. "What does this song do?"

"It will keep whoever is chasing you from following into one of the other worlds," Titania says, then quickly: "This is an important spell to know, and one that you must understand before all others."

"When would I use that?"

Titania stares past Niena. "In Cuiven's Lee, if we go there, and I think we may have to. That will, of course, depend on the next few days. You need to be prepared."

For the next few hours, as they move, she is drilled on the spell and little else. The light fades before she realizes, and twilight approaches. Titania withdraws into herself shortly after the last practice, saying nothing and offering no more knowledge. In the forested hill overlooking the river below, they set up a smokeless camp, and so more of Titania's power is used. Branches with their needles still attached are used as bedding. Together the women contemplate their next move as they settle into a short rest.

Chapter 8

Wildlife is driven away by Niena's shuffle. She tracks down a rocky trail, following the slope and spread of the mountain. In the heavens, the sun spills over an embankment of clouds, its morning rays tumbling down the steep approach. Below, where mundane things live and plot, a freeze from the prior night has made the shade treacherous.

Slush mimics the drifts of a previous snow. "Do you think it will storm?" Niena says. A misstep sinks her foot to just below her ankles, and she is forced to grab a branch to maintain balance. Despite this, she keeps her head in the clouds, enraptured by the touch of a strong western wind on a canopy of pines.

"I don't think so," Titania says. "There are two ways weather normally passes the Isfall region: one from the sea, the other, an easterly ley. They will meet north of here, at an ancient crossing. People used to call it the dancing witches." She rolls her wrist. "Superstitious and stupid people."

"Well, we will need to find shelter sometime soon. There are fires in the comb of a hill beyond the river," Niena says. "It could be a farm. Or another tower?"

Titania snorts. "Shepherd huts — can you not smell them from here? It's autumn, and they drive their beastly flock to the mountains."

The fairy queen's hand then covers and lowers Niena's, until the gesture marks a feature between the two banks: a natural land bridge. And upon that bridge, a ring of walls and bonfires in the early morning that make the others look like fireflies in a field.

"This I find much more interesting," she says.

"What do you think that is?"

"Trouble," Titania says. "And an opportunity as well."

Niena lifts an eyebrow. "What do you mean?"

"Mmm, you will see," Titania says.

Last night, when the veil hiding the chords was weak, Titania was able to perform an augury while her granddaughter slept. Aided by the passing of a storm northwest of them, she caught the scent of magic — Rein's magic. The hunters are close. *How did he learn the spellcraft for Hearth so quickly? He must have had help, he—*

"You mean we could ask them to give us shelter," Niena says, pulling Titania out of her thoughts. "Maybe we can convince them to let us stay the night."

"We'd only get fleas," Titania says.

"Maybe we can just go around," Niena whispers.

"There is no time for that," Titania stands. "Do you remember what I said about violence?"

"That anyone who resorts to it is a fool."

"Not exactly," Titania says. "Physical violence is for fools, and those who have been fooled. But what would happen if our dear Rein were to have a little rendezvous with these shepherds? Would they offer him tea and biscuits?"

An errant breeze teases the length of Niena's hair, and a loose strand tickles her nose. "I don't appreciate hurting other people for no reason." She reaches for the itch then, but Titania catches her hand as if to say: "Others may deem that gross."

"Will they be as noble?" The fairy queen then gently caresses the girl's hand. "The fox sometimes leads the hounds around a bear's den, the feyrloch lead the ship into a storm. They always have the choice of leaving us alone."

A gale smells of wood smoke. But in the distance, there is the sound of branches cracking. Titania lifts her hand and pulls Niena around, and around, then lets her go into a glide across a patch of withered grass. She curtseys.

"I know the perfect start to this piece." Titania's right hand sweeps the tree line, and the tops of the pines sway. "A song it is then. One about winter, and the long nights that follow." Her face sheds a grimace and her hand brushes against the Ever-charm. "

"The Evercharm." Neina hesitates.

"Sing of winter. Only this. Leave the rest to me." Titania says. "Focus on the storm and the snow. Drown all other thoughts, and then start your song."

"Drown my thoughts…I'd like to know that trick to get to sleep at night."

Titania smiles. "Your snore betrays you." She lets go of Niena's hand then, tilting her own down as she walks backwards. "I must attend to the rest of it. I am sure you will do fine here."

"Wait…You aren't coming with me, are you?"

"You don't need me to hold your hand," Titania says. The fairy queen dashes to the girl, rises on her toes and bends forward, speaking again, but to her granddaughter's cheek. "Babysitting is boring."

Branches shiver above, and a cascade of snow falls between them. Veiled by the fall, Titania sinks back into the forest. She laughs softly as Niena's awareness of her fades, and the girl's head sweeps left and right, looking for her grandmother.

"Follow that row of pines on your right until you come to a path," Titania says. "Take this, and by midday it will bring you out of the cold and around warm springs, and then finally to the river basin."

Titania fades into the forest as a memory of summer. Down the footpath, where the tread of animals is lighter, whenever the stink of men can be found. Down the very side of the mountain. Noon light breaks the clouds, and the slush again melts, but it does not warm Titania's flesh. No, it too passes before her, just like the rocks and trees. For, thanks to Oberon's curse, the fairy queen is little more to the world than the wind in the willows and the murmur of a stream.

I used to be the roar of the river.

Beyond a clearing, where the sun warms the grass, she pauses. Titania seeks the river, and the ancient stone whose stories bubble in the white water. Stories that are weak, like her, but remain.

I was the thunder of spring rain before the last gasp of winter.

A path opens on her right, marshaled by overhanging trees on one side, leading down further to the shore on the other. She heeds the song of the stone and passes cattails as if she were just another breeze, the plants already dipping their heads at warm winds blowing from the sulphureous springs in the hills. Then, at once, into the river itself. The water would be cold if the fairy could feel it. It laps at her ankles. It flows through her legs. Titania laughs once more — a dark thing, full of sadness.

A half-submerged stone lies midway through the mouth of the river, and the bridge bears the markings of a ritual way-point. The anchor for a spell. The steel, for her trap. A fine mist from the river sprays constantly over the edge as it hits the boulder, but it does not touch her clothes as she approaches.

The shadow of my past. Once, long ago, the people that dwelled would gather round and tell stories. Titania mimes running her fingers into the worn grooves cut into the surface. Her lips move. Notches, to an outsider. Words, to her.

"The trap stretches from here to the cave," she whispers. The charm is a simple one. Niena's playing of the lyre will be like a beacon. "If her plan works well, the party shall be split."

Titania looks up and shows her teeth, wishing she could taste the brine of the surging river. "The elf I will catch myself or drive him into the forest with vine and lash."

Yet, the risk to Rein brings her no comfort. Titania's mouth twists as she tries to work the beginnings of her spell. But the knot in her stomach will not let her. She swallows hard.

"Not my circus." She strains the words through tight lips. "Not my monkey."

Closing her eyes allows the rush of the river to take over. She focuses on the sound, on the spray of water. Her worries and concerns become pebbles. Flotsam. Debris the river carries away from this point, to be deposited in the vastness of an ocean, where such trivial things amount to nothing.

And Titania then tells her own tale, about a cave, three would-be hunters, and the separate paths their quarry led them on.

Chapter 9

New flakes fall where they may, drifting slightly west.

"Let's get this over with," Niena says. "One storm, and no more…chords. Does Sethlan deserve this; does Rein?" She pops her thumb knuckle by rubbing it up along the fabric of her hem.

Crack. Down, where her gaze naturally falls, the rock with the little fort stands out in the morning air. Niena watches her breath steam. These men had also done nothing to them. Rein was only trying to help.

"Or maybe I am just a…" she says, then spits out the word "fool" in a huff. "Maybe Titania is right, and I am being too soft on those who don't deserve it."

Niena crumples the dress's seam between calloused fingers. Titania had claimed many things, and how much of it was true? Perhaps it didn't matter, as it seems, she was stuck with the fairy for now. It has been two days since they have even caught sight of anyone other than themselves. Only by her "grandmother's" magic have they managed not to freeze. Convenience doesn't equal trust. "I'm not useful to her dead anyways."

Niena blinks. "I think."

She'd better keep these thoughts to herself from here on.

The road splits before her. Towards a greenway, where few have trod recently. Or south. Niena touches the Evercharm on her back and shivers. It is well past midday, and the early autumn's warmth remains a stranger. *But the snow isn't touching the needles here.*

The river contrasts against the pine, here at the top of the world. Brown against green, and blue mixed between. The air is still thin, and Niena's breath thickens on her lips.

Fairy magic. She releases the crumpled edge of her dress. *My magic.* If she could go back and tell the younger Niena anything, it would be that mythic peoples in her books were nothing like the stories. Elves were terrible. Fairies were to be feared.

I had better do what she wants, and then find a way out of all this.

With the lyre in hand, she scoots over the edge of the trail and onto a boulder, then sinks to shimmy off the rock. During the descent, her eyes do not lose the palisades. A crack in a boulder teases, but several logs and other debris have pushed up against a great oak that straddles the rear. Niena gestures at the exposed roots, mapping her planned route and the angle of the leaning oak with a wave of her finger.

Do you have something to say to me, fairyblood? Those were Sethlan's words. Not long after kidnapping her. She remembers struggling against the bindings, and the taste of blood mixed with the smell of trodden earth. Most of all, it's his dark, rumbly voice she recalls. This man — *elf. He's working with Rein now.*

"Then you get what you deserve," she whispers.

Stealth and measure. A hold on a branch here. A hand on a firm bit of grass there. Slowly and surely. By now the rush of the river is louder than the wind through the canopy, and she can see a stripe of blue widen, beyond more trees, more rocks.

Yet, when she steps over a tiny stream, Niena can't help but pretend that she's a giant in dwarf country.

"Let's try something." Her hands find a clump of moss and weeds. The idea feels preposterous. Cast a spell by using a story? Niena laughs, her hand touching one of the strings. "Chords, Marny..."

This was not what the girl meant when Niena asked him if she could attend a Sagonhallo and become a Sagenhort. A storyteller, and musician, and much more: a bard. In the old tales —

"Old tales." The girl snorts, then stands and balances herself on the boulder, letting the freezing cold seep into her bones. Old tales were for men, not fairies and fairybloods like her. Were the sorcerers in Shenan able to grasp winter's hand, and lead it in a dance? No, they only spoke their words. Many probably didn't even know what they meant.

With the wind swirling, Niena closes her eyes and focuses on this chill.

"Once upon a time, a bear and a wolf shared a den," she says, her head tilting dangerously forward. "The wolf and the bear were fighting over a rabbit that had wandered into their cave."

Niena opens her eyes, roots and dirt tugging loose as she raises her arms. "Wolf, said he: You can still hunt, while I must soon sleep. But the wolf was hungry. He could not turn away the meat."

Above, the skies darken as she jumps from rock to rock.

"So, they fought," she gasps, dropping too fast and scuffing her leg. "And as they did, the little hare snuck from their cave. Summer bear and winter wolf would both go without dinner."

A small clearing offers respite, and the slope below has fewer boulders and more plant life. She stops shortly before slipping around the first of the trees on the mountain side.

"Not really tying into the whole storm thing, and it's an awful story, but maybe…" A smile sneaks along the side of her face. Testing. Testing, then appearing in full, as it begins to rain. First in a drizzle. Then, in smaller, patchier spurts. Niena frowns.

"I don't think that will do it—" The Evercharm glows warmly in her hands. Playing it was what Titania wanted. "Almost demanded…" those words tasting worse than the one, "fool", that made her spit. She sighs and unstraps the lyre.

The strings flow, coaxing out the words. Niena juts out her chin. The sensation of playing the Evercharm is electric, rippling through muscles and touching her tongue with a metallic taste. Power fills her. Niena hops over a log. And the rhythm of her song pounds away faster, and faster — slower only than the flight of her feet.

Now onto the pebble-strewn slope, where the forest is thicker but unbroken. Now onto a field carved by will and the use of fire. Wild heather rules — the smell is at once in her nose and hair. Even while the roar of the river would take her mind elsewhere.

The storm writhes behind, trailing like a wayfarer's cloak. Building. Building. And crashing through the forest by her side. Niena keeps singing. The snow and the cold answers, but still, it isn't enough. Rain threatens to catch her as she runs on. Through a stagnant pool and the dead reeds within. Onto the edge of the river itself, white water thrashing.

She sings on, while rushing towards the fortress. She sings on. While the way inclines, threatening much more. The cold rain comes with her, spilling light like lost stardust and slicking Niena's dress against her body. The battlements loom as the bird song quiets. She gasps, and the sudden inhalation of freezing air is a punch in the gut.

♫

"Chords…" Niena struggles to get up, disorientated. Weak. Thunder booms around her. The storm rages. "How long have I been here?"

Excitement and spells. Both can take their measure, together, they are dangerous. Her gaze floats. The flames from the fires take center stage, sputtering, fighting. Men cast temporary shadows; a few. She can see through the storm, and the light along the battlements makes them appear as grim things from some ancient barrow.

"Titania?" Niena tries to cover the Evercharm's glow. "Where are you?"

The cold of the stone and the water lapping at her feet sends a tremble up her unprotected leg. She gulps the air. Wind rushes past, ripples the cattails — and, dusting everything in a fine layer of snow, it sweeps up, up the rampart lane. Niena moves, cautiously, touching a boulder half submerged in the muck with the tip of her fingers. Shouts on the battlements force her to hide in the water. *They have cut steps in the cliff face.*

"Do not cower now, child," Titania says, attempting to grasp Niena's arm. A second attempt from the fairy queen snatches the hem of a sleeve. "You definitely made a show of strength."

The return of warmth shocks, as does the hand around her waist. Niena tries to spin but is held firm. Titania's laughter meets her, high and barking, like those fat and lazy creatures that sometimes warmed themselves on Sunford's docks.

"Don't be so bloody dull."

"Be quiet!" Neina protests. "We are too close; they will see us."

"See and hear, daughter's child," she says. Titania then clasps Niena's left hand and pulls her from the boulder with a spin.

"What the chords are you doing?"

"Someone needs to teach you how to dance," Titania says.

"They'll prickle us with arrows," Niena whines.

"In this wind? If you are going to lead, you need to be more confident."

Fine circles in the clay enclose them; conspicuously, the toes of Titania's shoes are muddy.

"Count girl, count."

A single flake drifts with them, flipping in time to the sound of Titania's voice: "One, two, three. One, two, three. Keep your feet moving." The first flake is joined by another. Then a third. Then many more.

"Move your hand higher," Titania says. "And don't stare at your feet, now…"

Niena nearly stumbles as they spin. Above, the stars protrude from an embankment of clouds. Nearby, the fires on the wall answer a breeze, sending sparks up into the air to double the number of heavenly bodies as they gather on the canvas of dusk.

Wait. Stars? She must have looked stricken, or gawped, for the fairy queen's resulting laughter is jubilant.

Titania tilts her head. "You didn't notice? You spun a song. You spun time, and as such were wrapped up into it. You are no longer the ignorant little girl. There are consequences to knowing." She leans slightly forward and clucks her tongue. "So, what are we to do?"

The snow sweeps across, threatening to turn Titania's hair white. Niena shivers. Finally, when enough breaths have passed between them for her grandmother's spell of warmth to falter, and the chill of the night marks each with steam, Titania backs away and sings:

We gather near an apple tree,
And see the withered leaves,
Of hollow flesh and broken limbs,
Left on midsummer's eve.

Nature fights against the magic. The fairy queen wraps her hands around the girl's arms as the spell echoes.

"What are you doing?" Niena says, dress billowing.

"The cold has its hands on your storm, but they aren't really dancing yet."

Niena shivers, hunching her shoulders against the wind bounding off the wall to her back. Her grandmother pulls closer, smiling. When their eyes meet, Niena is hit by the feeling of a warm sun on a field of grass, and in this moment, she forgets the cold. A nudge turns the girl's head to the top of the battlements, and to its gate.

"It's starting to freeze over," Niena says while Titania begins the second stanza.

The unnatural heat has baked the land,
And murdered our dear wood,
So, bring the women and lay the tomb,
With holly and maidenhood.

The storm howls and bites like a caged creature. With the wind comes the distant crack of wood in the forest behind. The chill hits them, pushing Niena against the wall.

"Chords, it's going to be a blizzard," she whispers.

The song ends, but the storm does not. Niena's gaze is forced towards the shoreline, and the mountain they left. But Titania pulls her into the rock face, pressing the girl's back against it. The cold is shocking, causing Niena's shoulders to twitch even with the spell of warmth working through Titania's fingers.

"The spell will not last long," Titania says. The fairy queen smiles, a flash of excitement chased by pain. She dips in a mock curtsey. "Do you know the game of foxes and hounds?"

"Can we just go?" Niena says, shivering through clenched teeth. She looks west. "I don't want to stay here."

Titania's arm rises to snuff the girl's protest as if it were a candle, and the fairy's hand the cap. A hiss shudders out of the forest, and Titania stares into Niena's eyes. Her cold, strange eyes. The fairy swallows, turning back to the girl. "Not before I lead the dogs to the bear's den."

Chapter 10

"I wouldn't…"

Wind howls over the guards' heads.

"…do that…" Grimweld yells again.

Torches make the air between the two men crackle. With the draft goes the clouds, and with those leaving, the temperatures settle. This is the hour of the veil for the mountain folk of the Isfall region, dwelling in a nameless hold — an ominous ruin on the edge of the Huldhorn.

"Your breath is vile." Rogard winces in jest.

The older guard to his left fidgets, adjusts a strap that appears too loose for his bent frame, too thick for his thinness. Elsewhere, the faint glow of the ritualistic torches drives away the darkness. It also ruins these guards' sight, but the fires are not meant for them.

"Do you think they will let us turn in early?" Rogard chances more of his girth onto a low wall. Battlement. The stonework's crumbling façade barely remembers being anything more than a fence. Distant thunder adds punctuation, pauses.

At first, every four words.

Rogard stretches. "Or was that damn witch, eh, was she really expecting us to sit here all night?" Nearby, Grimweld shuffles. "Nothing to do but listen to the goats shit in the fields."

Then every five.

"Though I'd say your singing is worse, Grimweld."

Thunder rolls softly. The air is heavy. Rogard's compatriot, the old guard Grimweld, mutters something under his breath. But all sound between them is fouled. Time passes, takes the last of the thunder, and the storm as well. Neither of the guards are armed in the conventional sense, but Grimweld's fingers dig into an unlit faggot.

"Tried Brannin's latest?" Rogard says.

The old man spits. "No."

"You're not missing anything."

"Then why'd you mention it? Just like hearing yourself talk, eh?"

Rogard regards his scowling partner. Shadows highlight deep lines and an almost skeletal brow.

"Chords, what are they thinking, making—" The wind shifts. Sparks from the torch hiss past, followed by a volley of Rogard's curses.

"Told you not to stand there."

Off comes Rogard's patchwork gambeson. Off comes his leather gloves, while embers bite into his oiled beard. He stumbles, dislodging a stone from the wall. Next, he unthreads a brass ring that affixes his beard to a belt. The wind turns again. Grimweld's helping hand secures the younger guard while he snuffs out the last of the flames.

The old man's quick laughter falters, as something else wins over. Grimweld pushes past the younger and looks out into the black. His nose turns against the wind.

"What are you huffing about?" Rogard growls at the push. Below, their perch is a set of wide stairs, used more by the livestock than men. "Ahh, no, I am not cleaning that up. It can stay there."

"Fif." Grimweld grunts. "It is not the goats."

"Your wife, then?"

The old man inhales violently. When he speaks, he says only five words: "What did the witch say?"

"No, no, no, no. We are not getting into that," Rogard says. "You always get this way."

"The fires. Keep the fires high."

The elders follow her every word. All of them. Rogard remembers the dusty book that was dragged from recesses hitherto unknown. He recalls the smell of blood and smoke, of words whose meaning not even his grandfather remembers. And, of course, of the lighting of the fires.

"It's not the first time she's gibbered about portents, and doom," the younger guard says. Despite himself, he lowers his voice to almost a whisper. "Might be that she had too much sour milk tonight?"

"Never, not since…" Grim's voice trails off.

Menfolk of his age looked upon the old mistress with the same eyes that he held now — reverent, fearful.

"You confuse her with that milksop apprentice," Grim adds. "That farmhand's girl."

Most of Rogard's mates took it like they do everything: with mulled ale, and boredom. "That doesn't mean…"

"Stay close to the fires," Grimweld hisses. "The old enemy is here."

Time hisses like damp wood in a fire, or the harried breath of the two guards. And the two take different positions on the wall. Grimweld, crook-necked and wide-eyed, hovering over the battlements. Rogard languidly behind and further from the precipice.

The night is elsewise quiet between them. Rogard's mind drifts. He thinks back to other times, other duties, in other camps. Real jobs for a chieftain, or at least his own stock. He reminisces about watching the rain stream down the sides of old gates, flowing past rivets as if they were boulders in the way of a river. He remembers the warm, greasy mutton. The bitter ale. His other work those last years was not quite so cheery. The tombs, for instance. Many times, he was tasked with being the lone sentinel to one. Because the dead never sleep, and the people of Isfall fear them the most.

The dead have a lot of time to think on old grudges.

Those camps were lonely — lonely, in drafty halls where decaying tapestries flutter. The seasons would change. The time of day, too. But it was always cold. Always dark, and food then more a meager affair; dried meats, and bread. He prefers the rain and the mutton.

Amidst the howling of the wind, snowfall comes. Rogard barely acknowledges it with a raised eyebrow. Snow is common in this area, even during the summer. In autumn, it is nearly regular. He snorts, and leans on the battlements.

Yet the memory of Maro Unsterbbēriz is different. There was no warmth there, keeping watch in one of the few hospitable towers on the blasted plain, on the Drachzehr. Or inside the city itself. Just the memories of the nights he patrolled the city doomed by dragon's fire makes him shiver.

The young guard looks up, and scowls at the change in the weather now. "Looks heavy; just what we need." Rogard grumbles.

White upon white dusts the old guard's eyebrows. "Tssst! Do you hear that, boy?"

There is the wind. The torches — snow dying to the flames. Rogard shakes his head, but Grimweld catches him by the sleeve of his tunic. Their glares lock, but the old man's face seems expectant, and worried. And then Rogard hears it. The soft tones of a "…woman's voice?"

"Singing," Grimweld growls. "Demons."

"Women," pulling back from the old man's icy touch. "But close enough."

"Don't be a fi…a fool."

Through the glare of the torches, the snowfall intensifies. With it comes a bitter cold — a chill that sinks the heavy air and digs into the bones of old and young alike. Grimweld acts first, moving quickly to stock a nearby pit. The fire smokes and sputters over the dampened wood, and a stash of faggots nearby proves no less soiled. Rogard joins him, and together they work to pry the wood apart. In the end, clumps of it get thrown into pits, threatening the flames as much as the snow falling all around. And it is for little reward. A white sheen quickly separates the two guards from their vision beyond the wall, cutting them off faster than any blade. The battlements dust over, then the very ground turns treacherous.

"We need the charms," Grimweld shouts through chittering teeth. "The words in your satchel, quickly."

But the leather of Rogard's glove breaks and cracks as he fights with the drawstring. The chill marches through them in waves of snow, in translucent fingers of ice. A lump of parchment disappears into the snow.

"No time," he yells, "Quick, into the long house."

Upon the wall. On their person. More and more. A tug at his side is Grim, almost hidden by the storm, grasping his arm as he tries to remain upright. The old man's hand is rigid and needles into his arm. Rogard, though, is young, and strong. He heaves into Grim with his shoulder and lifts the man up and over, stumbling forward as he seeks the earth-covered center building.

One by one, the torches sputter in the onslaught on his periphery. And neither the warmth of their dwindling embers nor a cloak drawn closely spares either guard. Rogard crushes ice that has formed in his left hand, the crunch and crackle of his linen tunic quiet against the roar of the storm. There is a sound of something heavy hitting wood, and he wipes away the frost clouding his face to discover that the noise was the thud of Grim's body against the door of the longhouse. He tries to call out to the other guards as he stumbles through, but the words are stolen from his lips before they form.

♫

"Ao chem amac an dora…"

Sethlan flinches, his face bitten by a sudden and harsh wind. The squall takes the rest of Rein's spell-chant from the elf's ears and shreds it, throwing the pieces all around his face. Freezing rain cuts him in spirals as the Inspector's voice quavers.

"Agusa st… shagal ele…"

More of the frigid little needles scream in his ear. The air ripples. Biting back a curse against all E'tah and their drycraft, Sethlan forces himself to face the rift. Flashes of lightning from the portal show him glimpses of what's waiting for them on the other side.

"A river?" Sethlan's tone rises. But the scene morphs as if it were a cloud in the sky. "A cave. Your magic does not appear stable."

An unwelcome hand on his shoulder makes him tense, and he turns to glare at Rein's wide apprentice, Higgins. Sethlan's lips draw back, and the desire to slap the little man's hand away wells up. But he relents.

"Get ready man — eh, elf…devil take it," Higgins says, apparently oblivious. "Get ready to go through."

"I am always ready," Sethlan says. As he turns back, a dash of snow hits the rift and the flakes mist. "The spirit of the night trembles in fear. Not I."

Further tides of winter ripple down the sides of the mountain. Snowflakes spiral through the portal, making Sethlan raise his hand then stare on in stunned silence as they melt into beads on his sleeve.

"There is something wrong here," he hisses to Higgins as he passes. It's more than the portal, he's already endured two of those. No, his entire body feels like it is on fire, as if his instincts are trying to warn him.

"Snathad a taran sithlen a cruthaid."

"Rein's nearing the end of the spell, I think," Higgins says. "Best we get moving."

Sethlan hesitates, then ushers the apprentice out of his way as Christaan De Rein's voice gains a birdlike lilt. *This is not that pompous sorcerer's drycraft.*

"There is fairy magic in the air," he says to the Inspector — to the haggard, aged visage of Rein. Sethlan steps to the side. "We should retreat and track them as before."

"No," Higgin says, gesturing towards his master. Rein's fingers splay before the rift, and his lips work in increasingly heavier and more pronounced motions. "It's already too late to back out; stopping now could kill him."

The hour is late. The rift shudders, and Higgins motions for Sethlan to hurry through. The elf flicks at the string securing his knives and does as bid. At once the usual sensations flood him. Feelings of being stationary collide with the sensation of movement. There is a roving soreness. And bouts of fear, too, scraping the length of his body, directed almost like an errant sunbeam.

E'tahs. How much can they know of me, of the ancient Sethlan, who has hunted the worlds for an age? It is true, this. The incalculable years of service to his Matriarch. The long dedication to the hunt, and the humiliation of his one mistake: giving magic to mankind. He never had the cruelty of his brother, Culsan, but that will not stop him from testing his knives on either the Inspector or the apprentice if they dare to betray him.

The elf tosses back his head to laugh, but instead is suddenly thrown forward. All the former sensations — the fear, the strange twisting pain — end abruptly. Sethlan heaves upon exiting the rift, then swallows his breath. His past meal lurches in the back of his stomach, and he collapses into the snow.

Give me two eons, and I would still never get used to that.

Hand over hand, the elf pushes himself to his feet. Snow slides off his hair and face, and as he draws himself up, he encourages the rest of the flakes to depart his clothing with a few well-placed tugs. The air is clear. The sky as a thin layer of black silk laid over a dimming light. Sethlan takes in a deep breath, savoring the freshness as he flexes his fingers.

Immediately he again senses the wrongness from before as the clouds dampen the sky like spilled ink on canvas, ruining the dusk and dipping the land into complete darkness. The hairs on Sethlan's arms stick up, brushing against his silk sleeve. "We should be careful. I do not like—"

A squelching noise grabs his attention, turning him towards the portal — or where the portal should be. Instead, there is only a ripple in the air. Worse is the extreme lack of Mannelig presence thereupon.

Sethlan's finger traces the faint outline of the moon as it tries to escape the storm, south.

"I appear to have arrived under the tor on the western face of a joining mountain," Sethlan says. His head hunches down, then arches, and he sways this way and that. "The air is heavy."

There is no shelter nearby. Nothing else stands out from which he can gather his bearings. He scans the skyline, north and west. "There." His eyesight adjusts. The mountain he came from is a luminescent outline against the black canvas, but it is recognizable enough for the elf. Good news for once.

"No, good is different," Sethlan says. He then lifts his finger to the air and listens.

Snowfall rages around him, and the flakes that he shook off before are fast replaced. "There is a powerful song on the air. The chords are being plucked." White dusts his hair. On his vest. Face. The elf brushes away the melt from his lips. "I will learn nothing from weather craft this hour."

Something happened to Rein's spell, and Sethlan cannot rule out a trap. Therefore, a decision looms. Should he continue after the girl and the Evercharm or reunite with the party? The former seems sweeter, but the latter leaves a bitter aftertaste. Medicinal. Sethlan spits, knowing from many years of experience which path he should take. Still, it does not help it go down any better.

"To the river," he says.

The first foot onward nearly throws the elf to the ground. The second is hardly any better. The way is treacherous. Sethlan adjusts his rhythm instinctively, but still struggles through the shifting and treacherous terrain. Fast storms are one thing; it is not the first time he has been overtaken. Fairy storms are another. Those happen less. The crack of wood and the layering of the ice on the trees tell him it is also time for his own spell work.

So, he tells a story.

"Once upon a time, the gods and goddesses held council to find the truth of Baldr's dreams."

Sethlan shimmies over whitening boulders. Past the shattered trunks of trees. He stops, then slides under a thicket, and whispers the name "Othin," letting the wind pick it up and carry it away.

Much that fell in those moments remains, and a blanket of snow covers the ground so that no grass can be seen. Sethlan clears his throat. *"Othin, that enchanter of old, rose and sought the answer."*

Forging a way through the trees makes him face a decision, for a clear trail has emerged, heading south and around the mountain. It is a tempting prospect and could lead to the Manneligs. A gamble. Sethlan shivers and stops beside a tree split down the middle by an early storm. Meltwater flies from his head, but he is unable to shake the feeling that he, the eldest of his line, is being hunted.

"Through Nifel. To the high house of Hel. Unto the grave of a wise woman, where through charm and mighty spells he bound her, and she did rise."

There are no fires in the forest. No dry wood for the making of them. Sethlan tugs at dart from under his cloak, then draws it slowly.

"And the woman's shade did answer thus: who is this stranger that has made me travel this troubled road?"

At the mention of the word *road*, the trail along the path dims, but a new way through the forest proper brightens.

Sethlan turns towards the spell work slowly. *"I was snowed on with snow. I was smitten with rain and drenched with dew. Long have I been de—"*

Laughter interrupts his story, and the path dims. *Is it from the right?* Where trees march with trees, nearly hand to hand. *Or the left?* But all he sees there are blankets of white and more of the storm's soldiers flying around him.

"I have tasted your kin's blood," Sethlan yells. "Will you be next, oh queen?"

The crackle of wood is the answer, and Sethlan lunges just in time to be engulfed by a white cloud, avoiding a stricken tree but losing his weapon. He curses, wiping his eyes, only to be greeted with more laughter. He leaps over a snow embankment.

"Aeval, Lyerg," he yells. "Do you know these names? Uris—"

Splinters pierce the embankment, his long coat, flesh — the force throws him backwards, and he, too, falls. "*Bac*," cursing as he lays his hand on a dagger-sized piece of wood embedded in his side.

The remains of the tree groan as they collapse further into the snow. Laughter does not follow the attack this time, only the growl of the wind pushing, clawing, and rising.

Sethlan's head jerks up. The storm intensifies, a sheen of white fast covering his wounds before he can tend to them. Noise on his right draws his attention there, then back to the left and to the glint of his discarded dart. He takes a deep breath and closes his eyes.

Wind surges in the canopy, and the elf's eyes open. He lunges towards the weapon, narrowly missing a branch's fall hidden by the wind.

"How are you going to work this into another glorious hunt, elf?" Titania's voice slips in under the wind, rising in mocking tones with the gusts.

The forest is then quiet. Waiting. Blood slicks a thin piece of wood when the elf draws it from his wound. There are more, but this is the worst. With the same hand, he secures the dart, pressing it against the injury.

"I wonder how many stories about you are actually true," she says.

The sentence ends with another volley of biting wind. And worse. The wreckage of the two trees sundered by her magic rise from the ground and fly towards the elf as if tossed by a giant. But a lateral move mostly spares him from harm, the greater part of the tree smashing into a still rooted pine.

When Sethlan hits the snow, he does not stop running. Over snow drift. Threading the needle through a patch of thickets. Forward to the river. But more than the wind is upon him:

Trees shatter and fall all around, dusting the air with debris and fibers from split branches.

An inopportune cough steals his focus for only a second, but it is enough to force the elf into a tumble to avoid more sylvan projectiles. At the end, he rolls onto his knees, clutching his weapon close. The storm rages, threatens to steal the last of his warmth. And then there is another presence.

Not the fairy queen, though she must be here as well. No, this one does not hide, but is further away. Perhaps just behind him in the place where he landed. The elf has sensed this one's type previously, back among the Manneligs before the mountain. Back during the time when he and his brother Culsan made their deal with the Teamor. Sethlan turns left, then scatters towards a small field. There, he puts himself in the center.

The Udur draw close. "There are no trees here, fairy," he says. "Nothing for you to use as a weapon but your own two hands. Come."

"Bold," Titania says, her voice seeming to emerge from the forest canopy like a family of thrush after a crow. "Bold, but wrong."

The ground shakes. Sethlan falls to one hand and puts the dart to his lips. He looks past the forest to the mountain side, and his eyes grow wide before they shut abruptly.

"What marvel is it I saw before the Delling's door?" The elf whispers a spell to his weapon. There is a heavy noise, far up in that mountain, but Sethlan does not look that way. Instead, he stares ahead.

Perhaps the sound is a thump.

His eye twitches, glancing right. There was a brief image. A sudden face amongst the knots of wood. Could it be more than that? *"Upward it flies with an eagle's voice,"* Sethlan says, then twists right, slowly so that his legs are ready to spring. *"And with a hard grip, it claws the helmet."*

The sound intensifies. The description of it belies the point. It was a warning of impending danger. Sethlan jerks to left, then throws the dart right with a backhand. It flies true, striking the breast of a great oak, but not before passing through something else entirely.

He ignores the surprised scream that follows, and turns to a run — run, as the trailing edge of the avalanche rumbles through the forest.

Chapter 11

It is still night. Sethlan's eyelids flicker open, starlight barely reaching him in the tree wherein he hides. The elf twists his shoulder, careful of his many small wounds. Below, the ground is covered in mist. He strayed too far. Sethlan suppresses the desire to focus on every crunch, every rustle of leaf. To look over one's shoulder and spy the threat. The Udur are nearby, but they have not found him.

Yet.

He peers through the tangle of leaves and vines, feeling the ebb and flow of the Udur's dread: their ancient shroud. Sethlan does not move. His breathing is slight. Patience is something that comes naturally to a thousands-year-old elf.

One. He slides along a branch, letting his arms support all his weight. *Two.* He sucks in his breath, lowering himself along the slick bark. Then stops. A long *three* follows, as the spindly demons move soundlessly below. *Four.*

Wind rattles the branches at the same time that Sethlan's feet hit the undergrowth. He whips his hair back and quickly scans left and right after seeing thorns barring his way forward. *Five.*

A high wail behind him makes him wince, and the bay is soon joined by others, farther away. *Six. Seven.* His throat tightens. *Nine.*

Like a loosed arrow, Sethlan cuts through the forest. Fear rides his heels. His head swivels ever so slightly as he bounds over rocks, saplings, and into the thick of the forest. Only the goosebumps down his arms tell him the Udur are upon him.

At an overgrown path, he hesitates, sliding over a patch of wet leaves and filling his nose with the scent of their crushing. Sethlan sinks to the ground, realizing now that his mad dash has taken him further from the river and deeper into the forest.

A tendril of mist solidifies around a sapling, just to his right. At once thick. Then, in an instant, gone. He steps forward, teeth barred. Each inch is bought in painful, slow breaths as Sethlan finds his way. The dread of the Udur is almost palatable.

To his left, he catches the quick change from mist. Beaks, this time, erupt from an undulating mass, then disappear in a cloud. Setlhan resists shaking his head. *They are pulling the trap closed.*

The knife mirrors the inky blackness of the dark. Obsidian, and eldritch. Still, he carefully hides the blade in his hand. *Deep.* Blankets of moss hang from a nearby tree, and the sweet odor ruins his sense of direction. *To deep.* But the sounds of the river tickle his ears, and he tilts his head this way and that, as quick as a deer and as slight in his movements.

Something else. He stands up from his crouch. *Voices? Bells?* He cups his ear and listens. Outside of the night fowl. Away from the crickets, the chorus of frogs. And close. *Awfully close.* Pieces of conversations emerge from the thickets alongside, and singing in rough voices that can only belong to Manneligs. They bellow a low, melancholy dirge that travels along the roots and ruts of the old forest. Sethlan's heart lurches when he realizes the noises are coming closer.

He scans the forest, then remembers the path just behind him. The elf spins that way, seeing several shapes writhe in the periphery. *Trapped.* The old path is there, though, only a few feet away. But if the E'tah even come, it will be too late.

Sethlan swallows. A ripple flows along the nameless dark before him, and the obsidian blade is cool in his hand. Reassuring. While the handle of his long knife is too hot. Sweaty. The wheels of a cart squawk in the foreground. He draws the weapons and bares his teeth.

At once, the night explodes with the Udur's terrible cries. All other sounds, bird calls, the trespass of the men in the forest, quail before it. But Sethlan does not. Without a word, without a challenging shout, he launches himself at the formless mass.

The long knife slides out and into his lunge, dipping low at the last moment as Sethlan evades the beak of an Udur suddenly bearing down. Yet pain flares from every side as old wounds mix with new, and tentacles – emerging out of the once empty air — hit, pierce, and slash into the elf. Sethlan's lunge flows into a roll, which in turn sends the elf popping up and over another attack, and the thorny brush between Sethlan and the Udur, where he hits the ground on his hands and knees. Clumsily.

Sweaty hands slap the ground in successive heartbeats, and the elf wobbles in that split second to his feet, then staggering once more into a run. The Udur, unaffected by blade or thorn, have no such issue. They swarm, flow, and shift through the bracken.

The new wounds provide the Udur with a fresh trail. Grass, weeds, and growth softened by the mist — not all of it born from horrors — crush in sighs underneath Sethlan's shoes. All around him, the hounds of the Teamor pursue. *I must keep to the path—*

A gust of wind briefly forces his eyes closed, letting the smell of livestock, the decay of the forest, and his own blood win over his senses. But the tendrils of the void spawn close in.

Mist bleeds into the overgrown road. Sethlan lurches over obstacles seen and unseen, while the monsters in the periphery pursue. He forces breath in. Then another. The elf must keep to the path, but they already likely encircle him.

Silver bells, but why here?

A hidden root causes him to stumble. Sethlan throws his hands forward, as fatigue and injury hurl him to the ground. The racket of the humans passing is near, perhaps just on the other side of this thicket. He crawls, forcing himself to stare forward. The Udur's presence laps at the corners of his perception like an ill-boding tide.

For several minutes, Sethlan lies there, not daring to move or call out while the men shuffle along their road, the clear sound of silver bells preceding each step. Yet the Udur remain. Fixed. Sethlan looks down his nose. The way forward is ringed in mist, but as he turns his head slightly to the right, he notices that the path is clear — the way towards the road.

E'tah attract E'tah. I could use them, somehow.

Hand by hand, he manages to pull himself to his feet. The Udur's presence recedes. The noise of the coming human caravan rises. His options clear, Sethlan warily reenters the forest and slinks towards the sound of the Manneligs.

Their lights disturb the night. Ruin it. However, these torches seem like a barrier. Weak. Flimsy. The bells must be meant to ward off fey influence. Likely they will have carts made from rowan trees, and ash staves too. Sethlan considers. None of this is meant for the void spawn, which means some other power must be holding the Udur back. Still, it is a barrier, one towards which he cautiously moves.

I cannot join them. He grits his teeth. *I will not.* The shapes of men, their beasts, and belongings parade through the foliage, illuminated by the poor light cast from the makeshift torches, and seen by the elf as a strange menagerie in the deep. He waits, counting their numbers as they pass. Sethlan returns his long knife to its place, hidden in a fold and sheathed by ram's leather. The obsidian dagger remains, cupped in his left hand. *But I can use these Manneligs. Gather information. Perhaps they can even help him find Rein and Higgins.*

He could also prey on them. The Udur likely wait on their fringes — perhaps so commanded by the fairy queen, though the import and danger in that is not worth considering currently. He could prey on the E'tah, take from them, as his own range and freedoms are limited.

The dregs wind past. Those who are either too poor or too wretched to be among the rest. And the children. There is little play amongst these, the dour mood of the elders affecting them. Sethlan squints and slips into the brush, following the tail.

I mustn't be discovered. The obsidian blade is cold against his palm. The image of his brother's pursed lips pops unbidden into mind, and he almost laughs. *Yes, Culsan. It will indeed be a delicate dance.*

Through a crop of tall grass waving in the moonlight, and alongside a cobbled road — for he has truly found himself on a proper road — are several children. There is an argument going on among them, as their voices rise in angry tones. *I was always the better dancer, my brother.*

One of them is pushed to the ground, and something is taken. Sethlan crouches, gently sliding aside the leaves and foliage from a patch of saplings. It is a little girl, and a boy stands over her. The elf settles into the mud, watching as the prone child tearfully reaches out. The boy hesitates. Turns his head to the right, where the others, presumably his friends, goad and pull him away from the girl.

These older children leave, taking their laughter with them, but abandon the little girl in the middle of the road. And for a moment, the elf considers doing the same, until the memory of Culsan brings a thought, unbidden and uncomfortable, to mind.

My brother would seek to capture her first. Sethlan squirms and pops his neck, the sound to him as fire in a dry forest, but the little girl does not notice. The elf watches as she stands — *I am not my brother.* Though even by Culsan's standards, the usual sport of the elves was rather unpalatable. The two always stood apart from most of their kin.

The child dawdles as the last cart of the caravan creaks away. She stares intently at something in her hands. Sethlan hides. Her curly hair catches the starlight just so, but he can see little else of her features. *Once he had his information, he would dispose of her. It is the wise thing to do.* The knife is cold against his palm, while the presence of the Udur remains curiously distant. He steps closer, then stops, running his thumb along the flat of the blade. After a quick glance, he feels confident there is no one else. His shoulders relax.

But I am not my brother.

Sethlan cups his right hand to his lips. His bird call makes the girl drop whatever she was holding. He sniffs, and moves in.

Upon seeing him, she hesitates, watching him intently as he gets to one knee.

"What is your name, child?"

The girl lifts her face, dark as night but moon-kissed. "Abria," she says in a squeak.

"Abria," he repeats. The elf's movements are slow. Measured, even while wounded, and the wonder in the child's eyes reflects this. "Do you like riddles?"

Her nose twitches. "Riddles are stupid," which draws a quick huff from the elf, and Abria reflexively moves back. "You shouldn't be talking to strangers."

"Me?" The elf blinks, then relaxes his shoulders with a slight roll. "What do I have to fear from you, child?"

"I can scream really loud."

"So, no riddles," Sethlan says, smiling. "How about a game, then?"

"What type of game?"

He kneels, lowering himself to her eye level. "The kind that your other friends won't like."

Chapter 12

Something is wrong. The hem of Rein's coat tore away from Higgins's hand hours ago, leaving him alone in this space between worlds. Desolation, however, turns to fear as darkness streams away, replaced by a real tempest and a fast-approaching reality.

"Rein," Higgins yells before the plunge.

Dutchman!

A shock of cold smacks his body, then the river rushes over him. Touches of white and gray whirl with peeks of a near shore and the night sky — and in those few moments the stars appear, and he gulps air, only to spit it back out again when striking rocks, logs, and the river bottom. Higgins's teeth chatter, threatening his tongue.

Lord—

A chance of snatching at some weeds disappears as his head bounces on a stump and the breath explodes from his lungs. Broken sticks and muck seem to find their way into every opening in his trousers.

Under.

Save me!

The water deepens as he is taken further from the shore. He flails randomly, the motion popping his head out of the water long enough for only a quick breath.

Under.

A shadow rushes overhead as Higgins's back smacks against a boulder, knocking the last air out of him with an explosion of bubbles. *A log.* Seeing the opportunity, he kicks hard several times against the silt. His fingers glance off the slimy bark the first time, but a lucky spin sends the bushy end of a branch his way.

Under.

Pine needles slip from his grasp, and he hits something in the river, his ride snapping the other way. Higgins hangs on by the thin end of a dead limb.

This is it.

The log jerks sideways and then, together, both snap up. Log and apprentice collide with each other under the surface. He reaches out. The river throws a cloud between him and the fallen tree, but on the second attempt, Higgins manages to wrap his thick arms around it, both tumbling over, and over in and out of the water.

By God's blood, I am going to be shitting through my teeth. He then tries to say this out loud, but it comes out more as, "Mmmmph."

Under and over.

A chance snag on another large rock lets Higgins right himself, and he claws his way to a better position. Here the river slows, and for the first time in several minutes he can breathe and see more than water and mud.

The wine list on this rendezvous was lacking.

With a grunt, he pulls a twig out of his mouth. To his far left, an upturned tree has created a little cove. Ducks play about in this, oblivious of the man who floats by. Higgins spits out another leaf. *I have no Schistostega Pennata for the Forme of a full seeing spell.* Yet without some aid here, he could easily be swept away. *But maybe just the first part will still help?*

The apprentice scrambles to raise as much of himself out of the water. He focuses, drawing his breath in slowly, then speaks the Étincelle and Mort in two short, staccato huffs. *"Faican dorch."*

Without any strength, or magical ingredient, the best he can manage is to adjust his eyes quicker to the night. It is enough for now.

The log spins slowly, revealing wild land clutching to a shimmering blue in the night, like a ribbon winding around the flat of a bonnet. Mycah spackles a bare hill, catching the starlight and reflecting patterns of the night sky above — mockery in miniature, and looking all the while fey and dangerous.

Higgins, for his part, just clings on, his face partially buried into a mess of twigs and leaves. The night, the flight of clouds, and the passing of the last storm jealously hide most of the mountainous slope. What he sees further ahead is covered in deep lines of snow and ice.

Somewhere in that mess is his mentor. "This is a disaster," his gaze taking in the shore. Rocks and sand glitter. The current slows more.

"I'm going to have to find Rein — and the bloody elf, if we are to salvage any of this."

A tracking spell on top of the last, then. If the fairy wasn't tipped off before, she would be now. His mind takes a small trip, shaken free by the last winds of a dying storm. *Shi...* Higgins's clears his throat. "I've been spending too much time around Rein. It's not a matter of bad breeding. Lord knows, I am just a peasant. But those Dutch..."

He gurgles, and spits. The river rolls the log lengthwise after hitting a submerged rock. Over and over, until he manages to set his weight in the crook of its former bough, nearest to where it must have broken off. A second adjustment keeps his head above the water, but only just.

"Well, he's not at the bottom of the river," Higgins gasps. "Bastard's humor is so dry it'd soak it all up."

Cold seeps into his muscles. Deep and heavy. Higgins paws at the branches, trying to pull himself further out of the water. But the drowsiness settling in is so inviting. If he were just to relax...

Higgins's growl is helped by the water he sputters out. The apprentice takes one long look at the shore's outline and his log, then grabs on tightly. "If I bloody well die again," he whispers as he kicks, "that man will never let me hear the end of it."

The shore, however, is another two hundred yards away. And there is worse, for when the apprentice looks at where the river's current wants to take him, he is treated to the outline of what could be a natural bridge, and the passage under it is choked with ice.

"In bloody autumn!"

Higgins winces as a wave dunks him briefly again into the soup. He shakes his head, vision blurring, and bites down on the log. Here he uses the pain seeping into his joints to push harder, and for his efforts is rewarded both by closing half the distance and by the fact that the natural bridge is a fort.

Shapes scurry along what must be the battlements. Higgins groans but keeps kicking. The ice he saw earlier now materializes, forcing him to pick his way through the melting obstacles. At a small crook before the bridge, his log is caught in a glut of debris and Higgins abandons it, diving.

Under.

Moonlight filters through the floating muck above, only just. Everything aches, but he fights on. To a tangle of weeds and ice. Through flash frozen mud at the shore, until he can't hold his breath any longer and must thrust his head up for air. Almost simultaneously, his arms land on the bank. Ice crackles and snaps as he drags his girth along, wetting weeds and grass with the tails of his soaked coat. Here, next to a stump, Higgins collapses.

A bird cries, quickly followed by rustling nearby. More fowl join, gossiping. Higgins props himself up on one elbow and wipes his eyes. Everything is covered in a dismal pouch of snow. The apprentice mouths the words for a spell of light, then stops halfway to cough.

A quick breath. The feeling of his knuckles cracking. All pass before the rustling stops. But when it does, the shore falls into silence, so completely and without warning that it steals the apprentice's next thought. Higgin swallows. A vague dread freezes him, and a feeling reminiscent of his time on the resurrection table pins him down. *Right before the Udur were upon us.*

Slowly, he stands, fighting his own muscles for every inch. He takes a step, his gaze sifting through the few weeds poking out of the snowdrifts. There are voices. He can't make out what is being said.

"It's Rein; he's come for me," he whispers over his shoulder, half delirious. Higgins rubs his knees with one free hand, the other clutching the wall. "The man's as unbreakable as your mother's scones."

But as he scrambles through the mud, Higgins finds he needs more than just words to keep him going. Touching the face of a rock sends a wave of goosebumps up his arm. Higgins mumbles and pats his forehead with a wet handkerchief.

"Blath mo chaman."

Pinpricks of power light up along his frame, and steam rises off his coat. The hiss is louder than the sound of approaching boots, both of which the apprentice ignores to idly wring the handkerchief. He staggers, the spell having sapped much of his remaining strength for a little warmth.

He returns his hand to the rock. The cold brings back those bleak moments after death, like watching his body bob in the ocean.

"Rein?" he calls.

Shouts answer behind him. One voice low. One high. Higgins falls to a knee, and tugs at his days' old beard. The voices seem to shift as the world itself spins. Higgins closes his eyes. Their intensity grows, and one voice crawls along the left. The other almost echoes in his head.

"Bloody hell," he barks. "Is that you, Dutchman?" His vision never fully cleared, and now the shapes of three men appear to melt into a ruddy mess.

There is a sharp pain in his left shoulder, followed by a heavy force thudding into his midsection. The apprentice cries out as he crashes back into the murky river. "Devils," he yells again.

Men. Savages. Their red hair flashes over the brown of their wool as they rush to circle the apprentice. Each clutches a spear, and each wears a feral snarl upon their face. One by one, Higgins's hands and feet are bound, and he, cursing all the time, is carried off by his assailers.

Chapter 13

Snoring from a man-shaped lump of clothes sums up the company in Higgins's cell. The apprentice grunts while stretching. *Where the bloody hell am I?* Himself groggy, he turns over, hoping to wipe his nose on his sleeve. *Bound. Of course, those men.*

"Rein, is that you?" More mumbles come from the other cellmate. Higgins squints. *No, far too bulky, and those feet are just wrong.*

He tries to stand, but instead falls on his shoulder. *What is this place?* The closest wall appears irregular, and the others are shrouded. Where the other man sleeps, the darkness is deeper; only the flick of a torch's light touches man and stone.

"Can…It looks like I can …"

Higgins's meaty fingers inch around the back, digging into the grime of uncounted years. Then stop. The lump of clothes mumbles something indistinguishable. At first, it comes across as only gibberish, until he realizes it is, in fact, another language.

"Bloody foreigners," nodding to himself. Then, he puckers. "Wait, I'm the bloody foreigner this time."

Or worse. He looks over his shoulder to his bindings. *The bloody criminal foreigner.* Higgins shakes his head and pushes against the wall. From this new perspective, the young apprentice can now see the cell door, and the torch behind it. Beyond is an expanse whose length is only hinted at by the shadows.

Now his chest, arms, and more heave in panic.

"Rein!" at the darkness.

And he hears the darkness return: "Rein."

"How do I know this is real?" he mumbles. *Focus.* His interest then slides over to his cellmate, as the lumps reveal themselves to be a young man. A hairy, robustly built young man.

Higgins closes his eyes. *"Cotchan am masg theanga,"* his eyes opening in a flash to fall upon the rousing figure. The spell of translation, one of the few that requires nothing more than will, for it takes from memory itself. If the man's tongue is anything close to those Higgins knows, he should be able to communicate.

"Would you cut with all that yelling?" the man growls.

It worked! Another victory for the Gaelic derivative. "Apologies," Higgins says, letting his head fall into shadow. "I thought you might be my friend."

The man snaps towards Higgins and glares, his oiled, partially singed beard quivering in anger. "I am not."

"Do you know where we are?"

The man tilts his head so that his profile is caught by the torch's light. "Does it matter? We are both dead."

"On what grounds?"

"These grounds," the man says, blinking. "Or other grounds, once—"

"No, I mean, for what reason?"

"You are a wizard," the man answers, wide-eyed and ogling. "Or at least a foreigner. You're at fault for the snow whichever way you slice it, and that means I am as much to blame because I didn't kill you. That's the reason they are using to get rid of me. Not that I could see a blasted thing in that mess. I could barely find Grim."

Higgins presses his back against the wall to quell his shaking. "I had nothing to do with any storm," he forces through his teeth.

"Doesn't matter. You were here, and the storm came. Bad luck is as good as drycraft in this village."

Higgins stares intently at the man. Trying to find imperfections. Cracks, in a façade, something like Rein might do. Something he can use. Something he can discern in the gloom. What he receives is eye strain, and he jerks his head to the side. "They call me Higgins."

The man returns the stare. "Rogard."

"Rogard," Higgins repeats. "To be honest, I must say I am surprised you are even talking to me."

His cellmate turns his head, briefly treating his profile to the light. His lips draw in tight and sharp. "Snow happens this far in the roof of the old world. Last week, they blamed a goat of being a witch..." As he gestures at Higgins with a flick of his head. "Maybe it was a witch, I don't know. Bleated something hoarse every time I passed by. But, for you. Should I fear you? The wizard who gets caught by fishermen who lie with sheep?"

The light withdraws from his face, and Rogard settles back.

"I am not dumb, and I have seen enough to know that I have not seen enough. I think...no, I know have been in this village too long. I should have left with the foragers or with the traders. They and their bells that make my head hurt — but these people here, they have long wanted my head. They call me a drunkard, and a thief too! Words. I don't care, I don't care. Dead is dead, now, isn't it?"

"No, dead is not dead," Rogard continues. "There are better ways to go about being dead. Ahh, but the Seafield has old traditions. We were raiders, once, conquerors. The elders won't stop talking about it. Chords, I am starting to sound like them too."

I'm a better judge of horseflesh than of men, as he acknowledges the man with a nod. *Here we are, I shall find a way out of this situation.* Higgins's cheeks bulge and he puffs himself up. Then his shoulders slump. *The last jail I escaped was through the drop in the gallows.*

"Some traditions should be left in the past," Higgins says.

"Aye, on that, I agree. Especially those that involve drinking, and not that milk these people love…"

Traditions, Higgins mulls as Rogard talks on about mostly nothing. Memories, and *prejudices.* The French jail was not a picnic. The beatings. The squalid cell. He looks around, absently rubbing his fingertips. *No proper breakfast.* There was more than one reason for his antagonism against anything French.

"Where is this place?" Higgins says. Almost as soon as the words come out of his mouth, he realizes that he has perhaps said too much. Naturally, he tries to fix this by saying even more: "I was on a very important mission, I…"

"I don't care," Rogard offers.

"Would you believe I was chasing after a girl?"

"Bah." Rogard then leans over and coughs up something foul. He takes a moment to lick his lips, then turns one eye upon his cellmate. "Better." One of his eyes glints in the darkness as he tilts his head. "Keep your stories believable. That's what I always say. Now, Grim was never one for telling tales, but when he did, I—" That one gleaming eye measures Higgins, and he smiles. "Here I talk, eh? Though, on that thought, how would one such as you come here? Besides drycraft, I don't know." He spits, and the drizzle slides down his sleeve. "You're in the Isfall Mountains. Whatever name this place held, none here remember, nor none care to give it a new one. Though Grim once called it *Brunnbodr.*"

The cell door bangs open. Rogard raises his arm to the light, but Higgins can find no such relief before the guard's step —

steps — stops before the apprentice. He slows his breathing, waiting for the inevitable strike. Something else arrives on a tide of fear. Higgins blanches. A feeling of wrongness permeates the newcomer. The guard takes another step.

"Time for the slop already?" Rogard's voice slices the wall of fear. "Have you news of old Grim?"

Boots scrape as the guard turns heel. The apprentice mouths a Latin version of the spell for light, but an oppressive chill steals the breath from his lungs, even as the walls and ways bask in luminosity from the torch.

"Hey, come on. I'm just asking... Grim," Rogard repeats with a growl. "Tell me. Say something."

A bucket clatters to the floor, followed soon after by the deafening crash of an iron gate.

They are already here. The tide of fear recedes with the departure of the guard. *It has not been a day.* Higgings dips his head, pressing his neck against the wall to steady himself.

"Are we supposed to eat this or piss in it?" Rogard asks.

Higgins cranes his neck weakly to look, but the contents are murky and thin. The smell of pine trees and forest mud follows the spillage of whatever it is onto the prison floor. He can't tell what he is looking at. "Do not touch anything there."

For several long moments, Rogard only stares into the space, as if he could divine his future there. His blank expression then peels away, and he sneers, upending the rest of the contents on the floor with a kick.

Higgins pales. Remembers.

The nether is dark, but not lonely. No matter how much I would prefer it elsewise.

The bucket rattles around the room after another swift kick from his companion, and some of the forest muck splatters near Higgins. He retreats further into the corner, and into himself.

Was it always so? No. The first time I died, other spirits were there, other Artisans. That wasn't Rein's fault. Not then. He looks up, letting his bald spot rub against the stone. *I don't know when they broke through. When they managed to take the Nether.*

A thump from the opposite side of the cell heralds the return of Rogard to being another unremarkable lump in an unremarkable prison. Higgins squints, staring at the oozing contents. *It is probably harmless mud. The guard's mind is gone. He is doing what he does out of rote, little more. They must have fallen upon him in the forest. It won't be long—*

"Grim," Rogard mumbles, terse for once.

Those devils more than just touch to take a man. "We should sleep," Higgins says, finding his voice. "Tomorrow brings new troubles."

For while no sun trespasses, there is always a fresh torch just out of sight, so that afternoon or evening can creep up unnoticed. "Bloody Udur," he whispers, feeling suddenly ashamed. His fingernails then touch the rope. *They have my scent. They will find me, take me, with the rest of these poor fools.*

He looks to the man-shaped lump. "Unless I can enlist some aid," Higgins whispers.

Chapter 14

"Higgins?" Rein moans.

Time, they say, is like a river. If that is so, then this old Artisan must be stuck at the bottom of a raging one. The Inspector has no idea how long he has lain unconscious on the floor, but his breakfast has fouled on the tongue.

"I thought I heard a voice," he whispers. "Sofie's voice. But that is impossible, I left her in the Fairhome..."

The floor is cold and grimy. *I am not in the portal.* The air, stale. There is also the additional tang of blood in his mouth from the fall. Rein's lip is cut.

Inside his head, Rein hears the elf's chiding. The tone is clear and mocking, repeating, "You've fallen into a trap," louder and louder each time. The Inspector shakes his hands on the ground back and forth, peppering his cuff with spittle. "It's the ground. And I thank the Lord for it...The Lord."

He clutches his temple in pain, stifling back a scream. The room spins.

It is dark outside. The Fairhome is always—

"Dark," Rein whispers, completing his thought as he wipes tears from his cheek. Yet doing so does not rub away the void that surrounds him. He coughs, and pulls his head down towards his knees, and as such, onto his knees.

This is how his colleagues once found him in the early days of his career. Cultists had ambushed him in an ancient tomb, brought him low through a series of infernal enchantments. It was a turning point in his life, the day he decided to dedicate himself fully to studying the elder craft, and to the service of the Curatorium.

Rein fights not to laugh. "They could have been casting color-changing cantrips on their hair, it made no difference." The Curators do not like challenges to their order. The Construct was made for this purpose so that a few could divest the many of magick.

Hunting cultists was now his job.

Slowly, he retracts and struggles to his feet. Rein stumbles almost immediately. Kicks something. And this something rattles against the hard ground while the Inspector staggers forward. A wall stops him from falling.

"A job I hate." Rock. His fingers pick at the dirt of the barrier that saved him. "Where am I? There has been some mistake, some error."

The question disappears as if on wings. He grabs his head in pain, presses his eyes closed. What replaces is something different. Perhaps Rein falls into unconsciousness. Maybe it is madness. Either way, a malignant force intercedes on the psyche of Inspector Christaan De Rein. In this vision, he walks the dark lanes of the Fairhome.

The Inspector scans the horizon left, right. "This can't be." Weeks have passed since he left Sofie, back when they escaped Chancy and his minions. He inhales. "It has not changed."

It would not. Shadows whip across a dismal landscape, barely distinguishable from the gray-barked trees that oppress his view. Rein checks himself, clearing his mind as best as he can. There was no way he could have come here, not without a leyline present.

"I must be logical. I can still feel the wall," he says to his right hand. At first, he stares at the lines on his palm casually. Then, with intent, as if he can force himself to shift—

Black. Darkness. Void. He's returned, the evil force that took him, retreating into the recesses of his mind, waiting to resurface. The Inspector lets out a ragged breath, focusing on the feeling of the air escaping his lungs and the rank taste in his mouth. But there is more here. The smell of pine remains, cobbled together with the deepness of a tomb, its dank earth, and of things older than the shrouding canopies of trees in an open forest. He searches his memory for a spell, one that shouldn't work in the Fairhome: *"Sol an lochhrein aleanta."*

Light. "Rot," he growls, nearly stepping into a shallow pit of loose earth. "It smells like a tomb because it is. How did I come here, and where is here, exactly?"

He remembers the vision before entering the portal, of the cave and the river. The air was muggy — just like it is now. But it is colder here. His memory is fuzzy. There are flashes of Higgins's fidgeting.

"The cave." A draft of wind carries an odor foul as the mouths of aged men, gaping and ridden with halitosis. He staggers, sweeping his spell-created lantern left and right. "Why would there be a tomb on top of that mountain? And why am I getting these visions...Could the magic have had some effect on my mind?"

Over many pits are tall stones laid. And some bear faint markings chiseled into the rock, head high. "Grave markers, or...."

He approaches one, whose sign reminds him of scrawls near Lyon, attributed to a Gallic tribe. His fingers trace the runes. Searching. Probing. And in this instant, perhaps by reflex, Rein closes his eyes. Again, his mind flows away as if perched on a log in the middle of a fast-running river. The bleakness of the cave shifts, and Rein must again make a grab for something to right himself as his former reality is invaded by the dream world.

"Do you have any idea how ridiculous you look, fumbling around in the dark?"

"Who said that?" is what Rein wants to ask, but his jaw locks as if held by an unseen hand. What comes out is an unintelligible mumble as the oddly familiar voice returns to admonish him.

"But of course, that could be a euphemism for everything you have ever done."

This must be a dangerous foe. Maybe even a cultist. Like in the cave before, Rein's own thoughts seem to close in on him from all directions — bury him inside. Yet the Fairhome is vast.

Rein raises his arm and flicks his wrist. "Sol an lochhrein aleanta."

Light. Five shadows spin around the Inspector. "This is all wrong, that should not have worked."

Five. Six. A carousel of shade spins everywhere he turns. From the grotesque to the monstrous. Rein, dizzy, backtracks. "Is this a dream?"

The images move against the forest backdrop, first clockwise, then counter. He raises his hands towards them. Between each revolution, the gaps become smaller, and smaller, as if gravity were somehow drawing their forms together. Merging them.

Until all melt into one distinct figure.

"I thought even you could have learned something from the fairies' world," it says.

From this shade of a man, a magic green light emanates, illuminating the surrounding trees, rocks, and ground. Old mosaics are revealed below its feet, painting them in a sickly glow. And the figures feature begin to clear.

In the figure's hand there appears to be an umbrella. And this figure — a man — takes a step forward. Then another. The ferule strikes the ground in sequence with each step. Two. Three.

Clack, clack...

Crack. The snap of a bone pulls the Inspector out of his dreams. Rein's mouth twists, and he runs, his wail funneling in the halls, bouncing and returning to him like a forgotten part of his own memory. The presence does not relent as he runs. It haunts him as he careens around an ancient well. It oppresses him in the center of a clearing with a small dais. It tracks him as he crashes into an altar. Spent, Rein collapses, his back against the cool stonework.

"You are dead," Rein mumbles.

"Is that so, Inspector?" The voice stops at "so," then draws out the title as if it were on a string. Rein stiffens slowly, too, fighting with his knees to remain upright. The spell of light pulses, little rays reaching out to touch the veins of his arm, then retreating.

The figure has crawled out of his waking dreams. And now lives, here. Before him. Rein raises his hand feebly at the sound of an approach. "This isn't real."

Chancy of the Teamor grimaces. "You should have learned from your time in Fairhome: Reality and dream are all a matter of perspective."

And the apparition stalks towards Rein. Chancy' approach is slow, deliberate, but out of sync. The footsteps are not in time with the stab of the umbrella. One step, against the sound of four. Two, six. The man stops just above the Inspector, his smile uncanny. At once, his image flickers in tune with the surrounding cavern. The sound of rushing water bursts forth, then falls away in this brief instant.

Black coils slither out of Chancy's eyes, and each births more lines that stretch across the cavern floor like clawing fingers. The Inspector trips over a femur, falling on his hindquarters. Three, seven. He backpedals desperately, pushing bones and debris up against the altar. Still, the figure closes in, and at the sound of the last footstep, it is upon him. Shaking, he takes the femur and uses the jagged edge to cut his own hand.

Eight.

The vision of Chancy bends over, and Rein cries out: "*Solna nea, Oran cruchaid, an beath an tene!*"

An inferno leaps from the stolen femur, pouring over bone, tree and vision alike. Shadows disintegrate and the surrounding area is lit by sudden flame. The spell Rein learned from Higgins has a horrible pedigree. Horrible but powerful, and even as the twisting form of his rival persists against the onslaught, the Inspector gains composure. Fire dances across Rein's vision, and he stands up as if launched by a tensed spring.

"I am Christaan De Rein of the Princeps Inspectorem." Voice hard, lips trembling. He then points the makeshift wand at his foe and repeats the incantation.

The coils from Specter of Chancy widen, spreading out and replacing the shadows lost, shielding him.

"There are darker things in my past than the likes of a tramp, raised far beyond his station and means," Rein says.

Light meets shadow. Tendrils pour into the stream from Rein, and the edges of the phantom lose focus in the gloom, merging and moving out of the growing black — until the visage of Chancy looms large. Rein advances, but the power of the Teamor's agent is too great. Tendrils overwhelm the wand and the hellish light is snuffed out as Rein's mouth opens into a wordless cry of pain.

Yet the Inspector's stance hardens. His resolve tempers as the embers of his spell smolder. Rein recasts his earlier charm of light. Briefly, the shadows retreat, only to storm back and encircle the sorcery. And then, in the complete black, the two —

Inspector and rival — take a step towards one another. In that moment, all sound, all light, all movement falls to nothing.

Chapter 15

Shapes flit between the trees to Niena's right. She stops to catch her breath.

"It's too soon to rest," Titania says.

The girl leans on her knees. Packed ice crunches underfoot in the shade of a nearby trunk. *If she says one more word, I am going to sit down right here.* Everywhere else, meltwater muddies the ground and rots the leaves, turning their noses up at the sweet smell of decay. Walking through this forest so far has been a misery of red clay.

Morning has already escaped them. Now midday approaches. Finally, Niena stretches into a stand, and on the way back up she attempts to rub some feeling into her calves. "I thought I saw something in the trees."

Worry flashes across Titania's face but is fast gone. Concern, however, remains. And as the girl's breath mists in the air, Titania places her hand on Niena's shoulder and hums softly. The fairy's breath is shallow. Quiet. The hum slips into a powerful but limited spell.

"Better?"

"A little, but…" She holds her fingers up to the light as if she might catch the lost thought. Between the index and the thumb, she can see her grandmother's smile. Niena's right arm drops, but she peers past Titania through the skeletal canopy. A sudden warmth wiggles into her fingers. By the time Niena notices she is steady, her feet are already moving again.

Leaves are the first to join the trek, swirling around them in a green dance. Then the sun, and an early moon as the day tosses away the casual wear and shifts to evening. It is around this time when the slope of the land changes, to only thereafter rise in low sheets of rock layered like cake before the face of a great hill.

If it's cake, then Marny must have baked it, Niena muses while they mount it in a bid to dry their shoes on the warm rocks — shoes that are caked too, in an equally unpleasant way.

They rest here. More for Niena's sake. And here, high enough above the canopy, it is clear the forest curves west. Until, in the distance, surrounded by mist, only the glimmer of a road and a hint of a field can be seen.

Niena kneels and drinks from a puddle corked in a boulder. By a layer of moss, the water is cool, and clear, but doubt still tweaks her stomach — a doubt that grows when she looks at the fairy.

"Why are we still in such a hurry?" Niena asks. "Your plan worked, didn't it?"

"It did," Titania says, crossing her arms.

Niena uses some of the moss to wash her face, then stretches again. "You don't sound so happy about that."

"It's…complicated." Titania sighs. "I also don't think we are safe yet. We must keep moving for now; we can judge whether it was enough to evade our pursuers. Or if more desperate means are needed." She stares hard at the ground. "There is also something you need to know: I am growing weary."

"Then we should both get a solid day's rest," Niena says through a smile. "Not just me this time."

Titania lowers herself, bending over and kneeling to sit at Niena's level. "Fairybloods require sleep, but true fairies do not. We need…the dreams of men. Stories, songs, to replenish. Sometimes even faith and worship, or a place where such power has been vested."

"Let's find a town then," Niena says. "A good tavern, with a real bard. Not these country affairs. Something with class."

"How would you know what is what?" Titania shakes her head. "I daresay you would be just as irritated with delay now if we were to do so. Or do you deny the Evercharm's call?"

It is true. A strange wanderlust has been toying with Niena's mind. It started not long after being reunited with the lyre. She looks to the south; a curious desire to see what's beyond the next hill there sparks. Could it be the lyre's desire, as Titania said? Or just the old daydreaming?

"I don't know about that," Niena says. "I say we should go with my plan and look for a town. We must be close to one."

"As you say," Titania whispers, becoming distant. "I don't trust anything that passes as civilization here, however." She uncrosses her arms and finds her hips. "Barbarians with their mock tea parties."

A glint forces Niena to squint. The sun has taken the treetops as a sort of a shield, gray and barren though most are, and sheds its rays between them. There is red. Orange, and a scatter of purple. Niena searches her memory. Something about this place also pricks at her from the inside.

"This hill still remembers when it was a mountain," Titania whispers.

Her voice is like the wind moving through the dead leaves. Niena fidgets as the fairy queen walks over to where the girl is sitting. Her dress ripples.

"The old songs are here," Titania adds. "They dance to the music of the approaching winter. But autumn is not that old, and steps lively." A cautious smile crosses her lips. "If you can feel them, that means you are coming into your heritage, I think."

But the smile isn't returned. *Heritage.* Niena's dreams the previous night were dark. It was as if she were seeing the storm's working from a raven's eye. The ice has also shown horrors, like a child waking their parents with two words: "Guess what?" And the bodies of those who fell before the weather's turn did not settle in her dreams like the dead should, but stirred, lurching at her thoughts from the shadows of her mind. Is this also the sort of heritage she will gain?

"I don't want to think about that," she whispers. "So, do you even know where we are going?"

"Look to your west, for that is the last of the Isfall Mountains you will hearken upon. Look to your east, and think on the sea, for Sunford will remain a memory now. Beyond this little hill, there is a vast plain of fields that trots south, south, until broken by the shadow of low mountains, and then unto desert," Titania answers with a shrug. "So that is where we go."

Is she making fun of me, talking that way? "And then what? Are there any towns nearby?" Niena shakes her hands vigorously as if that could lose her the memory of the previous night.

"The devil if I know." Titania says. "I haven't been here in forever."

"Well, I guess there's nothing we can do about that. So, if there is a village, might be we could get a room," Niena says. "Two rooms. Then we can get some real information about what's around us. I don't like this whole trudging-blind-through-the-wilderness plan we have been running with."

"Why two?"

She pops her thumb knuckle. "You snore."

There is a long pause, more than enough for the ache to leave Niena's legs. She scratches her throat and watches her grandmother's face shift through the seasons — from the pale of confusion to the flush of irritation.

"Let's keep moving," Niena says, trying not to smile.

Dust from the rock face flies up around Niena as she takes the distraction, smile, and all, into the forest before Titania can react. The young woman's step is lively — for at least a few hours, until her feet remember the pain of trekking through the mud and the weight of everything that has happened until now. Against this, she hunches her shoulders and continues. The sun is high before they slow, with wide but thin clouds taking a measure of the light. It is still enough to see by, and plenty for them to share a meal in the shade without issue. Old bread and honey.

"There might be a road," Titania says as they walk on. "We should look for one, if only to keep it close."

A clamoring of birds on their right steals the moment for reply, clouds of them clustering and shading the sun. Day turns to a quick night, then back to day. Niena adjusts the strap to the lyre. *Something was moving fast...probably just a deer or something.* Titania doesn't seem to be concerned, her hands idly twirling the petals of a wildflower from earlier.

Fog rolls in. Slowly. Thickly. The gray bark of the trees around the hill doesn't make it any easier for her to see the way, and several times Niena's trip is nearly upended by a hidden root. She rolls her right shoulder and slows from a walk to a dawdle. Ever since those birds, the wood has seemed to tighten for her. As the sun dips, Nienas thinks about the flight from Maidenhill. Of the oppressive nature of Fairhome and the way the forest closed in. She shivers, and the chill reminds her of the sewer underneath the city of Shenan, and the prowling dragon above.

Despite Marny's warnings and Titania's actions, she'd rather stick to a road. *All roads lead somewhere, whether it is away or towards something. They themselves are not dangerous, outside of what happens when a foot lands upon them. If a book is a key to new worlds, and new imaginations, the danger of a road is that it may yet take you to them.* These are the sort of thoughts filling Niena's mind as she traverses the old way.

"I think we are coming around the bend," she says.

She takes a glance over her shoulder to see Titania effortlessly following. Or floating. *She is a fairy, just like Oberon. Chords. Just like me. I have fairy blood too.* And every fairy she has met has been manipulative.

The longer I am with her, the more she will be able to manipulate me. If the last days have shown anything, it is this. Niena starts rubbing her thumb knuckle absentmindedly, repeating the rhythmic popping noise from before as Titania approaches.

"Can you see the road from here?"

"You are the one with elven blood," Titania snaps. "If the ancient folk did build one, it would be nearby. Better to follow the mountain's path, the high ground, for the lower is marshy. If you were paying attention before, you would have also noticed that the trees at the western side were thinner. We have been passing through groves of birch as of late."

"Then we are close."

"You make that sound ominous," Titania says.

"It is when we are two women, alone in the wilderness."

Titania's brow flutters at her own words turned back. "So, now you understand? Still, we could follow the road for a little while, then leave it before it shows signs of dwelling." Her head gestures at the hill. "It would not be as hard of a climb as the mountains before, even."

Niena considers. "With your magick—"

"You should not count on that," Titania interjects. "Look to the strength of your limbs and the grip of those long fingers of yours this time."

"I am not as sure then," Niena says, pausing a few seconds between not and sure. She stares at her feet, then her gaze climbs the hem of her grandmother's dress. "I feel…" Her attention slips back to the floor, and she looks away. "Rein and them. What will stop them from finding me again? What's to stop them from just showing up on my door a year from now?"

Titania pauses. "Nothing." She hesitates, lifting her chin as if considering something distasteful. "Yet we do have allies," she adds slowly.

"And what will their help cost us?" Niena asks.

Titania shakes her head. "Much in one hand, and little with the other. Have you heard of Cuiven's Lee?"

"That is a…" She lets her arms drop. "Oberon talked about it. It seemed—it seems important somehow."

Titania nods her head slowly. "It is. I am sure he told you about the lore, but not much about what can be done there. What you can do there."

"With the Evercharm," Niena whispers. "What would they have me do?"

"They will ask for two things…" Titania says as she turns to her wildflower. "First, to sing the song of unbinding that I taught you, which will remove the connection between all three worlds. This is the start and needed for any great changes. But like everyone else, they are keen on the song of creation." She drops the flower. "The changes they would make would not be trifling, but they could give you the freedom you want. That is perhaps the best offer any have for you."

"I don't know; I don't like the idea of giving anyone that much control," Niena says carefully.

"We will have to burn that bridge when we cross it," Titania says too quickly. She then takes a deep breath, and slides around the girl to face her.

Titania appears guarded, as if there is something she is holding back. "Remember the name Maro Unsterbbēriz. Likely, every road that we take at least passes through there. If you are captured. If you take up these potential allies' offer. Or if we decide to skip to Earth."

Snippets of conversation flow between them on the journey around the hill. Back and forth, heaped in allegory or other subtleties. Never direct. At times, it is sparked by a choice word, or double entendre. Others, by a mere action or inaction. Such as resting near a tree, or while they shimmy down the muddy screen fields. To-and-fro. As clouds take the place of the canopy, darkening their overhead. Almost always it is broken up into a few strings of words. Or even just a word. Sometimes long stretches go by without any talking at all, only to explode in a torrent after climbing a rock. Or crossing a stream. In the end, the only thing decided is that they will talk more about it. Cuiven's Lee, though never mentioned overtly, hangs over this promise.

They walk on, rejoining the road. Leaves crunch underfoot. The dry grass too, and the smell of it is strong around them. Every so often, Niena takes a side glance at her grandmother. And every other step, she can see something bubbling up to the surface. It shows in frustrating gestures. In random swipes at saplings, or the fairy taking the effort to create footprints and kick up the dirt.

A distant horn attempts to steal Niena's attention, but memories of Oberon, and of the old riddle, wrench themselves free. "In Cuiven's Lee stand three thrones. One silver, one gold, and one of bone."

Titania narrows her eyes, and Niena turns away to peer through a line of storm-thinned trees. They are not so high up anymore, but there is still enough to see.

Tents come into distant view. A greater town looming over those, with tall spires, walls. There seems to be the hint of people, too. And the clamor of oxen laden with supplies. The trees where they stand now are wispy, providing even less cover than the thin forest before. Niena sighs, finally free from the oppression of the forest.

As her grandmother joins her, she says: "Do you know this place?"

"No. When I was younger, this was all fields and wilderness," Titania says. "Niena, I don't like this. We are taking a great risk."

"When we get to their tavern, I want to hear your take on Cuiven's Lee," Niena says, catching Titania's attention. "Maybe we can buy a map of the surrounding area then, too. We can also get you the rest you need."

Titania smiles gently. "While no one there will care about old fairy tales—" she says, then looks to her left, appearing to consider. "I do not think it will be so easy for me."

"Fine," Niena says, making to continue, but Titania's hand forestalls her.

"There is something else," she says quietly, struggling. "We cannot stay too long—"

"I know, I know. Rein will find us and—"

"Not them," Titania whispers. She hesitates. A battle appears to be brewing on her face. The fairy queen's lips thin and her jaw sets. Then, everything relaxes. "Something far worse is out there. Something which I cannot protect you from, alone." She ducks her head and draws closer. "How much do you remember about that village we fled? How much do you remember about what happened before I found you?"

Niena pulls back. "I remember shadows..." She shakes her head, frantically. "No, not just shadows. They moved. They spoke...I..."

"Shh." Titania slowly brushes back her own hair. "I have been hesitant to place this worry upon you. There are many powers in this world. Not all of them are...human anymore. Or fairy, or elf. They think in ways that are unrecognizable to the folks of the three. They all want the lyre." The fairy then pauses, as if holding her breath, and adds: "And you. These things are close even now. A town would be a terrible risk. They would expect us to go there."

"So is wandering around. When you admittedly don't know anything about the area."

The intensity of Titania's gaze fastens Niena to her heels, and she relents. Her grandmother keeps her jaw locked, though, as if quelling some inner torment. Finally, after several moments of this, she squints, and nods distantly.

"We have to be careful then," Titania continues. "There is no telling what we may find there." Her head tilts up proudly, and her eyes smile. "I think you can handle yourself, better than I ever could." At once, the playful visage disappears. "However, no games. We shan't get distracted and overstay. Do you understand?"

The interaction leaves Niena with questions. Again, she nods, though this time she manages to dig deep, past the insecurities, beyond where all her fears brood, and summons forth the courage to say: "I will lead the way then."

Chapter 16

The terrain changes as they approach the first of the fields. Meltwater has also turned the space between the crops into sucking pits. Niena sighs. A slow going. Dogged stubbornness keeps her moving now.

Sundown. The last fingers of light reach the beams of a barn. They tease out a blush in both wood and sky, and the view seems to liven the ladies' steps, from a march to a fast walk. Trotting past the tumbled stone of a farmhouse. Skulking over the hollow of a deserted fox den. Both women listen to the wind as sounds of town life find their way to them, and it is while listening to these, near a clutch of oaks, that they consider rejoining the road. Instead, Niena sees an opportunity in a line of barley fields.

A breeze carries some of the last snow with them. Titania sets her sights upon the lyre hastily strapped to Niena's back, and so she mouths a lullaby. Her hands work over the instrument's elegant lines. The outlines of the Evercharm retreat from view.

"This will hide it for now," Titania says. The fairy woman's cheeks are pale, almost translucent. Niena reaches for her, but Titania takes her hand and walks with the girl past a fence around an overgrown field.

The tall grass scrapes the mud off their shoes, letting Niena's feet finally breathe. And they tread through the next hour, keeping low, taking rest in a former orchard, long unattended. Here, when the weather shifts, a magpie's song comes to them piecemeal. At once high and piping. At once quiet, then back again as if never having stopped.

Under an apple tree, Niena reaches behind her back. Her finger follows the instrument's curves. Up the arm. To the crossbar. Touching the lyre does not seem to affect the spell. But when she moves to catch a string, Titania forestalls her.

"It is not so strong a working," she says.

The orchard leads to another field. Then to the farmhouse. Shade welcomes them on the ruin of the western wall, where mushrooms, saplings and ferns have huddled together, seeking respite between the parts that remain standing. There is a musty smell, and where the door used to hang, a tree has split the threshold.

"I can hear lots of people..." At the wrecked threshold, Niena watches Titania creep ahead. Here the woman pauses, ducking against being seen, then motions for Niena to follow, despite the girl's previous determination to lead.

Niena tiptoes through the debris. Visibility is low, as clouds have settled behind the mountain, taking them into darkness. Still, she can now put the voices to something more than just disembodied spirits. Even if here, between the bushes, they are little more than shapes moving against the backdrop of an impermanent camp. With her free hand, she pulls back some of the branches and leaves. The encampment appears to be no more than a couple hundred yards from them now.

"The clouds are so low, I'd bet they'd cheat at taroc," Titania quips without looking away.

"What do you know about these people? Who are they?" Niena asks.

For a moment, Titania is too distracted to answer, but shortly after she gives a quick tilt of her head, and says, "Are? If you follow the tents and lift your eyes, you can see some of the buildings poking from the treetops. There are two towns here, of a sort, it appears. That is as much as I know of what they are. I know a little more about who they *were*."

The fairy glances at Niena and seems to read something between the girl's temple and eyes, then sighs.

"You want to know," Titania says. She makes a gesture as if she were refusing cold porridge. "I will tell you what I can while we are still some distance from the tents. But let us make haste while there is some light."

Visions of knights, of fantastic battles, and horrible princesses from the many books she's read fill Niena's mind. These flood together with historic texts and the origin of certain words she read in the libraries of Sunford. The Southlands, never well known, have been forgotten in only one generation.

"Humans have always had their gods," Titania says, rolling her wrist. "And wants."

Niena lets her hand drift along the edge of a thatch roof. Her fingers trace a split in a batch of reed, down the breakage and as far up as she can reach.

"We learned to listen," Titania continues, ducking low.

Her explanation carries into the next field and beyond the old farm. This time their pace is slowed by their own choice. Broken carts become resting stops. Brush a place to muffle their conversation. While edging through the weeds, Niena learns about how the first fairy supposedly came from the collective want of mankind for something greater and the stories they told around the campfire. How Titania's kind were originally looked upon in awe by men. And how the fairies profited from this, first as a lark, then as something more serious. Becoming akin to gods.

Titania's voice waxes and wanes in patches as they progress. Hiding and waiting. Watching, and listening as the distance is closed, and the once indistinct shapes of the tents and people reveal themselves. Whenever there is movement, she falls quiet. The closer they come to the road, the more hurried the talk.

"My brothers and sisters never really cared much for these mountains," she says hoarsely. "Sacrifices were already a long-standing tradition when I appeared, and not all of them were…" Again, her voice drifts with the wind in the weeds. "Come on."

More of the shanty town lies along the winding road west and east. Niena listens hard, and as Titania turns to collect the girl, the faint plucking of a lyre or another stringed instrument rises.

"Empires rarely ever held these lands. Men like those in the deep south thought these wild places were too fey for them to maintain, always shifting, ever malevolent. They were not wrong, for Cuiven's Lee lies somewhere beyond, and many fairies dwelled long in these lands, taking forms that pleased their nature," Titania says, pushing down the stems of a thick patch of wheat. "The Red Hat, the Glaistig. So, it perhaps is no wonder that the folk are bloody minded." She lowers her head. "Do you see that storage building over there? Its front is long and comes close to the road. We could go around that building and come out the other side, maybe merge in with the crowds."

"Do you know many stories from here?" Niena says.

"History is boring unless you are the one making it." Titania says. "Don't give me that look. I told you what I did there, so you can understand the danger you've put yourself in, but I see you are stubborn." Titania shakes her head sadly and says, "People don't change quickly, at least not where it matters." She hikes her dress and makes to climb over the bramble before a fence.

Niena clears her throat. "Wait," she almost calls out, forestalled by a series of shapes moving parallel to the first line of tents they approach. The girl climbs over the briar hastily, then rushes to catch hold of Titania's dress but misses.

Laughter finds them. Titania ducks under a rope and moves to a series of crates and barrels, almost sliding to the edge. The laughter dodges between the tents, battens at the edges — forcing Niena to run, then fall, near the fairy. Concern shows briefly in Titania's movements, and she motions for Niena to hide and keep quiet. Then she mumbles something in a language Niena can't understand.

"You want to leave?" Niena says, uncertain. "Why?"

Titania nods. "Do you see this division? The tents and the town above? There is much danger in a place like this, for you and the Evercharm. We would also be trapped if your hunters are able to gather themselves." She lifts her chin, and gestures for Niena to follow.

Niena mulls an answer but keeps quiet. Her own reasons for coming here — the need for information and other resources — already being well stated.

They duck down a narrow space between two huts, eyeing a series of steps cut partially into an embankment and leading up into the village.

Screams coming from the village force Niena to join Titania in silence. At the same time, a boy ducks under a pole, and the two children — a boy and a girl — toss snowballs at each other, then disappear in a torrent of giggles and yells.

"I do not think we should stay here," Titania whispers, finally.

"We are already here; besides, you get used to hearing screams where I'm from."

A moment later, the little boy returns, followed by a girl and a gaggle of others. As the two watch, the children's shared laughter winds its way to the fence they left moments earlier, to more games, more—

"If you are determined on this, we need to move," Titania says, her hands gesturing frantically. She lowers her eyes.

With the wind at her back, Niena stands and shifts the weight of the Evercharm to her other shoulder, falling in step with Titania. For the girl, this seems like a normal town, if rustic. Children at play, people doing business. Someone being assaulted in an alley. The stonework hints at permanence, even if the tents ripple with a populace that drifts in on the wind. Even so, for Niena, this place has a familiar feeling.

"You are wrong," Titania says, as if again reading her thoughts. She stops them at the edge of the stairs. Her pose remains fixed, as if deciding where to go. Then the fairy's head bobs up, and she swivels around to regard her granddaughter with a weary frown. "Keep your wits about you. This is not Shena, or Sunford."

"Shenan, and there's nothing here to worry about if—"

"Shh!" Titania's hand seems to instinctively find Niena's, stopping the latter's attempt at a gesture.

"Whatever happens, child, heed me." She looks back at the stairs. "Do you see any guards? There are no laws in places like this. You must be careful." Titania's hands go to her sleeves, then under them as she crosses her arms. "You are going to have to do some things you won't be proud of ere the end. For I am becoming only…"

It is here that Niena notices that Titania's hand has no substance. She nearly stumbles as the edges of the fairy's outline fade.

"A dream," Titania completes. Her frown then melts into a small smile. "Who only another dreamer may see — a dream, and one that is soon to pass from memory." She leans and uncrosses her arms, gesturing for Niena to come closer.

"How long have you been like this?"

"Long," Titania says wearily. "It has progressed faster since the storm."

That fear once in Titania's eyes finds its way to Niena's. It sizes up the girl's form like an unwanted compliment. Suddenly embarrassed, she lets her gaze move to the clouds. The sky is overcast, and ash from newly kindled fires scatters like arrows loosed against an invading army.

While shifting her body away from her grandmother, Niena notices a procession in makeshift alleyways among the tents. More screams interrupt the quiet. Shouts. By now, she can even tell some of the words being flung.

"We need to get you to a tavern," Niena says firmly. "Maybe —"

"Listen," Titania says, and Niena does. That chill of fear returns, and as the girl watches, Titania's fingers ghost through the beam of a small shack.

"In the month that we have travelled together, I have guided and protected you from the worst nature has to offer," Titania whispers. "I have shielded you from terrors so that you can sleep at night. But I have no power here." She turns and stares down her nose at Niena, giving a small nod.

Niena brushes back her hair. "In Shenan, I stole the bread from the hands of my attackers, and plucked their manhood from between." She waves at the town. "What can a few drunkards do to me?"

"Terrifying," Titania says, raising her eyebrow. "Next time we are attacked by bakers, I will rely on you. For now, look at this."

The stairs loom, towering into the unknown. Titania moves away but continues speaking to Niena over her shoulder. "You lived on the streets, but you have forgotten your fear of the dark."

The red of a torch mingles with the sunset, and Niena hurries, trying to shift to the left along the stairs. But there is nowhere to hide. She drops to one knee and looks behind her while Titania climbs on.

"Wait." But the word catches in Niena's throat. She clutches at the edge and raises herself up another step. From here, she can see over the shanty. Niena keeps her attention on there, and the low murmur of the crowds finally comes.

"You will remember it before the end."

Following Titania's example, Niena mounts the remaining stairs quickly to gain the protection of an outbuilding. Here she slows, slinking her way through. Up and around the low rock shelf the town was founded upon. There is an out-of-place gatehouse at the top. Its stone archways juxtaposed against a warehouse and the remains of a palisade bridge another gap between buildings.

The streets beyond seem narrow. Niena looks up and squints. Whatever text was engraved on this entrance arch has long ago worn away. There are no guards, but plenty of people. Niena and Titania press against the wood of an outbuilding.

An old man limps past as Niena's back hits the wall. "What's the fuss about?" he says to someone at his side. Their voices rise and fall, joining with others to tut excitedly. More and more each moment, and from many directions.

You don't need to worry— the girl ducks her head again, mimicking her grandmother, and realizing the woman acts for her benefit: No one else can see the fairy.

The murmurs disappear around a corner. And as Niena waits, the last of the sun's red rays mingle with the flick of a torch in a farther alley. West, along the outer curve of the shelf. She peers that way.

"They're all ambling along the same path," Niena whispers.

"The town's center. Maybe something has happened."

"How do you know that?"

Titania huffs slightly. "Gawkers gawk."

Together they risk the inner streets. Unlike in Sunford, and Shenan, the buildings here keep their distance from each other, even where the way is narrow. *That's good, and bad,* Niena thinks, skirting the attention of an idle passerby to hide in a shop's porch. Good because very few buildings are taller than one story. The walls do not quite close in, and there is a clear view of the sky and the stars — if the clouds would let them appear.

Bad because that means there are less things to hide among.

The fairy quietly rejoins her as the girl waits in the lee of some crates. Niena rubs her thumb knuckle, thinking. The flicker of movement from a man skirting the corner of the crate makes Niena pause. Being seen now might be risky. There are too few people for her to go unnoticed, and she doesn't want to be called out as some thief. Especially if these folks are as dangerous as Titania suggests.

I wish I had a hood. The workings of the folk here seem strange. The movement of individuals speak of excitement, and when Niena walks around Titania to join the onlookers, none so much as look her way. *I'd take a burlap sack too.*

A woman calls out behind them: "Henrik, Henrik? What is it?"

Niena's eyes narrow as Titania joins. More shouts and jeers erupt, then a hush. Now the girl also hops on tiptoes and peers around shoulders to get a look.

"Oh, I wonder if another one of the wandering folk from the tents came up here," a man says. "Brave sod, if so. Or dumb..." The man clears his throat. "Or drunk with the festival and all."

"The boys probably took care of it," the woman says. "Let's go home."

When Niena instinctively turns to search for the speaker, a flurry of activity stirs in the throng. Shouts reach them from deeper in, towards the center. Men and women, who once meandered, now move more eagerly in the same direction. And Niena follows reluctantly. To the western face, where a solitary watchtower emerges in the deepening red of sunset, empty but guarding the town proper against the shanty town. To the center, not far from there, where the action stops.

In the retreating shadow of that structure is a small market. The excitement of the crowd echoes off the stone walls surrounding the spectacle. The shouts continue. The clear sound of cursing and fighting emanates from the mob. The desire to see what is happening ahead touches Niena here, but Titania stops her. Faded and pale, she spreads her arms wide like a ghost sent to warn.

"I told you," the fairy mutters. "There is no law in places like these. These people are barely beyond the warring tribes they came from, and the only thing they can agree on is they don't like outsiders in their little nest, even if they tolerate them outside. That means you."

The girl nods. She takes a breath. Then another, falling behind a young couple as they turn to leave. Evening gains the upper hand at this moment; the torches of the mob bloom one by one, passing from hand to hand.

Niena gently taps the wife of the couple, and when the woman turns, the girl moves past them. She glances over her left shoulder, watching a group of bawdy men as they waddle by. Chancing it, she slides in front of a gaggle of chatterers, and joins them. Just beyond the blood is a tavern.

Bless the chords, as the feet of someone is dragged away nearby. "Chords..." she swallows, looking up and beyond. Over the tavern's door, a worn sign hangs, hidden mostly by the thatch. There is no writing, but a carving shows that it must serve as a meeting point or way house. The back of the tavern, which they just passed, has more nefarious uses.

Titania walks beside her granddaughter. "You insisted on a warm bed. Should we get one, you'll have to lie in it." The fairy queen draws a deep breath.

A song scurries from under the door of the tavern. Niena pulls her dress closer as others pass by, seeking the same sort of solace. The melody is sung in an ancient dialect, and while she can only understand every second word, it makes her shiver.

Careful, child, else the bed they have for you will be more dirt than hay in the end.

Niena checks between a canvas window and the threshold. She holds her head. The voice that just spoke was not her own; no, it rose high, as if piped through two thin blades of grass. Or the sort of sound a grown man makes when he holds his nose. It's been a long time since she heard it. The last was ere her capture by the brothers elven.

Titania is suddenly at her side, face twisted in concern and worry. Niena tries to grasp the memory of the voice in her head. The long day has her imagination acting up. She takes a confident step forward, but Titania does not join her.

Niena looks back. "Let's get inside." The words falter on her lips as the outline of the fairy shimmers. Titania reaches out, confusion and fear racing across her pale features. And then she is gone. Where she was standing, now an old man walks. He spares one look at the girl's outstretched hand — and shoves his way past.

Chapter 17

Oil from a nearby brazier burns thickly as she hesitantly strides into the tavern.

"Tallow," Niena whispers. She squints as they walk past a table. "No, rush lights dipped in oil."

The villagers' collective stare at her darkens the hall, but none say anything, and most return to their drinks shortly after Niena passes. The smoke makes the air hard to breathe as she coughs. Behind her, the door swings shut. Niena ends up taking a table nearest the roast. Not ideal.

Several men steal glances at her. Titania can only stare, her ethereal hands following grooves in the table made by years of rowdy patronage.

The voice of an old man rumbles, "It is almost time for the harvest, I—"

Niena checks the back of her seat, resting just as the tavern's owner finishes serving the closest table.

"You don't look familiar," he rasps while waddling over. "Where you from?"

Niena smiles. "Quite so."

The man's eyebrows hang like the thatch at the entrance of the tavern. Between this and the podgy nose, his two little eyes light with clear focus.

Rubbing his jowls, he says, "Roast or stew? Onion and deer. The deer is a little old, so is the ale, but both is better for it, I say. That is all, nothing fancy here. Should I ready you, or are you waiting for someone else?"

"Stew would be fine for now," she says, avoiding further small talk. "And water."

"Will you be staying?"

Titania tries to take hold of the young woman's hand, but it goes unnoticed by the girl. Niena answers, "For just this night."

"Alone," he half sings. "Two bits, then, before you turn in."

"It is too late," Titania says with a sigh. She sees the girl hunch over, muttering something she can't make out as the fairy's hearing fouls. She attempts to rub her temple, another habit that makes no sense now.

Titania's eyes flutter open. *There's no way out, no easy escape.* The solitary window is made of oiled canvas, dirty and stained. No latch allows for easy opening. *Nothing I can do to save her.*

She regards her step-granddaughter one last time. "I'm sorry," she says. "If any part of you can hear me, travel south. There you will pass a wasteland, and the roads will take you further to a city called Skehfelthuz, or Maro Unsterbbēriz, as I hear in the dreams of men. There, maybe we can meet again."

A small hope, but not an unselfish one. The Teamor wanted Niena and her lyre. Their bargain was all the fairy had as hope. A deal wherein as much mischief went into keeping the other honest as fulfilling the terms. The cost remains the question, and she does not know the aim of their ambition. In their meetings, they expressed a desire to regain control of the silver throne, but this clearly was a lie.

Again she sighs, drifting away. This all felt wrong, a sensation as irritating as it was useless to dwell upon. *Yet another human weakness.* She had spent too much time among the mortals — time enough for their habits to pass to her, as well as their views on morality.

Guilt. Titania balls her fists, then releases them. Idle feet carry her to the oiled canvas window. Anger and joy are among the first emotions a new fairy learns. The more nuanced feelings usually come last — when a creature like her is doomed to fade.

"If you had just heeded my advice when I said we should move on, I would be with you." Titania growls. "So stubborn," chancing a look back to watch Niena enjoy her meal. "You must take greater care. There is no path that would be safe without it."

The thump of Niena's wrist hitting the table makes Titania raise her eyebrows. A fly comes too close to the girl's face, risking a swat. The fairy sneers.

"Else the Teamor will beat you, and you must fight for the scraps. Will your life be much different? Changed? Shall your choices let this world fall like Fairhome, into twilight with ever fewer fairies to tend the garden?"

Titania's translucent hands flash a sudden red, flushed with life. To survive is all — that is the game. To live, to enjoy the fruits of conquest. To love. "Rein…" His face winks across the window as if summoned, but it is only a daydream to a dream. Her anger fades into the numbness of reality. So, too, do her hands lose their color, turning pale.

A red-faced patron stares at the place where Titania was, wide-eyed and shivering. Titania, already moving away, smiles at him, and exhaustion from the effort drives the last bit of life from her hands. Resolved to what she must do in any case, she mimics a breath as the unnourishing energy from the dreams of the sleeping folk in the tavern overtakes her senses. She then moves through the closed window.

"Did I lie to the girl?" Titania says.

Night is no more the domain of evil than darkness, only the absence of light. But when the stars refuse to show and the fowl have fallen silent, grim thoughts echo the loudest.

"Yes, I did," she sighs. "What have I become?" A queer pain flows with her and the wind. Other emotions, faint as they are, join loosely on her journey. Away from the window. Away from the chimneys and past the smoke flowing around them in thick bands. Lastly, together they swirl against the night's backdrop, stirring the fireflies and starlight in a weird dance.

To the south. She forces herself through the pain of the guilt, what remains after the admission and the anger. *I know a place. Fates willing, below the waterfall, near the old barrows, I will find something that will invigorate me. Mayhap it will be enough for now.*

In the land men have come to call Earth, there are also many places of power, where ancient stories and songs are sung. Though by the time Rein came to visit her at her hut, few new ones were being created. As Sofie, Titania had drained many. To remain alive. To remain corporeal. She must do the same in this world, in Hearth.

Niena fell into that category. Oberon's granddaughter, not her own. Yet the last few days with the child have taken a toll. Twinged those new emotions and risked everything. For the first time in years, the fairy considers something other than herself. It is a thought she can't lose. Not by following an edge of trees, pine needles still clinging to the colors of summer. Or by threading through the eaves of a warden's home, uninvited. The dust that makes up the fairy ignites, and bursts through the air.

A league passes before her in a moment. Another in a second. Until the last vestiges of the forest fall back, ending in a small hill and grove. Upon flying near this landmark, Titania circles.

Spiraling down, down. The slight canopy envelops her, and she is granted visions of night fowl and flowing water.

Down, down. Pine needles give way to broadleaves. Down, down. The branches of the great trees dip and dip as if nature were shaking its fist. Down, down. Water tumbles over rock from a dizzying height. Titania looks up then, and catches the moon through the spray of a thousand droplets. There is no time for worry here. Not where the forest creatures come to bathe, and flowers from an ancient time cling to life as the moss and lichen cling to the rocks.

A chance wind takes her under the waterfall, hiding moon and canopy alike. The mist that is Titania drifts between the droplets and down into the silver bowl. There is no splash. No other measure of her intrusion. Above, the night is clear, and even through the cascade, some of the moon's light finds her.

Long ago, on a midsummer's eve, I once came into the company of a star watcher. He fled the ball for the quiet, so I followed.

Here, a young man held her. There, a young man kissed her. Titania touches her cheek and can suddenly fill the warmth with the Dutchman's lips. The memory forces her to freeze and materialize as quickly as if cold hands were thrust upon her unprotected stomach.

She remembers the feeling of his head in her lap. And so she can stand. She recalls the thickness of his hair between her fingers, and then she has arms once more.

An errant cry pulls Titania's attention away, past sickly-looking trees at the edge of the bowl and far beyond the boughs of the great trees. Behind her, water trickles from a waterfall, but she does not hear it. Nor does she feel the chill of the cool grass on her toes. Memories cling to the bowl, stewing, waiting for Titania to reach out and take from it. She glances at the sky; the high canopy blends with the grass.

The fairy queen's hand drifts through the water that sits over the ancient stone. She then places her fingers along her throat and tests her voice. A weak warble bubbles forth, ending in a cough. "Not good enough," she croaks.

Titania closes her eyes. And as she continues to speak, the fairy queen's voice slowly gains strength. Yet her form flickers. She shakes her head, watching her hands threaten to fade once more.

"I know what I must do, but there can be no room for error." And she looks west, where the scrublands start. Then south, and beyond a desolate land, a land that must still hold the city of Skehfelthuz, or Maro Unsterbbēriz, depending on who you speak with. "I will have to trust in her strength."

Ephemeral fingers glide over and through the worn edifice of the altar. Water splashes all around, but she still cannot hear it. Instead, Titania focuses her attention upon the power therein — power begat by years upon years of worship. She closes her eyes and whispers to the stone, hoping to draw what remains for her own purpose.

"In Seofuden, the weirding way, among the bird calls,
A gentle music forever plays in the canopy tall,
The rushing wind, I shall not know, to pass the endless hours
Forever waiting in the field below the silver tower
"Oh lady fair, oh gentleman bold, whose shoes are stained with mud,
Your lover's heart sits just below,
Forever pumping blood,
So where has gone your noble vow made with little toll?"
It lies under the silver tower, in a watery bowl."

Water drips from her fingernail, and Titania smiles. She can feel the cool touch of autumn. She can smell the faint musk of the moss.

With that, she climbs to the shore. Here, there is an old grove of willows gracing the waterline. Perhaps they are descendants of the ones planted eons ago. *Maybe*. This place has survived — and remained above ground, ever since the breaking of the world.

This, as she knows, is a marker. Beyond is the blasted dragon waste, and it is the city of Skehfelthuz. Where they shall begin their journey to Cuiven's Lee.

Chapter 18

The door to Higgins's cell opens.

"Good morning," he mutters, seeing two guards waiting, the slack-minded one from before not among them. His words are the spark, and the men rush forward. Rough hands grasp his arms. Swarthy fingers force something foul into his mouth, and a sack over his head.

"Get your damn hands off me. I know your mother," Rogard yells.

The wall rushes to meet Higgins as he is forced from the floor. At his side, his cellmate struggles, which ends with the sound of something hard hitting the wall. Rogard groans, but the apprentice can only choke on the rag as his binds are tightened. Soon after, they are made to walk on.

Blind, they stumble. Time and distance are counted only in the plod of their boots, or the venom of Rogard's threats. After running into another corner, Higgins thinks back to his time in the Forum Magicae, riddling out the maze underneath it when he was a student.

Those wanderings were part of the ritual of learning. Seek and find. Learn, and change your ways. Or paths. The riddle to their forced meanderings in this case must have a simple answer: to keep them from learning the route, or so Higgins figures.

A shove from a guard sends his shoulder into a door frame. He grunts. *Bastards.* In his early days in Liverpool, not long after Rein took him as an apprentice, Higgins had to endure just as much. The guard continues pushing them along.

New apprentices were made to walk through the tunnels under the forum, with only their master to guide them. Symbolic of their future doing the same in study, moving from catacomb to catacomb. Reading treatises. Listening to half-mad sorcerers. Both in his studies, and the initial ritual, Rein's mentorship resulted in many knocks on Higgins's head.

Higgins flinches against a backhand.

They are redoubling, trying to confuse us. He takes the blow unflinchingly — an action that earns him another elbow to the side. Once he is down, the guards say nothing, and after a while he is prodded to his feet. They continue forward. Down a long corridor. Up a flight of stairs. Around. Around. Rogard's cursing duels with the prison. Then they stop.

"You won't find a rope big enough for me," Rogard mutters.

Higgins turns his head to his cellmate's voice, this time earning no rebuke. The guards' breathing is hard. One of them calls out a man's name. There is a click, a creak, then a shove forward.

Chilly air, colder voices — the stench of cattle hits them immediately. To add further insult, the bag is thrown off, and the apprentice is blinded by the sudden reintroduction of light.

Torchlight. Higgins blinks. *Is it not morning?*

It is indeed. Not enough time has passed for madness to take root, so when the apprentice chances a look, he is relieved to see that the sun is veiled. Turning earthward, Higgins sees faces that make him long for the greeting he received from the guards.

Wherever he looks, he finds the effects of the flash blizzard. From the buildings wrecked by the ice and the roofs buckled by heavy, melted snow. To the haggard faces with signs of frostbite. And the livestock still lying where they fell. Worse, no one seems to be interested in setting things right.

It is a small village, and for this affair barely two score appear in the center. However, despite the few occupied buildings, there are several stone structures in ruins. Also houses, storage shacks, and huts set into these. Other shelters, and a lack of adult villagers. *There are many children.* But these seem to stay close to rows of wagons resting in a greenway.

A rush of blood to his head is followed by a tinge of nausea, a sickness which is not helped by rough guards. He rights his head just in time to see the long, bony finger pointed accusingly at him.

"It's the Heggri," Rogard whispers.

A feather pokes out of matted hair that wreaths around two piercing eyes. To the villagers, she is called Heggri, owing to the nose that curves like a beak. But this is not her name. Nor, if you were to ask, would any of those who live here remember what it is.

The crone's neck hooks as she arcs a claw-like finger at Higgins. The apprentice's knees buckle. He fights this, turning away from the fire burning in her heathen eyes. His legs weaken and the world spins until rough, unhelpful hands, the same that dragged him from his hole of a prison, force him fully down.

"She says if you repeal the curse, she won't flay you," Rogard grumbles, joining him at the crone's feet. "Today."

You would think my nerves would remember dying. Dirty faces rush about to meet him. Men, women, and children. Some are angry. Others seem just tired, but all are touched by a pall of doom. Higgins drops his sight to Heggri's feet.

"This one likes skinning men," Rogard says to the apprentice's cheek. "She also likes to prattle on, so pick your poison."

Higgins's head droops lower. The spell he cast before has long faded. However, it became clear at the edge of the magick's working, that Rogard spoke something close to the Gaelic the Irish still speak. *How is it I can't understand her?* He thinks as he grits his teeth.

"...Because you are an idiot apprentice," Heggri cackles. She then shambles forward and speaks again in a hoarse whisper: "Mannelig, I wonder if you have always bumbled your way towards doom?"

"Then you know I am innocent?"

"No point talking to her wizard," Rogard says. "Unless you just like pissing in the wind. These kinds are for theatrics, where the smoke and mad women—"

The old woman's brows then lift, and a raised hand quiets Rogard. "And he says I like to prattle."

Mountains of crag and wrinkles rise in the few expressions as she returns to the apprentice. She speaks softly then, and with a not unkind shake of her head. "You have trespassed, Mannelig," she says. "Innocent? Hardly anyone is that. Doomed? Obviously, and kin in kind." The crowd around grows silent to hear her words, and even Rogard's head tilts to the side as if harkening. So Heggri speaks even quieter.

"They are here," she says. "The dead walk the fields, which is untidy. It is said that the old masters too have come. This I do not think is truth." She slips in closer, coming up to his right ear and breathing so heavily that Higgins can smell the ochre on her teeth. "You are not their desire, but a rabbit caught in a snare is still dead, eh?"

"Do you know what they are after?" The rattle of the woman's breath catching is all the answer he needs. "I do know, and I can help your people."

"That time has passed."

"They still live," Higgins stammers. "My master—"

"Is lost. You should not look to him, Mannelig. You should not look in many places, least of all behind you."

"What else am I to do?"

The crone hisses. "Do? The only answers the old know for truth is how to get old." She smiles, and here Higgins wishes she hadn't. "But I say this: Do whatever you must, and don't look back. Else, when the night finally falls, you will hold up hope as a candle, and step out into a darkness so thick, you will never find your way out again."

"Prophecy?"

"Truth." She backs away, smile black-gaped and wicked. Flapping her hands like a bird to the crowd, she cackles. "Tomorrow night I shall have a new coat."

But there is no cheer among them, and Rogard and Higgins are dragged back to their cell in silence.

♫

Higgins's fingers alight upon the cell wall, tracing the marks left by a former prisoner in the stone. The gouges grow shallower — weaker, as the days pass. Until the last is only visible at certain angles and when the torchlight is strongest.

He tugs at another string with his teeth. For some reason, the guards left his hands bound forward. Perhaps a mistake, but iron bars are harder to overcome, and tomorrow they die. The gesture is unlikely to be due to kindness.

"Have you heard the tale of the prince and the raven?" Rogard tuts when no answer is given; apparently, the relative quiet of the cell offends him. "Once, a prince was traveling through the southland forests with his servant. Far, far to the east of here."

The old woman was right about one thing. Higgins furrows his brows at the man's geographical knowledge, but the gesture is silent.

Rogard continues: "They delved deep into the wild, until chancing upon a hut nestled in the roots of a cliff's stone. No sooner had they arrived at the door that a maiden came to them, trying to shoo them off with a warning that her stepmother was a witch who disliked strangers. A witch, who was known for being a poisoner."

"My aunt was a poisoner. At least when it came to fish, and anything that didn't walk on four feet."

Rogard grumbles. "Maybe you heard the tale of the sheep and the three horses?"

"I probably have," Higgins says. "Who are these stories for, anyways?"

Rogard hums as if considering. Finally, he says, "For me own self." He looks at the door and throws back his head. "Or maybe that some bastards can hear we are still in here."

"I have not seen anyone in many hours," Higgins says. "Have you seen anything from your side?"

"No, but I haven't been looking."

Both men lift their heads to witness something scurry across the floor. Rogard stretches his legs around their bucket. "In my village, stories are important. Here, though, they have a different taste to 'em. Might be the witch is right, and if so, I want for a fairy to hear its own tale and look favorably on me."

"There are very few of them left," Higgins says.

"Hrmm. I will then settle on the hope Grim's sour milk will not be the last thing I have tasted."

"This Grim is a man?"

"Aye," he says. "What of it?"

Higgins squints at Rogard, who is little more than a dark blob against the torch's glow. "You folk are strange."

"Says the wizard," Rogard snorts. "Wearing that ridiculous… What do you call that thing on your head?"

Higgins wrinkles his nose. "You mean my hat?"

"That's not an honest hat," and he can imagine Rogard shaking his head.

"I never knew there was such a thing as a liar hat."

"Oh, there is; there is, wizard. Yours is too odd. A wizard's hat if I've ever seen one. Not that I have." A pebble pings the wall at the far end. Then another. Each time, Rogard makes as if to speak, then falls quiet.

"You're worried about tomorrow," Higgins says.

Rogard grunts. "This is what I mean about a dishonest hat. The truth, wizard, is that it is you who has this fear."

"I hardly think my hat has anything to do with it."

"You don't know this," he says, stretching his legs out. "Have your kind spent any time thinking on it? Or maybe you have, but the hats have taken over your minds."

"That's ridiculous." Higgins snorts.

"No more than us facing the axe tomorrow."

This sends chills up Higgins's spine. Rein could not save him now.

"Chords," Rogard laughs finally. "To die so, after so many years of…You can take some pleasure knowing that their blades won't be able to take that ugly stump of yours in one hack, I think."

"I am not sure that I will — take any pleasure from it, that is."

He crooks his neck towards his cellmate. In the gloom, Higgins can see Rogard's barrel chest rising slowly. Up. Down. He huffs, or scoffs, then furthers himself into the shadows of the dimly lit cell. Away from Higgins.

"Do you think hanging would be a better way to go?"

"Now we are talking about something I am familiar with," Higgins says. "I…didn't mean it that way. Just that I have become accustomed to death."

Rogard pops his knuckles. One. Two. Then clears his throat. "And?"

"Hanging is one of the worst," Higgins says. "Rarely does it ever break your neck on the first drop. It's also a nasty way for a loved one to find you…" He rubs his own neck. "You get all distended and… doesn't look nice."

"Hmm. If I had been smarter, I would have just let the cold take me. That death I do know; it's a quiet one," Rogard says. "But I did not think I would be dragged in here and blamed for this. And why? Because I did not re-light the fires? They say I was drunk…Grim told them that, the bastard, to save his own… Now, that is a neck that needs stretching."

"You know, Rogard, I had nothing to do with this snow?" Higgins leans on his bound hands. "I know what it looks like, but it is the truth. Honest hat."

"If you did, or didn't, what does it matter? I am a proper Isfall man. They came here from the east, from their boats made of reeds, so we are told. My mother used to sing to me, at least. Through honor, I was bound to come here, defend this very tomb we sleep in, but they put me on a wall." Rogard slams his back into stone with a heavy thud. "I am not theirs to so command. I do not belong to their tribe. By the chords, and the old pacts…" He then quiets, and Higgins can hear his wheeze fade into a chuckle. "Oh, wizard. These people are clever ones. They have killed my people off slowly, and are never at fault."

"You aren't from here?"

"Who would admit to having come from this hole?" Rogard brings his face into the light, turns his nose up as if the words he spoke have fouled the air, then falls back once more with an audible slump. "I do not call the mountains my home. My village lies far to the…" He halts abruptly, then coughs.

Higgins tries to stop himself, too, but the words still come out: "Do you ever want to go back there?" He clears his throat, laughing to himself at Rogard's expression. "I mean, if you didn't have an axe over your head."

"No, I don't," Rogard says. "Well, not much to go back to. It is quiet, I give you that. They at least herd cattle." Then, with a dark expression: "I will be going back though, it seems."

"That's better than goats?"

"Sheep," he says. "Are a little over three and a half feet from hoof to their curly head. Cattle are about five feet or so."

Higgins tilts his head, and Rogard answers: "When women become scarce, which do you think they'll go for first? Not many men here are so tall."

"Most of their sheep are dead now," Higgins says, hiding his face.

Rogard wheezes and hooks his thumb into his belt. Straining. "Oh, chords. Well, we must escape now."

The air is cold and humid. Stale, too, full of the musk of two unwashed prisoners and the decay of things unmentionable. Yet it is still a pleasure to Higgins; the dead envy the living, even their pains. "Do you have any ideas how?"

"I've got nothing," Rogard whispers. "If I could just get a good, solid club. If only, but I am no wizard." The last part coming out almost as a question.

Higgins lets out the breath he was holding. Slow and quiet, with a timbre that is measured. His words are rough. "I have some thoughts." Then aside, as if in a long sigh: "Magick will only do so much; there will be fighting, and killing."

"I'm last of the Isfall Galenian stock. Broad of chest, strong in arms, I have borne the honor of guard of the tombs before any of the other whelps of my village's brood," Rogard proclaims. "First with the spear, and first to blood. Last to leave any fight. I have entered the dread city, I have seen Maro Unsterbbēriz. I have walked the streets of the temple of the moon and read of their heathen ways."

"I will take that to mean you have no moral objections."

Rogard barks a quick laugh, then drops his tone. His voice is unsure at first. "Aye, mayhaps, mayhaps." Then grows in confidence. "It would do me well to know the measure of our potential alliance. How did you get yourself into this mess, wizard? The wilds are not for someone like you, so caught unawares. What were you really doing out there? If you were not cooking up a storm like you claim."

Higgins shifts, settling with the binds. The air is still stale and musky, but there is another odor here. "Me and my mast— mentor and friend, Christaan De Rein, were chasing a thief."

"A thief," Rogard bellows, then quickly lowers his voice. "A thief," he repeats excitedly. "Oh, this sounds like a tale, but is it the truth? Or another dishonest hat? I would love to know which."

"It is the truth. Also, quite a tale, in that you are not wrong," Higgin says. "One with terrible monsters, unspeakable evil, and heroics. Mine, my master's…and maybe yours?"

"Ahh, ahh-hahaha, I see what you are doing," Rogard bellows. "You are calling to my wandering mercenary heart, and I approve, wizard. Though I am not so easily snared. At least not without the proper bait."

"Grim's milk?"

"Pah," Rogard spits. "Not that, anything but that. What are you going to offer me that I haven't heard? Gold? Jewels? Women? Those are more trouble than worth, I will have you know. They also like to take the other two."

The tone was defiant. Full of the bravado of youth, and for a moment, Higgins is taken back to his younger days, playing, wrestling, fighting in Alford. Before his family moved to London for better pay.

"A chance to save the world."

That cold air is pushed roughly aside by Rogard's laughter. "You sound like our witch," he says. "Let's save our necks first, wizard."

"Everything big must start small."

"I can tell you would be a hoot at a wedding." Then, with a quiet laugh, "And a funeral. I will let that one pass," Rogard says. "Let us be serious, we have much to talk about tonight."

So it was that this day Higgins became the storyteller. He told Rogard of the Udur, their origins, as far as he knew. He spoke about Rein and some of their adventures. Between tales, they planned. Hope was kindled. Even as their agency was whittled away with the passing of the hours.

Chapter 19

Twenty years of studying lore. Twenty years of trespassing through crumbling ruins at the behest of his master — and this barbarian from cattle country has the choicest bits served to him on a platter.

"There is no recourse for it," Higgins sniffs. "If he did not understand the spell work conceptually, this boat would sink before it lost its moorings." As it was, the man had trouble comprehending the concept of the Étincelle and Mort, the beginning and end words that create the mental formation of a spell and termination. The Forme was easy enough, as children here are apparently told of witches and the ingredients of their spells.

"I've already been in a sinking boat once."

The morning is now a stranger. Noon passed without greeting. The afternoon stayed overlong, allowing Higgins to idle in his plan making, and Rogard to steal the reins. Two hours is all it took for the Galenian to make the apprentice long for the axe. He rubs his wrist. At least the last of his bindings is broken.

"Fey is the golden throne,
Cold as the elven bone..."

Higgins drops a pebble he'd been using to scratch the wall.

"Held in silver land,
Rotten upon the hand..."

"Udur. A spell song," Higgins whispers, eyes searching for his cellmate, who lies asleep nearby. A chill seizes the room, fast moving and biting.

"Fear the moon, the wolf's howl.
Fear the night, death's cowl."

His cellmate's hand swats empty air. The second time he is shaken, the back of it catches Higgins in the face. The man rolls over when Higgins grabs him and slaps back.

"Blasted man," Higgins froths. "Get up, we've got to get out of here. Out…God. Devils—"

"Fey and elf and man shall die,
And in the black to forever lie."

Higgins should have anticipated the return of the Udur.

Rogard tries to sit up, face moving from confusion to rage in lightning fashion. "What are you doing on top of me?"

"Quiet, listen."

Between each line of the repeating chant, there are whispers — shards of pleading and terrible curses. The cellmates look at each other.

Rogard leaps up and crashes against the door just before Higgins. The men's combined desperation rattles their cage, scattering dust that has been lying for ages.

"Those bars are made from pig iron," Rogard growls. "It's old and rusted — we can break it. Keep up, keep up."

Rust? "Could you scrape some of that off on your side," Higgins says. "I can make a nasty surprise with the iron dust."

"For what, the guards? I bet they are gone. I could just break off one of the bars for 'em anyways."

"No, listen." Higgins's voice cracks, and he accidentally kicks yesterday's bucket. "You aren't going to fight the Udur with that. They aren't fey, they do not fear iron or bell."

"Bells, what the ever-loving—? Bah."

"Forget it, I have gathered enough, I think."

Together they watch in shock as the lock clatters to the ground.

"It was never set." Higgins answers the unasked question, then answers another: "The old woman. We were so caught up in our misery, we never noticed."

Rogard raises his trembling hands. "They must be gone. Left after tossing us in here." The cell door creaks at his gentle push. "Or are dead."

Higgins grabs Rogard by the shoulder, hands clumping the man's tunic. "No thinking, acting."

The torch's light is dying, the flames having eaten most of the jute. They take it anyway. Into these rough-hewn tunnels, through which their captors marched them to meet the crone the day before. Fumbling their way into disused sections of the jail. And the tomb.

"We're not getting out of here by morning at this—"

"Shh," Higgins interrupts, shading the torch in a corner.

"Fear the moon, the wolf's howl.
Fear the night, death's cowl."

The apprentice peers around, expectant. "Devil…" The hallway is empty. "Morning would be good right about now." He glances over his shoulder. "Won't save us from the Udur, but at least we can see."

Rogard puts his hand on the corner to peek, and as if taking offense to this, the torch sputters out in a huff of smoke. Higgins mutters something under his breath, then: "Doesn't matter. I think I know the way. Just like school."

"Fey and elf and man shall die,
And in the black to forever lie."

"Keep your hand on my shoulder," Higgins says. "Don't look back. Block their song from your mind now. They are hunting."

"Are these the Udur you spoke of?"

"Yes, and the dead they drive."

163

"The dead can be broken," Rogard says, but sounds unconvinced while doing as bidden. "What are these master creatures — are they ghouls?"

"Worse," Higgins whispers. "Do you not remember our conversation yesterday? Predators, older than the three worlds. They are not mortal."

Magick, balefire, is what they need. Yet that spell requires too much of the spirit, the key Forme aside from blood. *Would I be able to run out of here in my current state if I fought them?* One of the narrow thresholds he must have bumped into presents itself then, and thereafter Higgins leads them down a long corridor. The stone has been worked, but not recently. Guards have passed here, and he guesses, from the rate of incline, so have they. The ground is dust-free.

"If only the nature of their housekeeping could lead a better hand in our escape," Rogard grumbles. "There are plenty of rat droppings. Can you use those?"

Higgins tilts his head, feigning a reply. What magic could he use against the Udur? Iron dust is useless without straw. Sheep droppings are good only to ruin someone's clothes. "No. Dirt can be combined with a pebble for a fortifying spell, but that won't protect against them," Higgins says. "Was there something I may have missed?"

"Chords."

The shock in Rogard's voice causes Higgins to swing round. He steadies himself, reaching out, searching for the edge of terror that always comes when the Udur are close — or the pressure when they have touched your mind.

There is only the first. Powerful, but not overwhelming. Or directed. "Rogard?"

"The elves and bone." Rogard's muttered answer drowns under a high wail. "I've enough of this." He elbows off Higgins, and the back of the apprentice's head slaps the wall.

"I told you not to listen," Higgin snarls, grabbing where it hurts. "I told you not to bend your mind to them."

The passage echoes with the thunder of Rogard's boots: *thomb, doom.* Rushing on, making a course towards the deathly wail. Higgins tries to stall the man. A hand is shoved away. The grip on the tunic torn free. *Thomb. Doom.*

Barreling on in a wild haste. New ways open right, left, but Rogard rushes straight. They pass doors so rotten that most of the wood lies on the ground. And sections of the tunnel that have caved in, further on. These slow the Galenian, but only the confrontation with a dead end finally halts their flight.

Higgins bends over, nearly collapsing into Rogard. "What are you doing? You idiot," he wheezes, but Rogard doesn't seem to pay attention. In the darkness, Higgins can hear the man fumbling.

"What is this place?" A grunt from his cellmate forces Higgins to quickly add, "I don't think I've seen any other building of theirs made from stone."

"Used to be a tomb." Rogard spits up a gobbet of phlegm. "There has to be something here."

A tomb. The longer Higgins dwells on the word, the thicker the air becomes. Disturbed dust from the ages summons memories of the other side, of life in the realm of death.

"Mortal weapons are no use," Higgins repeats.

"I'd still rather have a good sword in my hand." He kicks at something, adding the clatter of bones to the Udur's screech.

"I'll have that."

Rogard's laugh falls into a dangerous chortle. "Must have been a child, can't use that as a club."

"I'll still take it." The token of mortality tugs further at the apprentice. The possessor of this bone departed long ago. Gone to where the dead wait, or maybe beyond. On that realm, there were many shades that wandered, neither seeing each other or themselves.

The hunting Udurs' voices carry down the tunnel to them. Rogard spreads out his hands and pushes Higgins behind him.

There were worse things than the stillness in that realm, Higgins thinks, lowering the man's huge arm. *There were worst things than contemplating droplets in an ever-growing sea of death.* Higgins brushes himself off. The Teamor were there, neither forgetting who they are or their hate. Where they weren't, their hounds hunted.

"We are trapped. I have led us to our end," Rogard says, voice cracking.

The wail draws closer. "The Udur," Higgins whispers. "I am not ready for this," as he eyes the arm bone. "Yet I am still strong enough for bad ideas."

Their song returns, freezing Higgins. He peers into the dark, straining, then uses the jagged edge of the bone to slice his hand. The chant is neither close nor far, but the wail is almost upon them. *"Solna nea…"* he falters, nearly falling from the strain.

"I'm the last of Galenia. I have faced the dead of Maro Unsterbbēriz," Rogard yells. "You will not take me so easily, wizard's demon. I will fight you with everything I have."

If the beast were stalking them, now it must be running. Higgins looks through bleary eyes at the man. "So you shall," he says and strikes, grasping Rogard's arm.

"Solna nea, Oran cruchaid, an beath an tene!"

Spirit fire leaps from bone, eliciting a cry from Rogard and Higgins as the needed Mort is drawn from both men's souls at once. Flames engulf the charging Udur. Higgins throws back his head and laughs. "From hell's heart," while Rogard adds, "And from my mama's glare," screaming.

The Udur reel, and twist again. The flames seethe through one, then another, and black flesh bubbles and boils under the torrent.

"Demons," Rogard says. The still living remains of the Udur drip and quiver on the walls. "Demons and wizards."

The apprentice ambles forward and drops himself on the wall nearest to Rogard. "More will come," Higgins says, pushing the man. "And these will join. They cannot be killed. They will not stop."

"Don't you ever do that to me again," Rogard growls. "I may not be able to harm those bastards, but I will kill you."

The Galenian snatches at the tomb's alcove, and shakes loose another arm bone, and from these and others the two make new torches. He spares one glare for Higgins, then stomps back through catacomb and tunnel. Once more, they retrace the path that was run in panic. The worm-eaten doors and divergent pathways return right, left. Down one of these they decide to travel, finding another corridor. They continue, meandering along forgotten tunnels until the old stonework gives way to newer carvings.

"I knew my nose had the right of it," Rogard says, stretching.

Between the two of them, it is his spirits that seem to be the lightest. Yet, it is a façade. When the light from the torch dwindles once more and bleeds into the next room through a cellar door, and a new noise is heard, it is hard to tell which is darker: this, or his cellmate's frown.

"What is that sound there?" asks Rogard. "More of those things?"

The apprentice tests the way forward. He pauses and places his hand on the door. "I don't hear anything; I am going to open it." A creak of wood. A flash of light and sound. And then?

"Rats," Higgins says with a sigh. "Lots of them."

"This doesn't seem real," Rogard whispers over his shoulder. "This whole mess. Nothing of it can be real, right? I am mad and gibbering in my cell. You're just my fungus-chewed mind getting back at me."

"Get ahold of yourself, man."

But echoes in the empty hallway are real enough, as is the draft. Braziers hang lifeless from the ceiling, offering nothing. Higgins rubs his jaw. *Something isn't right*— his breath catches from an unexpected trick after an errant footstep: a click from a trap, metallic and dull, resounds off the stone walls.

Somewhere deep in the dungeon there is an answering *thomb*.

"Of course, we are still in the tomb," Higgins says, then swings to Rogard.

"Traps," Rogard says. "Or fiddly things that close doors elsewhere. Useful things. If they are traps, they won't work. Would have been removed a long time ago, like in other tombs, else there would be many dead guards."

Higgins nods. "There was another branch in the passage; let us go right this time."

Retracing swiftly brings them to the other passage, which continues straight for ten meters, then forks. Ahead, a few lit braziers remain, dangling from the center of the ceiling. Black rules right. The apprentice can feel the will of the Udur in his bones, but nothing stirs. The drip of oil, and the limits of the dying torch, try to fill the gaps. They turn at the skittering of tiny feet, or the flirt of a shadow.

With reason. "Do you hear that?" Higgins says, as he traces a finger along the edge of an architrave.

"Singing."

"God, I hope there is tea at the end of this adventure," Higgins whispers. The old passage inclines. The cold now has seeped through the soles of their boots and clothing, sapping their strength. At another crossroads, they head right, seeing that this way continues the incline.

"Fey is the golden throne,
Cold as the elven bone..."

Rogard reaches out, batting the edges of the wall with the torch. The apprentice forestalls him from continuing, dragging him by the elbow elsewhere, to the other passage, left.

"One's close," Higgins says over his shoulder. The two turn a corner, then stop immediately.

"Held in silver land,
Rotten upon the hand..."

Through the grate of a closed portcullis, mist and a long, slithery form wind through what must be a corridor that this entrance intercepts. Higgins holds his breath and quickly passes the torch around the bend to Rogard. Together they slowly back away.

"We will go straight this time," Higgins whispers, then snaps his head around. "You are a tomb guard — why am I again leading?"

Rogard hesitates, then passes the torch back to Higgins. "You think I'd get us any less lost? The deep places weren't made for trespassers." Then to Higgins's back, as he faces forward. "Or sane men."

The way straight ahead reveals itself in time to be newer and lit by iron braziers above. Several passages dot the sides, leading off into crude storage rooms, half of stone and half of a rudimentary type of brick. They pass more crossroads but proceed forward. At their back, Higgins can feel the tell-tale approach of the Udur's mist seeping from one of the former branches. And the many eyes upon him. Unsteady feet push him forward, forward. Then up. Gaining confidence when the floor rises in a slight incline.

An unwholesome, shrill cry from an Udur sparks a rampage. Furious hordes of rats flee their way. Rogard stumbles along, the crunch of bones adding to the cacophony. Another wail is all it takes for the two to join in terror. Their footsteps drum, faster and faster. Sweat sticks to Higgins's sleeves, and their torch expires.

They feel the way forward. The narrow stretch gives way to a widening. At the end there is a pair of doors set into the angle of their incline.

"It's the exit," Higgins yells, slowing down as fleeing rats pass below the gap in the door. Rogard, however, does not slow enough to keep from landing hard against the old wood. Iron handles jingle at his effort to grasp them.

Sweaty hands grasp and paw for a way out. Tired minds keep them from coordinating, and three times when they take hold of a handle, and one pushes, the other falls upon it to try the opposite way. Finally, on the fourth try, a breach is managed; Rogard opens a crack just wide enough for each to shimmy through at a time. Even so, more than a moment's worth of heavy breathing is spent, back against wood, braced. All the while, their terror is peaked by the keening.

Once through, the expected tinges of morning's light are missing. It is black, as black almost as the tunnel. Only the gasp of air wanting to find its way into the passage behind tells them they have left the underworld. The wooden door slams closed at their back.

"Devil—"

The warmth of the fire dies quickly with the wind. And Higgins spoke loudly; too loudly.

Heavy, plodding thuds answer around them. Their brief calm ends, and they reel about, desperately trying to find the next steps. Higgins bends low and searches the ground. The next cry is also his, as he lays hands on something that may aid.

"Sol Lochrein."

A light just bright enough to both illume and instill terror kindles in a ball above the apprentice's head. Shadows seem to move everywhere. Wicking, dancing. Around the mist emerge the shapes of huts, of barns and other buildings. But these are not what they focus on.

"Couldn't you have cast that earlier?" Rogard whines as the first of the shambling figures enters the radius of the light.

On the walls of a barn to their right, another silhouette lengthens from a fence post. More join beyond, wrenching themselves out of houses and outbuildings in jerky motions. A low sobbing seems to come from everywhere.

Higgins holds up the rest of the straw to the air. "I had no grimoire to cast from, and no straw for the Mort." His shaking hands toss dust then, and his voice carves the firelight-touched motes into the next spell. "Shut your eyes! *Sleah grian.*"

The sobs turn into an explosion of angry wails as the light crackles. Higgins's fingers flit about the softening embers, spreading them and their light through the doomed village. Phantom shapes appear from the misshapen dark. Hands, arms, and fingers crawl towards them.

A clanging of iron doors behind them makes him turn his head, which he quickly turns back. "No, wait—"

Rogard tenses and springs, kicking the first figure in their way, then spins to meet the others. The wail of Udur in the tunnels rises in a crescendo as the second undead monster joins a third. But Rogard does not back away. Instead, he charges towards them and Higgins, the latter ducking just in time to avoid both the lurch of the monsters and Rogard's fist.

Teeth splinter and ribs crack just under Rogard's hearty laugh as knuckles meet unarmored flesh.

Higgins boggles. A cold hand stabs out from a rolling mist, clambering for his neck, just missing it, and grabbing his shoulder. The apprentice flails and the effort ends up dragging both to the ground. The chill of the creature saps him.

"Off me, you devil," he screams, his fist meeting cold flesh again and again.

A warm hand this time grips him by the shoulders, pulls him violently to his feet. His gaze swerves. From body to body. To the catastrophe of a face below him.

"Devil take this," Rogard says, stealing one of Higgins's curses. "Let us flee this place."

Ahead of the spell light, shadows show on the side of an old barn. One. Two. The exaggerated forms of spears and helmets, framed against a wall like some child's puppet show.

"No, not that way. Forward, forward," Rogard yells, and dashes ahead, with the apprentice fast on his heels.

Flashes of spells flip through Higgins's mind, as if they were on little cards and spun by a crank. *First things first, to stop shaking.* The words spin, spin. Then slow, settling on one quote, from his favorite author. Virgil. He closes his eyes and reaches deep within himself. To the root of his heel. Trying to find strength. Into the ground, and the mountain.

Lord, the reagents. What the bloody hell am I doing?

Rogard's shout is neither a proper war cry nor a scream. It hits Higgins and the shambling horde simultaneously, like the yell of an angry cat whose tail has been trodden.

Clumsily. Wildly as a bull, in Rogard's case, they charge. Into the chaos. Stepping on a prone undead. Pushing through flailing arms. Towards the barn. Higgins here takes the lead, and upon seeing the wraithlike soldiers, spears in hand and shields raised on the left, both men turn simultaneously to veer around the far-left side instead.

"Where we going?" Rogard screams over the undead cries.

In flight, few can outrun Higgins.

"To the gallows," he yells.

"Wait. What?"

"We need the forest," Higgins repeats, rumbling into a path between buildings. Rogard crashes into him soon after, and both seem to find the same uncovered mosaic and the same slick spot that sends them to the ground, slapping and sliding.

Behind them, the sounds of heavy footsteps approach.

"Quiet now," Higgins says. "There's not much between us and them."

Together they skirt open tent flaps, collapsed ruins. Left at a crossroads, then past one of the few chamber doors. Higgins brushes cobwebs from his head. The footsteps come closer.

"There's no surviving in the wilds of Isfalmaren, not when the night has come." Rogard says at his side, shaking his head. "Will these things not chase us even then?"

Higgins peeks around a hut built into a ruined wall. For all their hustle, they have only come halfway. "Just keep moving," he says heavily. The apprentice checks on his comrade then, catching the wild look that flashes on the man's face. "Always forward."

Their attempt at stealth becomes a trot as shouts and commands rumble behind them. Then, upon breaching the main road into the village's center, they break into a run. Here they encounter the first living resident of the town: a goat loose from its pen.

Over the footsteps, over the groans of the undead, Higgins can hear Rogard sucking in his breath. Ahead, a twisting mass of both undead and livestock stops them.

One. Higgins's flexes his hands. He searches his memory. The best spell for this would involve something with fire — *fire always works.* And those reagents, he has.

The apprentice rubs the remainder of the rust from the iron bars in his hands. Rolling it over the straw.

Two. Rogard's wary tread shakes his train of thought. Higgins recovers. "Menippus's *Remedy for the Unobligingly Fey* has the answer, I think. Fast spells, as quick as one can muster. That is the way. Though…his best work was with vampires."

Rogard bursts forth before the next count, screaming his nail-biting war cry. Higgins scrambles, his mind racing; he utters the first spell that comes to mind: *"Dus na mair."*

A chorus of terrified bleating joins Rogard's shouts as several sheep are simultaneously set on fire, sprayed with the splinters from an incinerated stall and introduced to a chord of menacing strings as if pulled directly from Haydn's *Die Worte des Erlösers am Kreuze.*

It was the same spell that Higgins once used to wake all the professors at the Curatorium in Liverpool. Sheep flee every which way, some of them on fire, breaking fence, paddock.

"We are still in the middle of the damn village," Rogard says weakly, beard apparently singed. He then snaps around to face Higgins as confusion, bleating, and chaos reign around them.

"Run," Higgins shouts.

The flaming quadrupeds rush to the supposed safety of the village's other flammable buildings. Thatch roofs light up here. There. Then, just as the bleating dies down, the fire torches the buildings.

Higgins and Rogard, however, do not wait around. They rush through the fires, dancing around the undead lingering at a well, even as some try to grab hold of them.

"Dus na mai!!"

Another round. More fire. More chaos. Rogard uses this to bowl over a reduced rank of now possessed villagers, with Higgins following fast. But they are not free yet. By now, Udur have been roused all over the village, and as Higgins looks back, he can see a score of the monsters beginning to pursue.

They press on, gaining the forest. Here, their running turns frantic. Shapes rush at them from the left, right. Bounding over their heads. Crashing into trees and brush. Only when they reach the top of a small hill does this onslaught relent.

"Just keep moving," Higgins says, pondering which action to take as Rogard disappears into the clutch of trees, up and over the underbrush before it. Higgins narrows his eyes and spins to face the oncoming assault.

A bob of black swishes in the undergrowth to his right. Higgins bites his thumb, sucking in his gut considerably at the same time. Half a score of the undead have entered after them, the brass studs in their belts glinting through the foliage and their wizened hands clawing their way up the hill.

"Bugger!" Higgin gasps in an explosion of pent-up air.

The out-of-place cry of an owl briefly startles him, but he shrugs it off and steps to the side, gauging the distance between him and the approaching creatures.

Trees sway on a distant hill, their bright green tops clashing with the sky, brushing off any clouds that want to mar the perfection of the day. From one of his unbroken pockets, Higgins pulls out a smattering of black dust. *Gunpowder.* He raises his hand and starts walking forward. The undead push forward, closing the distance slowly thanks to the underbrush.

"*Bas,*" he intones the Étincelle, flitting the gunpowder, the Forme, between his thumb and forefinger.

With each tread, the land and sky around him changes. At first, he only notices a switch in the music of the undergrowth. From the low background hum of insects emerges the hunting cries of creatures that should not be active in the morning. The owl again.

"*De ten agus.*" Power touches his tongue, makes his skin itch.

Then come the alterations an altered man such as himself cannot shrug off. To the sky. To the feel of the land underneath his feet.

"Deg a—" He stammers, the spell flitting away in his mind.

Darkness suddenly hangs halfway on the horizon, titled, like a picture badly hung. His shoulders hunch under the weight. "What?"

Higgins's eyes swing left and right. He looks up, following the movement of the undead villagers' own heads as they suddenly know fear. The other half of the sky is heavy with queer clouds that carry a green tint. Higgins grumbles and lowers his head, then smiles.

Fey magic.

Vines strike up and left from the undergrowth and from encrusted trees on all sides of the guardsmen. They wrap around legs, torsos. Necks, arms, and armament too.

"Damn," he thinks as he listens to them screech, twist, and turn.

Leaves rustle behind him. Higgins spins. From the same clutch of trees Rogard fled to, Sethlan emerges, pushing the Isfall man before him. And with his lips still working the spell story, the elf draws his bow and sends a single arrow to the chest of each of their assailers.

Thunder crackles in a cloudless sky. Then dissipates, while the sound of rain pelts Higgins without dampening the ground. This happens twice more, then stops, falling away as the last man dies.

"Sethlan?"

If wind were an answer, Higgins receives plenty of it. A gust nearly takes his hat, and Higgins covers his face as it ripples around the elf. He bends over to pick up a small, curly-haired child.

"Come," Sethlan says, and disappears into the forest without another word.

"Come on, lad," Higgins says, taking Rogard by the shoulder. "It'd be in your best interest to stay close this time."

An unsaid agreement passes between the three, and a realization: This is only the beginning. For Higgins, the priority has turned from finding the girl and whatever consequences that entails to saving his master. And surviving. He shares a concerned look with Rogard, and the two men follow the elf.

Chapter 20

Dawn finds Niena rather unwelcoming to its sudden appearance. Ruddy light, filtered through the canvas window, teases one of her eyes open. One. Without Titania to move her along, the girl does what any teenager might: She rolls over and goes back to sleep.

When time and a more persistent sun ray finally do stir her, the wakeup is a more painful affair. For the weather is turning, and the last heat from summer's wrath has left a parting gift: an oppressive headache. Winter is knocking at the door.

"And way too loudly," she groans. Lying in bed for so long has left her with the usual dry mouth and a back that also aches. She moves gingerly, and with a purpose, what would make Marny smile. Niena shields her eyes. "Titania?"

Not here. The girl stretches lazily before rolling out of bed, the shock of the cold floor eliciting an "I'm awake, I'm awake" groan.

"I missed breakfast, didn't I?" she says to the floor.

It is, in fact, a late morning in this unknown town. The birds are still repeating their song for those who slept in, and the market is busy with the noise of commerce. Life tempts from outside, begging Niena to explore, while inside it is musty, cold, and the smells of straw and body odor come together in a one-two punch that makes Niena sneeze.

Now what, taking in the room. This is the first time since meeting Titania that her grandmother isn't there when Niena wakes. She runs her hands through unkempt hair and squints, scanning the room for anything the fairy might have left. Nearby, the oft-repaired remains of her dress, the almost empty money bag, and a belt that is little more than a leather chord are draped on a chair. There is also, of course, Marny's old coat. *My coat.*

She shakes her head. Fabric and a needle would be a good start — and she nearly repeats this out loud as well. However, a protest in her stomach reminds her of other pressing concerns.

Boards creak in the hallway adjacent to her door. "Probably should get something from the kitchen—" she starts to say, then stops, sucking in air as if she might reverse time and take back the words spoken. The footsteps halt. For too long a minute, neither step nor breath is taken. And then the creaking returns, turns a corner, and continues down what might be the stairs.

A rush of last night's memories flood in with the rest of the blood to her brain as she slips the dress over her shift. "Chords," she blurts out. Niena hesitates, taking a step towards the window, and looks back to the door. She takes another deep breath.

Everyone is after me. Rein. Oberon. *Shadowy monsters.* She clenches her shirt closed along the neckline. "No worse than before. I had a bloody maniac who thought he was my husband from the future chasing me down."

Unbidden, a memory resurfaces. The walls of the little room fade, and she is back. Back near the Bastille, where her grandfather died. Back with the dragon and Calem.

The wyrm raged. Buildings, the keep itself, toppled to the flames. Stones fell to the ground like rain. Yet Calem seemed to be preoccupied by a conversation with himself. Niena squinted, staying out of sight.

"You underestimate me," he said calmly. "You have from the beginning." He wiped his face as if to pull off a part of his beard. "I may have let hope blind me, but I am not harmless. And I have your girl."

"Oberon," she whispered.

Calem's lips contorted into something close to a smile. "I know what you do value, Oberon, you damned fairy." His laugh ripped the air. "What if I were to intercede? The girl could kill the dragon. And I might then control that girl. And through her, I would salt this earth, and turn everything you remember, everything your people touched, to ash."

One foot. He didn't seem to notice her. A second step, third. There was a glint in the green, just where she was searching before. Niena walked lightly towards it and snatched the knife from the field.

"I was a druid of the Graystriders!" Each of his words bounced off stone to return, one by one. "Did you think I did not plan, research for the possibility of your betrayal? I may lose my wife, but I will still gain. I have the charms and the secrets of the Drel'nu. No one will be safe. I have a new destiny."

Snarls filled the air between them. He rounded, and upon seeing Niena, his face alive with rage, he said: "There is magic in dragon blood. Enough to find a way to the Fairhome."

Chatter invades the common room downstairs. It is this that rouses Niena from her recollection, and when it does, she rises from the chair with her belongings, angrily gripping the handle of the peasant blade she stole so long ago.

"I left home to be a bard, but my dreams were taken from me." Niena scours the room, as if she can find some purpose or direction there. "Never mind that it was a dumb dream, it was still mine!"

She huffs, lifts her bag, ties the belt around her waist. *South it is.* The lyre she straps on slowly and storms around to the door. *Wait, this thing bloody glows. What did Titania do to make it...* The words of the fairy's spell are recalled then, as if summoned by need. She blinks, reaches back and runs her finger over an exposed arm. The story comes naturally to her lips.

She shifts her weight, pulling off the bag holding the lyre — a stretch of leather that appears empty; the deceit is revealed only upon inserting a hand into the folds. With a budding smile, Niena reshoulders the pack and leaves, entering the common room with a cacophony of stomps and squeaking boards.

Daylight may not in truth chase away the things that linger in the shadows. For light creates shadows, and they will remain whether we want them to or not. However, light does manage to trick the brain — illuminating enough dark corners for us to relax. Here it is that the girl finds herself: full of energy, and unafraid. She steps through the threshold, her head turning from the barroom table to the fire pit.

The common room is still buzzing with the news of last night. A door, kept open for the sake of airing the place out, allows the morning to visit. And in this light, Niena's confidence grows, even if the eyes upon her are just as unfriendly as before.

I'll solve my problems one at a time. First, I need supplies. Swerving around the patrons trickling in for an early meal, she presses against a table that angles near, just as two dayworkers push past. In the tight press, and emboldened by the smoke rising from the roast, her hands lightly rake across the passersby's belts. One of the two purses she touches unfortunately acquires a new hole, and a few of the coins decide to come with her.

Niena secrets the knife back into a makeshift pocket amidst the tatters of her dress. The weight of the money in her hand steadies her spirits, even if the crime causes the girl to shiver out of fear. Outside the door of the tavern, she releases the breath she has been holding.

Life rushes to meet her. The air is crisp, though laden with the activities of the thriving village. There are shops, small and with few offerings. Sheep muddle about a central fountain — though more of a trough with a spring — ignoring the lazy and listless commands of their shepherds. As she rounds the fountains, she almost walks into a stand with vegetables, bright and orange, that she's never seen before. Then also right into the shoulder of a woman wearing a dress much like her own mother used to wear. Untrusting stares keep her from thinking too familiarly of the villagers.

I do not know what Titania is up to. Should I stay near the tavern to wait for her? A cart stops her from turning a corner, giving her another moment to ponder the warnings Titania left her with.

*Or, is she really...*Niena swallows, *gone?* She clutches the coins, once more feeling their solidness and their reassuring weight. *Chords, this is not the time to fall apart.* The little market now seems far too open for comfort, and she nervously hurries ahead. *This is just like old times; you can do this.*

There was something else, too. The pull Titania mentioned. It was beginning to weigh on her mind. How often had she looked south for no reason? It seemed like an easy explanation before: that was where they were headed. But why not east, or west also? The truth was somewhere in the deceit.

The Evercharm. The lyre. She idly runs her hands over the leather-covered instrument. *Is this thing really influencing me? Maybe I should just get rid of it.* Not if Titania is correct, she knows. Not if they are also after Niena. Rein could show up at any time. *Or those things.* It is inevitable.

A man's face pops up around the opposite corner. Right where she would expect to find someone shadowing her. Ahead, the wagon driver is engaged in conversation, and another cart, moving the opposite way, threatens to cause a scene. This she also notes.

"Good morning," she says to the wagon's driver, squeezing around his oxen. Her brief greeting is just enough to distract the man away from the pretty spinster at his side. Long enough to notice the other driver.

"Hey," he yells. "Back that up, don't you know this is a one-way crossing?"

Titania is also manipulating me. The fairy had lightly pressed, whenever a moment turned quiet, about the possibilities of a bargain — about leaving this world entirely. *She wants something more than she lets on about, power?* Despite the grand talk of the Southlands, and of adventures to be had, Niena knew it was a farce.

I would have given her the lyre if it meant freedom, she knows this. However, the lyre is worthless to anyone without me. So, Niena will gain nothing by ditching it. *But what will she have me agreeing to, in that last moment, when everything closes around?*

A breeze takes a strand of hair and tussles it. Wet hay mixed with the scent of freshly baked bread wanders in from a side street that leads to the tents below. Niena goes the opposite direction and keeps an eye out for further watchers. She swings around a mule, then ducks to the other side, crossing the patrons who crowd the steps of a small temple in the process. Past this, she slips into an alley where one of the temple's modern outbuildings straddles an ancient cistern.

I will have to decide, and soon: to make a bargain, or find a way to turn the tables. The Evercharm, whether I like it or not, is the only hope I have of salvaging my life.

Over her shoulder, she spies the suspicious profile of a man and sinks under the shadowy lintel of a bricked-up door. Niena smiles despite the danger, watching the back of his head until it disappears into the traffic.

"Like old times."

She sighs, letting instincts pull her round a corner and on to the back of a courtyard and a wall separating the streets. An unusual garden for city folk peeks from gaps in the courtyard's fencing. The smell of thyme, of sage and other autumn herbs hits her, and the views of the garden remind Niena of a shop near which she used to hide in Shenan. Here, Niena's strong fingers grant her access to the wall's edge, and then the second story of what she determines to be an herbalist's garden house.

The sun has baked the tile, and the feeling is warm and pleasant on her back. "If it was night..." She would have slipped inside. Tile was a rare roofing, where thatch ruled almost exclusively, here. The merchant who owned this business must have been wealthy. Niena takes in the horizon for a moment and makes herself small on the roof.

Over the town, a haze thickens, smoke bumbling in with the same breeze that brought her a taste of the lower market. From that direction too comes the gentle lilt of strings being plucked and songs, words, scatter over the rooftops. She angles her body, then crawls to the far side of the shop. This leads to the other end of a street that once connected to the small alley.

Using a soot-blackened gargoyle — an ornamentation left over from some older building — she helps herself down to this street. Rubbish provides a hiding spot then, until an hour passes, and the opportunity presents itself to again merge with the crowds going to the temple.

He must think me an easy target, she thinks, closely following a troop in priestly attire. Niena's eyes widen, finding the man from before, ahead and staring back. *A young foreign girl.*

No, he doesn't want to invite me for tea and biscuits. She freezes, then bolts as the man observing her reacts and moves.

The first hurdle proves to be two slow-walking women. The next, barrels in a street market. Shouts follow her, and the sound of heavy pursuit nipping. Niena swings around a post, tossing fruits from a nearby stand. Protests follow her beyond, past curious onlookers and shops re-opening for the afternoon crowd. Niena takes another turn down a side street, then stops, catching her breath against a wall.

Two ways from here, looking ahead. *Left, or right?* Chaos echoes in the street she just left.

Chords, Niena veers careens left as angry voices turn the corner. The choice at first seems poor, as the narrow passage ends abruptly. The girl, though, quickly scuttles up and over some garbage left out between two buildings. From there, she leaps onto a hanging gutter, and shimmies her way further, using this to gain a high window.

Please be open. She grips the frame. *Please be open.*

Wood cracks and the frame shudders. Niena strains, pulling herself up with all her might, while also maintaining her balance on the narrow sill.

"There's the bitch!"

The wood holding the lock snaps, the window flies open, and Niena tumbles inside. A quick scan tells her this is the upper story of a cobbler, and she is on a landing at the top of some stairs. *He's probably already coming back around.*

"Who's there?"

Wasting no time, Niena barrels down the stairs, knocking over tools and pushing past a surprised man on her way out the front door.

Empty, except for his damn screaming. Gotta find a hiding spot, or get the chords out of here. She disappears into the shadowy passage, his shouts and little more following her. Debris clogs the way, making her wonder how the cobbler gets any traffic. The little passage curves again back to the west, which she imagines is exactly where those men will come from.

Getting on the roof means I will just be target practice. Most of the buildings are one-story affairs, backing upon the street instead of opening. Niena's hand drifts towards the lyre.

"No, chords no," she accidentally cries, and hears in answer the commanding shouts of her pursuers. Panicking, Niena retreats through the debris, past the cobbler shop, where the only signs of the man's anger is the rattle of his swinging door.

If I can't go up, or around, maybe between? The gaps are regular, unlike in the other streets, if tight. She clambers over broken crates, under garbage that has been wedged between the walls as if tossed from a non-existent second story. Wood and other unsettling things crack underfoot.

This one. Niena removes the lyre from her back and squeezes into a V-shaped wedge, plaster flaking off the structure as she does. Footsteps thump somewhere behind. More than the one pursuer she had expected. She hurries, scraping her arm along the lime plaster facing as she does. After a third of the way in, the walls of the two buildings almost meet, something she did not see from the shadows.

"I am cooked," she says, staring back the way she came.

"She's hiding in one of these buildings," the voice from earlier says. "Did you check the cobbler?"

Niena struggles, pulling herself back out as the two men argue. Her breath mists the side of the right wall as she does her best to avoid making any sound.

"He ain't seen her since she ran."

She swallows and gets as low to the ground as possible. The garbage and debris from before still block the way through — lying undisturbed since —and Niena uses them as cover.

"Maybe she passed us and went to the bakery."

"Ain't no way; no way, I say. I would've seen her."

"Well, maybe we should check again."

"Yeh just want a roll…"

Niena exhales and peeks her head over a broken crate. Seeing the back of the men who chased her isn't enough. She looks up as the cobbler's sign swings. She sneers, hands reaching for a hidden knife. "To Dunos with this town." The plain wood handle is cold, but the steel is colder. "To Dunos with these people."

She sighs. Shenan. Sunford. This was nothing new.

"Things will never change," she says with another sigh, then straightens. "Not without a little help."

From this dingy alley, Niena retraces her steps to find the street and the stairs to the lower level. South. *Maybe there I will find answers.*

She reaches behind her and unstraps the lyre. The Evercharm feels heavy in her hands, the weight reassuring. "This is a bad idea."

But a bad idea, that is her choice. The song she plays then is a familiar one. Tinged with doubt, the insecurities of someone who desires above all else to remain hidden — and something else: hope. It isn't the greatest of spells for hiding, but a first step towards something more. It is also a very familiar song.

If only she knew who was watching her from the shadows.

Chapter 21

First, there is a twinkle — a wink of light from beads peeking between the dancer's braids. Heads turn away from the stalls and wares when dancers spill out of tents nestled against an oak grove, and as Niena places fruit into the merchant's hand, a trill of music lifts the face of a little girl shopping for apples. It is no birdsong, but the expert mimicry of a flutist hidden in the tent market.

"Did you see that, Grandmother." She shuts her mouth, and frowns.

This place is so different from Shenan, and from the walled town. Niena's eyes rise to look at the mottled walls of the village above. *I thought the tents would be depressing, the people even worse. But it's not. This little shanty is so welcoming, charming. Like night and day.*

Niena steps back from the one stall, and slowly ambles over to another. Between them, she pauses, listening to the flutist's shrill playing, a signal for something new.

A burst of color follows a trio of dancers as they flow out from behind an oak. Their long hair sparkles like gems sewn into a raven banner, and their limbs stream with lines of blue, red, and orange fabric, twirling effortlessly into the market promenade. A different cadre of figures follows them. Fewer, and less elaborately dressed. These men and women are also clapping and dancing, all the while trying to keep close to the other performers' flowing bands. However, these men and women quickly disappear into the crowd. *Thieves.*

With effort, Niena returns to the wizened lady heading the stall.

"I was wondering if you could tell me about the Southlands," Niena says. "I am trying to figure out the best way to get there."

"South?" The woman's wrinkles. She then cups her ears as if not hearing. "South?"

"I've heard stories about cities," Niena lies. "Cities in the sand that flows like the sea and..." She frowns, then leans in closer. "We have family there. With my parents gone, I thought to start my life over."

"There is no easy way south," the woman says. "Not in many years. West, west, then south, maybe. One who comes from there does so only once in their life. No more."

"Where does that road lead?" She is pointing to a winding thing topping the reeds of a nearby pond.

The woman shakes her head. "South. Wasteland. The living does not take. Maybe...Oh, look, child. The Equistrans!"

On the other side, in yet another line, shouts from a squadron of men peel everyone's attention away from the dancers. These too emerge from their own set of tents, but on the opposite side and away from any trees. *Equistrans?* She thinks of her books in Maidenhill, and the tales of those olive-skinned people. Looks of concern disappear on the faces of those shopping, quick as magic, when the Equistrans begin their own performance — a hearty song full of bravado, stomping, and laughter.

"Ah, we should have stayed here," Niena says, forgetting that night's priorities. She shrinks into her coat and from the stall.

"I should have," with an emphasis on I. Titania is gone. *No need to look crazy. Er.*

The flutist from before steps onto a stump at the fork of one of the little lanes; this time he is not alone, but flanked by drummers. The girl ducks under a branch, watches a young man be swept into a dance by a troupe that follows the musicians. They swirl and jump. Stomp, then scatter into the crowd. Spin right, spin left, the man's laughter as vibrant as the song. And the thieves' hands as quick as a dance partner. Niena checks her own stash.

A glimmer signals the reappearance of the dancers. Niena, remembering their fine dress then, and the smell of wildflowers that follows, suddenly feels like some savage thing that crawled out of the wood. She clutches her sides, mutters something intelligible, silently promising to see Equistra, their rumored home, for herself one day — not just see, but to live, and experience all it has. To go there and buy her own silk dresses of the colors she chooses, and to learn new songs and dances.

If I survive.

Niena frowns. With a resigned huff, she opens her eyes and pats the folds of her dress. Just as her fingers touch the knife, a strange feeling overcomes her. By instinct, she scans the crowd, then freezes.

There is a man. He lingers in the distance, and his features shift between distinct and indistinct. For a second, this figure with a long coat and strange tubular hat appears to look her way. But when Niena raises her hand against the sun to get a better look, he is gone.

"That's not one of the men from the village that were following me, is it?" She reaches again for the knife and slowly pulls back. *I never got a good look, but it doesn't seem like one of those thugs. It sort of reminds me of Rein.* Niena's eyes widen, and she lays her hand on the Evercharm.

The market has lost its welcome. *South by southeast, there is a mountain.* She makes to leave, cutting through a tent to reach the crossover of two other paths. *Southeast of this, there is a glade, and a waterfall. I shall follow the old road.*

"That hawker said it was a wasteland?" She stops behind a couple arguing over the price of some sweetmeats. "West, then west from here, she said was safe." Niena winces. "Kind of."

Her gaze settles on a road leading south and the forests that promise to hide her.

♫

Morning ends and noon chases out the last of the cold, allowing the sun's heat to settle. A temporary respite. The afternoon brings a scent from the west, smelling of salt air and heather, running what would otherwise be a warm day. For the westward wind in these parts breeds with the northern, and their offspring is ever bitter.

Trees intrude upon the fields. The winds blow against her profile and the sun sweeps, warming her hair — until the canopy comes to claim her and darkness steals the light of the day. When this happens, Niena looks up and sighs, and pulls her coat around to hide her tattered dress.

"I should have bought fabric and thread," with an irritated tug on her belt. Money has been an issue from the beginning, and the lie can't live long out in the free air. "I would have had to steal it."

The unwelcome thought lingers overlong, and to keep her mind otherwise occupied, she strips a sapling to make a walking stick. Niena checks the lyre. "One day I will make right with the people I've taken from."

The girl departs the road soon after finding it, as a stream has retaken the former bed, and lain in an abandoned pond that fed a long-forgotten mill. The dammed waters swallow much of the forest around. The road crossed here near the mill, and while the cobble of the old way was overgrown, the forest is completely wild. Coppiced trees disappear into thickets, and herb gardens are shaded under brushes. The few visible patches of farmland are covered in wildflowers. Niena collects dandelions in these places, for later eating.

By late afternoon, the westward breeze falters. Under assault by leaf and bough, the air has become still. Stale. Even so, fresh things can be found. Rose hips are plentiful. Blooming chicory more so. Niena collects what she can on her way towards fresh water. Frogs lure her there, to a small pond with a stream. The croaking stops when she wades through the cattails to refill her waterskin.

The disquiet Niena felt in the market earlier has slowly been creeping back upon her since the loss of the wind. She checks her knife and makes a quick prayer to the westward lords, like Dunos, who are said to pluck the chords of fate. The roots and flowers are secured inside the folds of her dress. Birdsong startles her next step, then quiets as she clambers through the cattails and back into the brush, eyes mindful and searching for the previous road. She does not find it.

Daylight leaves her shortly after the thickness of the wild breaks. Red touches the white in the clouds, ruby lips, a last kiss of sunshine. Niena listens to the forest. In an hour, the best light will be gone; the forest canopy will win against the intruding rays, and the night song will begin once more. Owls will hunt, and other nocturnal creatures will emerge from their dens. Prey, hunter. The canopy, though thin here, will cover them all. Even visitors, such as the other sort of intruders, the two-legged variety like Niena.

Those clouds keep coming, riding a warm wind from the south as the early autumn rolls. Niena sits with her head between her knees, watching dead grass get blown this way and that. Hills dominate the west, but it is the other shapes looming in the wastes that concern her. From this angle, some look like towers. Niena discards the sapling.

"I don't know where I lost the road," she says to her knees. A woodpecker interrupts her thought, tittering about after insects. Niena pulls her legs closer but also lifts her head and laughs. "Well, I mean the forest, obviously."

The girl has climbed high or taken a route that brought her here. And from here, a haggardly way down begs attention. "It shouldn't be too much of a problem," she groans, climbing once more to her feet. "Just a steep hill, not a mountain." One lie and a truth. She breaks off a piece of bread, preparing her strength for the descent. An hour of light is still an hour, and her nerves demand more distance between them and...*Rein. If that is Rein.* She shivers. She doesn't know why the memory of the man who helped her affects her so. He was hardly scary, but this new appearance has shaken Niena.

The sun was ever a friend when she first strode into the patch of trees, a ward against the unknown. This sentiment is gone. A nameless fear stalks her mind in these hours, and she fears to linger. Niena angles her head, juggling between scanning the horizon and watching her feet.

The hills west can never be confused with mountains, but still, they manage to lay a finger on the course of the southernly gusts. She closes her eyes with effort and leans into a scraggily tree, still expecting something to pop out from a rock or patch of grass and attack. The old woman made it seem like south would be a fool's journey.

Her shoulders slump, then straighten, as she once more finds her nerve. It doesn't last. Blinking her eyes open, she peers into the wild. *I'm being manipulated, every way I turn.*

A hunting bird cries, distracting her. Niena's hands shake, and she clenches her fists, pushing them against her side. The rage swirling in her stomach is a real, palpable thing. But this rage dies fast, and anger digs into her stomach, exposing the truth: fear. She steps back, rolling pebbles underfoot.

The lyre's compulsion was a small thing, a ship set against the backdrop of a huge ocean. "Is the wind filling the sails natural, or..." she whispers. "Or fate?" Though this fate feels real enough. Maybe it is not Rein that hunts her, but something that has put on his face—

Niena draws her knife. Trees bend. Branches thrash the air with browns and greens, in every direction around her. But there is no sound except the clatter of the rocks. An overriding desire to flee grips her. She spins. From the forest to the cliff, and back again — the knife trembling in her hand.

"Rein," shaking the knife at the trees. "Or whoever you are, leave me alone." Niena slips the peasant's blade underhand, secures the lyre, and lunges towards a boulder, sliding it to descend the hill. Shrubs and saplings help keep the path from being a quick descent, and she takes these slowly with her free hand.

A shape sways in front of her path, and she stumbles, scraping her left hand badly on the ground. The shape proves to be only a willow, but the feeling of unnaturalness overrides her good sense. Niena tears a strip of her dress to cover her hand, wrapping her wound, eyes darting from tree to rock, from rock to open sky. Much of the rest of the way can't be walked. She straightens and lowers herself.

To the right, scree and brush hold court. It is a tempting option, to try to scurry or slide down them. A week ago, she might have. *Thank you, Titania.* The appreciation of solid rock is a true gift, as a broken leg or even a sprained ankle out here would be the end.

Even so, her imagination alters the way down, picking out the next spots with flair. In Niena's mind, the rocks grow bigger, the brush wilder, and everywhere there is birdcall and the signs of potential prey.

This I can walk, identifying a less-steep incline and sturdy brush. Noises from the forest swirl in a flash of wind. Niena looks up in time to lose that last pure ray of sun to the canopy. Twilight reigns, and she sets back to the track to make the most of it.

The daydreaming gifts the girl a strange sort of calm, pushing the buzzing questions in her mind into the background, on a level with the chittering in the trees from the locusts. One last drop remains. A sheer cliff five meters over the hill's root. A difficult maneuver, on uncertain ground below: scree and other debris held loosely by grass and weed. She takes a breath, then works her fingers around the ledge. The knife here acts as an anchor as Niena lowers herself, hold by hold, down. There's a lesson in this somewhere.

"The elf treated me like prey." She shakes her head, then swings her left leg down and slightly to the right. "That's not the lesson."

"One," ignoring the soreness in her muscles. "Two…" she slides the knife up, pulling hard with the right hand on a shrub. Then, with a quick breath, she twists and pushes herself off the side. A rush of air whips her hair back, but the fall is brief, and Niena lands on all fours.

"I must be vigilant, like in the old days." Niena brushes hair from her eyes and stands. "Back to relying on just myself."

In this moment, caught between danger and reverie, the girl's mind lies between states — as only that of a child of fairy might. She searches the trees and path from which she just came. The presence remains, like a wall of fear, taunting her at the edge of the cliff. Worse, all birdsong has stopped, and it seems as if even the wind is holding its breath. She narrows her eyes. Between the trees, shapes sift and shift. "There is a…Oh, chords."

On the heights, a monster from Niena's past slithers out from the trees. Its visage is a terror of maws and appendages, surrounded by mist that hides none of its horror. She reacts instantly, readying the knife with one hand, and reaching for the solidness of a tree with the other.

The creature preens, as if sensing her fear, or so Niena thinks — but something else happens then. One of the maws stretches on a long neck, and from that twist of malefice, a hand reaches out to stroke it.

"Rein," she again attempts to speak.

It is then, faced with uncertainty, that another intercedes. A voice touches Niena's mind. A familiar nasal hum. It buzzes, warming every corner it touches and firming her resolve. She grips the knife close, no longer feeling alone as the presence helps her confront the man standing next to this nightmare creature.

"Hello, Niena," Rein says. "We need to talk."

"You thought it was a good idea to let me know by stalking me?" Niena takes a step back. "And by showing up with that?"

Keep your chin up child, the voice of Oberon says, just before Rein takes a step forward, dropping and landing right in front of her as if the fall were only of one meter instead of twenty.

"I believe honesty is the best policy," Rein says, bowing. He takes a step forward. "We do not have to like each other to do business."

Be strong, he cannot harm you, the voice reassures.

197

"After all," Rein continues. "Did you not like Oberon? How has that turned out for you?"

Stay focused and repeat after me. Niena raises the knife to meet Rein.

As she struggles to say the words forming on her lips, the beginnings of a ward are already humming in her throat. It is no story. Nor is it a true song, though melodic enough.

Rein smiles. "I have a proposal for—"

Sutr ferr sunnan, echoes in her mind. "Surtr moves from the south," she repeats.

Meo sviga laevi. "With the scathe of branches."

Niena blinks, expecting a rebuttal from Rein. Instead, a look of shock is frozen on his face. *Look at the creature above,* the voice says, and she does. Where the mist was slowly creeping towards the two, it now retreats as if pulled back on a string. The monster from before is nowhere to be seen. *Now say this...*

The impression of Oberon, her grandfather, mentally turns her back to the workings of the spell, tipping her chin up like a child's. She swoons, dizzy.

Skinn af sverdi. Niena swallows, her voice choked. "There shines from his sword."

Sol valtiva. "The sun of gods and of the slain."

The last of the spell falls away. Whatever was holding Rein then releases him, and he rears back.

"Now we can talk," Niena says, taking a step forward.

Rein straightens his coat, then glances behind him. "Aren't you full of surprises?" he says, and shrugs. His face quickly becomes a mask. "About my proposal."

"I know what you want. What are you going to offer me — gold, jewels?"

"If that is what you want, I am sure we can come to some terms."

"What I want is to be left alone by people like you."

Rein removes one of his gloves and examines it. "That would be impossible," turning towards Niena. "As I am sure you are aware." A smile slithers across his features. "You are terribly important; doesn't that make you feel great? Small folk like to be important. No? Well, what I can assure you is that once our matter is finalized, my benefactors will gladly acquiesce if that is what you wish."

"Alone," she says to his nod. "And in the dark." Again, he smiles.

Rein laughs. "If you cooperate, we can make all your dreams come true." He pauses and pulls on the fingers of the other glove. "And my benefactors know all about dreams."

Nightmares too. The Teamor's bargains are more dangerous than any fey, Oberon cautions as Niena narrows her eyes. *You are too much of a danger to them to keep around.*

"What will the others offer you, anyway?" The smile leaves Rein's face and his tone hardens. "The elves? You will be lucky to get a shallow grave once they are done." And then his eyes twinkle, and a lilt returns to his voice. "A clever woman like you...ahh, no. A clever bard in training, should be able to word her demands properly. Why, there must be so many new riddles in this world, and you must know them all, am I right?"

"How do you know about..." She straightens, holding the long knife in front of her. "What I want right now is for you to go away." Niena pivots, and at once the knife is swapped for the Evercharm. "You know what I can do with this."

He takes a step forward. "Do you really think to threaten me? With what, folk music?"

"One word, and you won't be able to move," she says calmly. "One song, and I will wipe that smile from your face."

The last glove comes off. He looks at the dwindling light, then shrugs. "Of course, you misunderstand me. I abhor violence…" His gaze flickers from her foot to her eyes. "And rudeness. However, before I go, can you do me one favor?"

Niena inhales and grips the Evercharm as his eyes follow her movements.

"Tell Titania that I send my regards." That smile, the same acidic, dangerous grimace from before, returns.

Rein tips his hat. "It has been lovely becoming reacquainted. Until next time."

Don't listen… Yet, the buzz of Oberon's voice is taken at the same time as the gloom of the forest envelops Rein. The Inspector's profile withdraws, taking the twilight with him. And as his top hat disappears, and the moon appears over a rise of trees, Niena releases the breath she was holding.

She opens her mouth to curse, but the words are lost in an angry growl. Instead, she walks defiantly into the thinning trees, still south. Moonlight seems to follow her, until a dust hazes the sky, drawing a veil between her and the heavens. And as the birds and sounds return to her, and as she stares out into the shaded horizon, not seeing a thing, nor caring, Niena collapses onto the tall grass in a hollow.

Somewhere between the setting of the campfire and an hour spent staring skyward, she falls asleep.

Chapter 22

Dandelion roots sit on a flat rock, uncooked, untouched. An attempt to reproduce Titania's spell succeeded only in frightening squirrels. Niena pops a chicory bloom into her mouth and watches the last of the embers fade.

Dawn is hours away. Rein, or whoever that was, is out there. Watching. She tugs on a lock of hair. *Time to leave.* Up comes the lyre. The roots find their way once more into the folds of her dress — walking food.

Unless that old merchant's idea of a wasteland is different than mine, I won't be finding much to eat there. With that thought hanging on, she kicks dirt over the remains of the fire, but only a half-hearted attempt is made to break the bed. Her father would have done differently. Bits of charcoal she has moved aside to let cool find their way into the tattered sleeves of her dress. The bloom of the chicory is salty-sweet and lingers until the last of the camp is broken and left behind.

As this traveler marches through the sparse forest, she considers everything that happened the day before. Over and over again, only occasionally contemplating the horizon between patches of the thinned forest. In less than two hours' walk, the forest quickly cedes the land to gray grass and dead shrubs.

"What the chords am I caught up in? Oberon, Rein...I don't remember Rein giving me the chills like that before." Niena says, breaking the silence of her hours' long trek. A sharp wind takes the last word, and she raises an arm against it, cursing. She sees hills under the shade of her hand, to the southeast. Dust, and an oft-blackened, red sort of dirt, uninhabited by large fauna, mars what must have once been a beautiful scape.

"Is this the wasteland?" It must be. More mounds rise west, and unlike the others these are small and their ascent more pronounced. Niena squints. "They are flat topped–" Her voice strains with excitement. "Could that have been a watchtower?"

The last of these high places, crowned in flowering trees and broken towers, borders an expanse of ruins that rise, far out, under a red haze. The same she saw from the hilltop during the confrontation with Rein. This is the devastation of Drachzehr, recalling the same beast that Niena encountered in Shenan. Drachzehr, the dragon that felled the empire.

Midday arrives with dust swirling, stirred up from the southern city, and she shelters underneath a march of fallen columns and the walls of an old cottage built against them. The wait is excruciating.

So, these Teamor must be the others Titania warned me about. What did Rein mean by the last thing he said? If she were paying attention, she might have heard the whisperings of Skehfelthuz from the stones, or perhaps even the name it came to be called after: Maro Unsterbbēriz.

These are yet the outskirts. It will take her the rest of the day to make it to the city she saw. Where Titania should meet her. Strips of her dress writhe under her coat, and Niena bends over, huddling close to the ruin of an arch. This feels too much like the situation with the dragon: herded along, with little other choice but to endure. She runs her fingers over grooves worn into the stone by ancient flooding. *This time will be different.* She has the Evercharm. She has the knowledge and the capability to use it — and not to be used herself.

The winds whip. A bird cries, circling a nearby hill. Niena teases her head out. *Stormhawk?* Legends in the Sunford library tell of them. *How many people have seen one?* Dust stings her eyes, and she crawls back to the overhang. *Well, heard...*

The legendary bird is not enough to pull Niena out of her brooding. *Sethlan, Higgins, Rein. Titania and Oberon. I can't trust anyone, yet I must. And even in the best situation, I will be running from one hole to another, always looking over my shoulder. This is my life...* She settles her head into the crook of an arm. *Isn't it?*

The hawk's call is clear, even as the midday sun lies shrouded behind the wings of the tempest. "Stormbird, I am not like you," she croaks. A sip from her waterskin alleviates a little of the dryness. "I'm the stupid little mouse running into an open field."

Niena coughs. The taste of iron hits her tongue as the wind finds holes in the stone. The sound is fearsome but lonely, rolling through the empty spaces. Soon after, the shadows around her feet deepened as if following the gusts, or as if the ruins themselves were breathing in. She moves back. Watching, Waiting, but nothing comes.

With a sigh, she settles against a wall. Her eyes hop from one leftover to another, some half buried in the strange red-baked clay. Sand, she read, should be orange. Or white, on some beaches. This looks more like rust mixed with soot. Thunder in the distance makes her lift her gaze. "One, two, three—"

The flash of lighting briefly illuminates more of the debris. A broken table. Remains of a shelf, an oven. Near to this is the fallen arch of a door, looking east.

A shock of thunder follows, and Niena clutches her chest. She hides her head once more. "One, two, three."

Pillars stand beyond a bank of ruined houses — to the west. The remnants of chimneys and other mundane wrecks too. The wind occasionally comes from this direction, and when it is not fouled by decay, it smells of the sea.

A low rumble passes east by northeast. Niena crosses her arms, not bothering to count.

"Chords, I wish I was strong or..." Niena buries her face into her hands, suddenly feeling very drained. "Just not pathetic. Marny was right. I should have never left home."

"You are much stronger than you think, Granddaughter."

"Oberon?" Niena bolts up, ignoring the wind trying to knock her back down. "Grandfather, where are you?"

Oberon's voice reaches her through the holes in the walls. "I once heard a story about a young girl named Niena. Whose mother took her own life, and she, a child of only eight, cared for a broken father until drink took the rest of him.

"Have you heard of this girl?" His voice is shredded by the wind as Niena staggers to the arch. "A girl so strong, she refused to die."

Through the arch there is only the storm and the gales that bite at every piece of exposed skin. Niena grimaces, forcing herself to look. "If I was so strong, why couldn't I save him? Why couldn't I stop my mother—" In the twist of sand, and through the crackle of lightning, Niena sees a vague man-shaped figure to the south. She reaches out, but with one more blink, the visage is gone.

"Alone again." Her whisper is taken. Niena crosses her arms, and yells into the gale. "Grandfather, how are you here and not? And why now?" She stares at the horizon. "I am heading into danger, aren't I? East, west, south, it doesn't matter, does it?"

For the next hour, she calls out to Oberon, her grandfather. Until the storm no longer howls back at her and the sun is freed from its cloud-shaped prison. Fungus has reclaimed much of this wreck she shelters in, and without the storm, the stench is powerful. Niena covers her nose, shrinking from the strange mix of decay and iron.

"She knew," Niena says. "Titania knew, but can I really escape through unbinding the worlds? Or is that a mirage, offering poisonous waters to a man dying of thirst?"

Leaving, Niena takes a last glance back. There was a time, back in Sunford, when she was truly happy. There, watching the waves crash against the rocks. Yes, she spent many a night looking after a cantankerous old goat in Oberon. Yet, most days were her own. Days she would now like to have back.

Seeing a road poke through the dirt, she takes to it, sliding over a toppled column. Though it may pass through more of this village's ruin. Though the pass seems to be cluttered with all sorts of wreckage. As she does this, her fingers trace some of the rubbish. There are more than pots and pans here.

"So much is just sitting here," Niena says while freeing a pole from a broken cart. It is a bit long — no normal shepherd's crook — but she takes it up anyway. Few hours remain in the day, and there is much she may pass through before reaching the city.

Who knows what pitfalls await? The girl slides around another cart clogging the road, following the path she set before. That is, no path at all. South, south into many unknowns.

Buildings become more numerous as she treads. The everyday castoffs of people in flight continue to litter the ground. Baggage. Carts, chests. Other items that, while not terribly valuable in the scheme of things, might be a prized possession to the families that left them.

"This isn't right," she says, wondering aloud. "What happened here to make them just leave it all, and why hasn't this place been picked clean?"

The howling returns, and Niena quickens her pace through the shadows cast by the many arches and tumbled walls around her. The sun stretches higher into the sky by the time she can wade past the rubble clogging the area. Twilight again threatens.

For a time, she forgets the earlier worries, losing herself to the rhythm of cobble crunching underneath, and the sound of dust carried through empty doors and windows. This takes her far, until the sun sets and day passes to twilight, and dusk threatens. And as dusk does approach, she sits down in the shade of an aqueduct to make her camp.

Fire sparks, the light loud in the gloom. Even so, as the flames rise higher and higher, it affords her a different security — a bulwark against the dark, even if the dark does not fear the fire.

"Doesn't feel safe here," she whispers. Niena unstraps the lyre from her back and sets it down near the campfire. "I must keep moving. I need to find Titania." She shivers and hugs herself.

She adds under her breath: "And then trick her."

She's the one that is the most useful to me, right now. Niena looks left, right, and finds what she is looking for a little further ahead. A toppled column, lying on its side and half buried.

"Up, then." The words spur her to spring towards the column. There, at the edge, she measures the gaps in the broken monument and the spoilage of other, taller works. With a vigorous jab of her new pole, she manages the first jump.

For a moment, Niena is again just a girl and not the young lady she's grown into. She hops from broken piece to piece, using the pole when needed. Eventually, after more than a hop and a skip, she reaches the top.

Squinting. Outside the reach of the fallen city, there is a silver blur of the moon smiling back. The sight stirs the other memory of that adventure: of wonder, and escape. She hops to the next.

"Fields," she mouths. *Golden waves kissed by fairy silver, and I am here like a beached boat on the shore. Could I set off again?* She half twirls, clasping the pole to her chest, then must brace herself to keep from falling. The top of the broken column is wide, but not that wide. Tentatively, she skulks again to the edge.

Now, as she peers around the blasted landscape between her and the winding road, she can see that this land is still alive, though wounded. The feeling of wonder is fleeting.

Tailwinds swirl. She looks for the traveling stars, but either it is too early or clouds hide their faces from her. Niena's feet drag her reluctantly back down, down into the culvert between the buildings. Even with this protection, she is forced to wrap herself tightly in Marny's old coat. The night is chilly, colder than it has been in several days.

Traveling after sunset always reminds her of her father, Graham. Poor as they were in those years, somehow there was always something to eat, and always a story to share. "Stories," she tsks. "He had those to spare. Too bad he could never tell the truth."

When Marny, her other grandfather, brought them to live close by, Graham promised he would make things right. Promises for that man were a credit he never intended to pay back. It didn't take long for him to fall back into his old ways. Niena hugs herself, wondering not for the first time why she always wanted to take after him: to be a bard, traveling from town to town, was more his dream. She did, however, like to tell his tall tales…

"Then he died."

Niena wasn't even ten years old. The last evening, they moved to the cellar of the tavern, and her father, by then, was far past his dues for rent. And drunk. He was always drunk. The tavern's owner was a kindly man, though, and let them stay till morning. Only, for her father, morning never came.

Niena leans into the pole, stifling the tears. "Is this strength?" Her grip on the wood is hard, knuckles straining.

The road winds on. Past towers. Past the ruinous town's first wall, massive even now, and alien looking. Blackened stone litters the ground, and the enormous blocks that make up the gate look almost melted together.

"What sort of fire could melt stone?"

She can think of only one thing. "Dragon." And *dragon fire.*

"Marny," she says in a breath.

Decay from an alley, overgrown with mold, hits her. Niena closes her eyes, to picture the man who truly raised her. He was well known. A plainspoken military veteran. Captain of the Bluecoats, and seemingly always the same age and mood: old and grizzled.

"Grumpy was his middle name," she says. "And..." Scars hid kind eyes. Rough words and a crude manner protected his soft heart. She could not see it when she left, only the moment he, too, gave up his life. For her.

For me. "The best person I have ever known." Niena chokes back a quiet sob and secures the lyre.

The breeze before was more than a remembrance. West-leaning winds bring the sea's love closer, marrying with the fields that lie in between — a bracing clash of earthy odors and salty pleasure. Once, this place must have been quite beautiful. Sight, sounds. Birdcall atop crumbling ruins. Visitors to the town would have seen the towers, crowned in flowers like broken crowns on tall kings. With a blue sky, and fair winds, Niena could imagine herself playing in the fields around. With friends and family around. Maybe a picnic? Maybe the place would have been her home. Now, it dwells in the misery of those who died here.

"Home," she says, finding the word hard to say but somehow filling. The word has a life of its own. Much like the salty air, and the birdcall, it strives for a true meaning. Slowly, it becomes an idea.

And this idea carries her away into a daydream. An ill time for such. Niena could not be in any greater danger.

Chapter 23

The deed is done. The arrow, loosed. Ash from the hamlet's fires drifts past Sethlan's eye as he stares forward. Observing.

"Cuiven's Lee," he says with a sneer.

So, truly, this is the end game. The elf shifts his weight to his left leg, and slides from the stump. His returning steps into the young woods are silent. His pace, wide and deliberate, disturbing nothing more than a shadow might in the noon sun.

The Udur have returned. Two of the caravan folk he rescued were taken. The others disappeared in the mad rush. Perhaps alive. *Perhaps.* His hand cups a broadleaf, still green and untouched by the creatures' foulness — a sign that their party has gotten ahead of the hunt. Hopefully, the child remains among them.

He dips low and stops at a beech. Apparently, the white bark has been rent by the claws of a large mammal, dangling soaked from the onslaught of snow and a previous week's rain. He sniffs, breathing in the musky air. *I must be careful.* Then, thinking of the Manneligs he has allied with: We *must be careful. I have told them all I have heard of Cuiven's Lee, and of its resting place, Skehfelthuz. I hope it is enough.*

Treaties with humans hold about as well as those with fairies, though at least with the fairy kind there is a certainty of mischief. Oaths are of course different, like the one he swore to his queen.

He leans into the bark, rubbing the rough patches against his cheek as he thinks. "If the fairy has indeed aligned herself with the Teamor…" he whispers. "If—"

Something flies by his neck, striking the tree just where his head was. The elf rolls, then slides to a stand, dodging appendages as they shatter the woods around him. Hissing, Sethlan unsheathes his knife in an arc and drops the bow. The bronze blade misses the Udur just barely, and Sethlan ducks low and bares his teeth.

A second creature lunges at his back, its appendage glancing off as he swivels in reaction. The move still catches the elf off-balance, and he falls face forward, rolling to the side while angling his weapon for a parry. The two Udur fall on him, flooding forth in a tide, striking left, right. Sethlan rages as lesions well up on his arms and legs from the thick, rope-like appendages that swarm him.

His screams twist as his body does in their grasp. From a low, guttural cry to a high, strained song. It is this that harms them the most, not the blade, nor the thrashing of his arms. Joining their own wails to his, one of the Udur takes Sethlan and throws him into a tree, where his blade is shaken from his grasp.

And then the elf, upon taking one look at the two Teamor nightmares re-forming between the trees and undergrowth, snatches the weapon and runs.

♫

Higgins sneezes. "Bloody elf," he says like it's punctuation. "Been gone for hours now."

The grass rustles behind him, and the apprentice turns. What pops out does have leaf-shaped ears. The squirrel chitters at the two men standing around the campfire, then scatters, disappearing up a beech.

"Looks like you scared off dinner," Rogard says.

"You didn't even know it was there."

"Yes, I did. I was waiting for it, and I bet I could have gotten it with a rock, or maybe just caught the thing. Rung it's little—" Rogard curses under his breath.

Higgins probes the forest's vanguard, seeing only a mash of reds and yellows. *Hope the others found safety.* He rolls up the parchment, narrowing his eyes as Rogard disappears into the briar. Scratched all over the leather are his scribblings — observations and calculations bent on rooting out the details of the Udur's actions.

A windless chill finds him, and he shudders despite himself. *A false hope for our new friends. The creatures that dwell beyond the Netherworld do not let things be.* He bends over to pick at his socks, removing a leaf stuck between shoe and foot. *They will make this world like theirs.*

Higgins holds it up to the light and twirls it by the stem, marveling at the rich orange, autumnal colors. He flips the leaf again and again between his thumb and forefinger until the stem breaks. *Just like this, so ends Hearth.* Higgins pauses. *And what of London; there, too?* The apprentice grimaces as his attention turns to the other end of the clearing, where Rogard went scouting. Or foraging. From here, he can only see a miasma — a dark veil that could be nothing but the shade of the forest, or something more sinister.

From all directions, there erupts a high-pitched discord that reminds him of children babbling. Leaves dip and shake. Higgins slows his breathing and pushes all his emotion, all his thoughts, out with each breath. The winds immediately cease, letting the rustling in the forest flow to the apprentice. He lifts his hand and barks a short incantation. Between his right index and forefinger, a flame ignites.

This he snuffs accidentally when, from the bushes, Sethlan appears.

"The Udur come from the east," the elf says.

"Bloody—" Higgins alternates between clutching his chest and burnt hand. "Bloody elf!"

"It is old blood, and not mine," Sethlan says, eyes snagging at the parchment. "You have made progress?"

Excitedly, Higgins flashes a corner of the scribblings at the elf. "Science. I can explain on the run."

From the opposite direction, Rogard bursts out of the thicket, marked by briar and fuming like a roused boar. And for the second time in as many minutes, Higgins jumps.

"I found acorns." He beams.

Sethlan angles his head. "We must leave. Now."

"Well, then," Rogard says. "We must see the rhythm to this journey. Have you've ever been told the story of Old Mac?"

Sethlan walks past. A whisper from the elf slips to Higgins' ear. Offering nothing further, the elf strides into the forest thicket.

"Right," Rogard says.

Bluebirds trill a greeting when they enter the thicket. Squirrels and tits shadow their movements, the latter's song a welcome escort. They are not the only creatures about. Beetles buzz when they're not calling, lazily wandering — often into their eyes, or else where bugs will forever deem worth delving. And during the few quiet pauses, they manage to catch sight of a deer.

Through this, the elf leads the party. It is, in truth, Sethlan's skill alone that rescues them from the worst of the briar. The apprentice shades his eyes, looking ahead at the fey. *Is this the same creature Rein was tracking in Liverpool?*

A beetle whizzes by his face and earns a slap. His master told him things, terrible things. And he himself had witnesses the chaos from the other side. This is the person that commands them now. From the lumpen scape, as if this were Scotland, or God were an Irish mother making potato mash of everything. Into false streams, those that are born of quick and heavy rains. Spring streams.

Where the briars do not follow, other plants take up the thorny business, until the elf guides them to another hollow and a shallow marsh. Water threatens the inline of Higgins's boots.

"Sod it," Higgins growls, which earns him a nasty look from Sethlan.

Rein. Where are you, my friend? Without you, we are lost. Higgins removes his hat and wipes his head. Leaves blanket the ground ahead, hiding an easy way forward. *Rein was our magical bloodhound, and my compass for years uncounted.*

Rogard trudges by and pats him on the shoulder. "Chasing women always leads to rotten luck, eh?"

"Rightly said there," Higgins says, turning to the man with a forced smile. "What was that story about Old Mac?"

"Old Mac?" Rogard's face lights up. "Why, it's one of the oldest tales of my kin. Once—"

"No stories."

Both men turn to see Sethlan glaring at them.

"No more chatter," he says hoarsely. "Do you not hear?"

Higgins scratches his head, looking from tree to root, root to stone. Beyond the sound of Rogard crunching leaves as he fidgets, he can't tell what the elf is on about. "I don't hear anything."

"Precisely," Sethlan says. "We are alone. Now we must fly like the birds that left us."

"Double the pace," Rogard says, striding past. He looks back. "Double the noise."

Higgins smirks.

Two leagues fly under their feet without stopping. Sunlight bothers them on high, as the hours fleet away unabated. Here, Higgins finds another reason to thank his master. *Hats are for growing older, and bald spots are kisses from the angel of death*, he would say. *You don't want to be one of those ungodly sods always fussing over their lost hair now, do you? Have faith in the Lord's plan.*

After a brief respite, they trudge forward to the base of a hill. Here the trees are even less numerous. Grass sprouts along a rocky natural terrace, and wildflowers are plenty. Higgins shades his eyes, to see the elf already climbing. Even fewer trees grace the incline, or top, taken by some recent fire. *Or the land's just balding; have faith, good hill.* What does return are more of those blasted thorns, and the apprentice has already prepared some of his best curses for the climb up.

"Bloody," he starts off as a snag rakes across his hand. Several volleys of execrable oaths resound after. *Lawks* finds its way in, as does a subdued *zounds*. But when Rogard inquires as to what some of these are, and after one particularly nasty thorn rips Higgins's sleeves, he gets called an "addle-pated blunderbuss."

"Speak more of what you have found," Sethlan calls down to them from the top.

"Finally. You have not made it easy on me to explain." Higgins struggles past a sapling while Rogard barrels ahead. The next stone proves to be challenging for the winded apprentice.

"Though Newton's *Principia* would say otherwise, Niena is the center of the universe," he continues, stopping. "I theorize the Udur are herding this child towards some unknown destination, and if we stay within their leading edge, we can figure out what this might be and then act. I am also starting to appreciate Rein's hatred of nature."

"Sounds like you mean to stay just in front of the wolf's teeth," Rogard grumbles. He reaches out to Higgins, offering a hand up and over a final boulder.

"And what course of immediate action does your science suggest?" Sethlan asks slyly.

Higgins grasps Rogard's hands, and the two men strain. Shortly after, they join the elf at the summit. The sun lowers on the western side, and light has broken through the canopy here, at the top of the hill. The apprentice shades his eyes, then turns and raises his finger to the wind, nodding to himself.

"Are you sure this Skehfelthuz is somewhere in these mountains?"

At the mention of the city's name, Sethlan's shoulders tense, then he nods.

"Then, if my theory is correct, we are being drawn into a tightening noose." He bends over, sketching a circle in the dirt. "I think we are on the outer right quadrant, hmm."

Sethlan narrows his eyes. "You think? Is this a guess?"

"An educated guess — one that makes sense based on observation. If they were trying to capture the girl outright, I think they would have already. So they must have some other goal," Higgins says.

He points at abstract marks in the distance. Forest surrounds them as far as his eye can see, but the apprentice knows the elfs are keener. Sethlan leans forward, interested.

"There are too many for them to be wary of Titania," he says. "No, I am a fool. The slowness of their movements shows this is deliberate." A grunt from Rogard earns his glare. "They are slow, compared to what I know they can do."

The elf focuses his attention solely on Higgins. "We have not seen things from the other side to be assured of a noose, or a circle."

"Then it is a jaw," Higgins says. "Or horns. Does it matter? We must continue south then southwest of here to remain on the edge." He breathes in as Rogard stumbles down the other side.

"Mist," Rogard babbles. "Mist is rolling through the forest behind."

Higgins turns to Sethlan. "The Udur. We must run; let us make haste, elf!"

"Haste..." The elf's eyes scan the horizon, and he sneers. "There is no such thing as haste with you two. Nor stealth. I will do what I can, but we must act with wisdom. South by southwest is our mark."

"Do you see that?" Rogard nervously exclaims.

On a hill at their left is a hoary shape, as discerned through the skeletal branches of a tree. Backlit by the fading sun, it oozes over the scenery as a nightmare made flesh. Higgins tenses, biting back the fear and pushing it instead into a fierce growl as the many pincers, maws, and appendages shift and flash in the revealing light.

"Yes," through clenched teeth. "There is a sort of beauty that can be found in the terrible."

Rogard stumbles against Higgins's hand. "Beauty? What sort of man are you?"

"One who is familiar with death," Higgins grumbles, then pushes Rogard.

"Cease your endless babble," Sethlan says. He disappears down, leaving the two men fast in his wake.

Side by side, the apprentice and the newcomer follow, the former's eyes dragging along Sethlan's tracks on the ground. Higgins only deviates from his endeavor in those places where the canopy dims. In these times, he can sometimes see the profile of the elf plainly. Waiting. Watching, and always disapproving of their slowness. At other times, only a glimpse of Sethlan is caught, shadowy, and vague, like a phantasm trying to decide if the world around is real.

At an outcropping of boulders traversing a cliff line, the elf stops. Higgins opens his mouth to call out but closes it with a *clop*. Instead, he regards his fellow man, then waits as the apparition of the elf solidifies.

"Why are we stopping?" he asks the approaching Sethlan. The apprentice's knees shake.

"There is a narrow lake after the cliff," Sethlan says.

Twilight makes ready to depart, leaving only the moon and the stars to watch over them. Silver threads touch the fringes of Higgins's frock then scatters, reflecting off a lone button as if he were a dragon in the middle of a hoard. The apprentice fidgets, understanding. "We must go around."

"I shall not risk swimming in the dark," the elf whispers. "Night is nearly upon us."

"How long and wide is it?"

"A few hundred meters and half that wide."

"It will be narrow," Higgins says, aware of the closing circle. "Lead us around the right of it; if our luck holds, an hour's march will give us safety."

"There are many of the enemy that way," Sethlan says. "Yet hope remains, so long as our path is true. Place your hand on my shoulder, and I will guide you ducklings." He smirks, teeth unnaturally white in the darkness. "Consider it as an exercise of faith."

Higgins grimaces. His chest heaves in what at first is a chuckle but ends in more of a sigh. There's something profoundly unorthodox in that, as his former pastor might say. Before he can decide, the elf turns, and in silence both men clasp the fringes of Sethlan's tunic.

The last red of the sunset and green of the canopy mixes, turning black — the horizon settling into the normal hue of night. Sethlan leads them in silence, step by step, the lone hunter guiding his pups through the wild.

They are close. Somewhere, out beyond the hills and between the mountains and the ocean, a lone wolf cries. Only it is not a normal bay; it's more reminiscent of the horrors that surely surround them as they inch along, and Higgins shudders to think on them. *And they are everywhere.*

Yes," the elf whispers, not turning. "They are indeed all around us now."

An answering howl catches them, and suddenly the elf spurs into action. His footfalls dance around all obstacles. Leaf and bough. Twig and branch. The men are not quite so fluid, and Rogard is the nosier. It is all either can do to keep their hand upon the elf's back.

Leaves and branches tear at Higgins's hair and face. He passes the edge of the lake fed by a quick stream, only noticing that his legs are soaked to the knees after they breach the other side. The apprentice glances at Rogard as his pant legs slosh. *He is wood-wise beyond my ken, but is a hare's jump to being wild... The Udur's song is upon his mind!* For the apprentice, whose thoughts often touch the realm the Udur name as home, the calls take on a different meaning:

"Cold, colder the hand that wields the blade,
Dark, darker below the farmer's spade,
The Stag's horn grows nearer the bed,
It is not with the living, but dwells with the dead.
"Never sun or moon to see,
Never to live, but simply be,
Till the Teamor stride the thrones,

That of silver, gold and bone."

Not just a chant, *but a spell.* Higgins clenches his teeth, and in that instant the elf jerks to the right. Panic sets into Rogard, and both men rush to keep pace. Over the howl of the wind, over the unnatural cries, the crash of their pursuit humbles all. Peering once over his shoulder, the apprentice sees a flash of beak and talon in the moonlight, and then something strikes his face and chest hard enough to make him reel. Higgins slumps to the ground, tumbling into a log and scraping his face against the bark.

Dimly, he becomes aware of an itch and a trickle of liquid that fouls his sight. Higgins swoons, just as a heavy hand grasps him by the neck and peels him from a brush, thorn and all.

"You'll not leave me to this alone," Rogard growls. Ahead, the elf's cloak whips in the wind, his figure cut against a cluster of bare saplings and the waxing moon. As the two men struggle, Sethlan's profile shifts towards them. From his direction, but as if drifting from the canopy, comes a song.

Higgins frowns. *Elf work.* Behind him, where the Udur must have been, there is now nothing. No rustling. No otherworldly terror, but the chant remains.

He stumbles to his feet with Rogard's help and checks himself. "I am whole," he mutters, patting his legs. "Thank the Lord, the creatures moved on."

"I do not think they truly have," Rogard whispers. "We are being watched. Time to leave."

The cadence of their march beats to the rhythm of the elf song, pushing them through the brush. Over the sounds of danger lurking on the periphery. The bay of the demons dwindles, but remains sinister in the suffocating darkness. Even so, Higgins finds himself heartened through it, lowering the collar he once raised against the encroaching monsters. Rogard, too, seems different. His furtive gaze is firm, no longer darting around as the forest thickens.

At times, their quick march stops. Sethlan remains in profile, his hand directing and pointing out dangers. In one such moment, Higgins follows the finger like a snake once followed a charmer he saw in Jaipur, to spot at the end a dark mist rolling down from a hillside.

Not just mist. Higgins squints.

They continue, slower than before. At a fire-thinned space in the trees, Sethlan mounts a crop of stone, allowing the men to rest. Tendrils of fog ebb against the lowest rock below, like the start of some cliffside horror story. Far behind, the river's blue is clear, wrapping sinewy arms around a protrusion in the water.

The elf turns to the men. "We are nearly free—"

Somewhere behind them, deep in the mist, a low, haunting wail scratches its way out, as if clawing from an ancient grave. Higgins's shudders, dropping down just as the moonlight, assaulted by the clouds, drowns like a wick dipped into water.

Sethlan turns his attention to the men. "You must do better than this. Rogard, I expect you to set the rhythm here."

The Isfall man beams under the elf's gaze. Once more, the party sets off, this time in three. Sethlan, as before, leads, with Rogard falling right after. His long gait has more purchasing power, and the distance between them lengthens fast.

The bugger's been holding back.

Twigs lay underfoot, and Higgins's formerly soggy leggings now stick to him by sweat. Once more, they climb a hill. Then once more they descend. Rogard acting as the bull, to the elf, whose grace is such that he melds into the stone and wood of the forest. Night fowl have not returned. Nor have the chirping insects or amphibians of the waterways. Higgins stares, but the low light allows for little more than to note them on the field. He looks back. Nothing.

Eventually, the elf leads them into a closed dell, with trees and other vegetation hiding them from a land what has tapered and leveled.

"This is not the camp I would have chosen, but it must do." Sethlan turns abruptly to the men with a raised finger. "Do not lose your wits."

The Udur continue their hunt. Woe betide those they cross, Higgins thinks, unwilling to whisper their name, close as they might be. He in turn looks at the elf and pulls out the hide from earlier. "Are we—?"

"We are through the gap," Sethan answers.

"Where on—"

The elf grasps Higgins's hand and drags his finger to the outer circle on the parchment, which draws a heavy sigh from the apprentice.

"We shall follow the edge in the morning for around two miles," Higgins says. "You will keep an eye for a chance to break west?"

Sethlan nods, but it is Rogard's relieved groan that draws their eyes, as the weight of the last few days appears to send him to the forest ground. "What now? What the chords now are we supposed to do?"

"We rest, and tomorrow we save this world," Higgins says, rolling the hide and slipping it into his belt with a flourish.

"What of the girl?" A question which earns Rogard a challenging glare from Sethlan. He shrugs. "When we catch her, we will need to take her to a stronghold or such. A safe house?"

"No home is safe, for her or us," Sethlan says.

Rogard leans forward. "What do you mean by that?" He turns to Higgins, his voice rising. "What does he—"

"The Udur do not have mercy," Higgins whispers. "They will never stop hunting us."

"There's only a few of them, though," Rogard says, dropping his own voice as Higgins did. "Just those from the village."

"There will be more," Higgins says as Sethlan withdraws food from his pack. "They will not let a fruit go unwithered on the vine."

"What are we to do?"

It is Sethlan who answers. "Bold moves, Isfall man." He looks at Higgins, eyes cold. "We shall save all the worlds or die trying."

These are the last words spoken. They settle down to a wary, fireless night. Each takes a turn at the watch. And each finds his own problems sleeping.

Chapter 24

The air in the dell is stale and smells of sweaty men. *And worse, much worse.* It is also humid, and grime from the previous fire is on everything. Sethlan lifts his nose. He will be happy to leave this dell behind. And when the time comes, the men.

Sethlan tilts his head, considering. *What of these Manneligs?* He shakes his head. *One oath placed against another. My queen, to these oafs?*

The elf waits just beyond the entrance to their camp, the cold from the storm pressing against his back like a lover. A natural pillar obscures him from the others. He takes a step forward, then stops. Snow licks at his heels but goes no further.

"I'm trembling," he whispers, his voice curious. Beyond, a mockingbird calls — a song that would be soothing at another time. Sethlan takes a step forward, into the arms of a young tree, the leaves shaking in the wind and the moon straining through, making his feet look as if they were set upon by a ghostly fire. Dawn threatens to wake the forest as Higgins gathers wood nearby. The Mannelig turns the corner to where Sethlan stands, and upon seeing the elf, the apprentice jerks back. The branches he was carrying fall into the snow.

"Higgins," Sethlan says. "Your plan doesn't allow for much rest."

"Why'd...Don't jump out at me like that."

"I barely moved."

"Well, you've got to give a man time." Higgins wipes his eyes and bends over to pick up the kindling. "Where are we, yes. My plan — my plan is little more than organized fleeing. One leg up from chickens in a coop defecating all over themselves when they see a fox. So, of course, it doesn't allow for much of anything."

Sethan's lips pull back. "That was... I did not think the lack of sleep was affecting you so."

"Yes, well. That's my father getting through." He stops, re-arranges the kindling in his arms.

"All roads lead to Cuiven's Lee," the elf says. He waits for Higgins's reaction, then continues: "I am now convinced the dark ones and the fairies seek it together."

"Or that could just be happenstance, on account of everyone wanting the blasted thing."

"Perhaps," Sethlan says. "The danger is behind us, for now. Until the field of play narrows and—"

"And we are face-to-face with it," Higgins interrupts.

"Yes." Sethlan crosses his arms. "It won't matter that we aren't the goal of their hunt then. If a rabbit is flushed, its fate is sealed, even if it is the fox the farmers are after."

"That is an interesting way to put it," Higgins says. He studies the elf, who remains unmoving. "Something else bothering you?"

Sethlan hesitates. "No, I..." His gaze drops, and the elf shakes his head. "My people do not die, save by foolishness or maliciousness. Yet here I am, fighting against time." His eyes drift to his own feet. "It is ironic for an immortal to be so constrained. On Earth, the Construct would always pull us back into our prison. Here, I must constantly be on the move, never having the chance to appreciate what is before me." Now his eyes are level with Higgins's. "There is no promise of a future," Sethlan whispers. "If the Teamor get to the girl and the Evercharm, it will be all over."

Higgins nods as Sethlan turns, and they stand side by side. A moment is shared in silence, staring upon the camp and upon Rogard, who sleeps. "It is a very…mortal condition," the apprentice says. "To know you only have a little time left. To know it, and yet strive against it despite the odds."

"Yes."

Higgins sighs. "I understand why Rein drinks so much." He pats Sethlan on the back and laughs as the elf's face twists into a sneer. "Let's get Rogard up."

The camp is broken, and the party moves on. The creaking of trees and rustling of leaves replace banter, though a persistent breeze stirs up coughing and sneezing among the mortals. The willows and elder trees, with little mercy for the Manneligs' condition. Sethlan raises his chin and regards Higgins. Rein was useful, his apprentice less so, though grudgingly he has come to admire this one's resourcefulness. His eyes fall upon Rogard. At the beginning of their hunt the three — Higgins, Rein and he — were besieged by the attack of the Udur. Would this new Mannelig be of aid if that were to happen again, or just get in the way?

The elf breaks his pace. A great oak shatters the monotony of pine — a reversal of the day's trend: a thickening. He walks slowly, dimly aware of the rest of the party. More oaks emerge, and other trees that steal his breath. At a break in the roll of the landscape, he slows further.

"These trees…" The row of tall oaks hint at a change in the forest. "We approach the sylvan heart. Here, they tell each other stories."

Near him, Higgins and Rogard recover, their heavy breathing telling of a lack of sleep mixed with the constant pressure to keep up. Sethlan bends his head.

"What sort of stories do they tell?" That is Rogard, though he cannot see the man's face behind the tree. "Like those meant for a roaring fire, or something else?"

"Elsewise, I think. They...are and are not similar," Sethlan says. "Your stories come from your parents and are meant to teach lessons. When a tree talks to another tree, it recants everything that has passed from root to seed, and beyond. For the lives of trees are very long. Do you understand?"

Rogard grunts. "No."

"Elves are immortal," Higgins says, smirking. "Is this why you tell stories too?"

"Must I answer every child's request?" And yet, he does. "Yes, but not only, for ours can become, as opposed to just inform of what became. Manneligs such as yourself have your drycraft. Fairies like to sing. And our stories play for the continuance of what is, and the delay of what isn't."

"That tells me mine are at least faster," Higgins says, and then under his breath, "And more useful."

"*Barna,*" Sethlan says, catching the subterfuge. "Do you wish me to sing for you?"

Higgins smiles. "No, but you can tell me what you bloody well mean by the continuance of things."

"The preservation of spring, in a world that doesn't understand it," Sethlan says, waving his hand as if to push away the question. He then spins swiftly towards Rogard in the act of breaking a branch. The elf narrows his eyes. "Yet, when in need for quiet, and stealth, I can tell a tale of the Redhorns, and their plight south of the Einbury Pass. It will hide trail, sight, and sound — and like all things of the Huldfolc, it shall last."

"Titania's songs will be as powerful," Higgins says. "Niena's, more so, if she is aided by that Evercharm. We will certainly need your stealth."

This place. Those old oaks, and the story playing out, make the elf anxious. And spark memories. "It shall be a perfect hunt," Sethlan says in urgent tones. "I am not my brother and do not love storytelling anymore. Yet, for this, I shall tell of a storm to hide our scent — fairy or not, we will have the advantage."

"No more storms," Rogard says. "The last one, I nearly lost my beard in." He grips a sapling between his hands and sputters — as if more words desperately want to come out. Finally, he looks at Sethlan. "Chords, have you all heard yourself talk? This is all so very mad. The world ending, undead, demons? If I hadn't lived through…whatever the chords that was back in the village, I would have thought myself drunk and dreaming." He whispers in awe, "And you, an elf? All the old tales. All the nonsense I've already seen. Now we are to rush off, into Dunos knows where, and face fairies, and these Udur again? I haven't said much, but this whole thing could be a trap — have you not thought about that? There comes a time when even the heroes of the story must look back and say, nope, there's no way I am going to live through this; this is silly."

"Hwaruh lokode kuningaz wezun skildiwiz isarnas bindanai midi baromiz," says Sethlan.

Rogard balks. "What in the what? Is that Elvish?" The sapling cracks in his grip, louder than the crickets in the background.

"No, it is the language of the men of the old forest, with whom my kind still had dealings after the betrayal." Sethlan stares south, avoiding the holes in the canopy that swallow his vision. "Everywhere the king looked were leaves of iron bound with bars."

"Traps and danger are everywhere," Higgins says. "If we had any other choice, we would not be doing this."

"And there are dark places beyond which your eyes can see," Sethlan says.

Rogard throws his hands up. "I get it. I think I will just talk to myself for now on, to regain my sense."

"Well, let us continue, and make a proper camp tonight," Higgins says.

"Watch the fire," Sethlan says. "I shall look around. But his voice is drowned out by the whisper of the trees.

The elf walks tree by tree into the forest, letting the wind take him where it may. The tension that seized his limbs earlier lessens only slightly, though he is able to bound over the landscape like a shadow against a quick sunrise.

The storm that hit this area was weak, but he cannot truly feel the nature of it. Long have been the years since the betrayal, and the land has forgotten his kind entirely. Now he is alien. This thought causes the elf's lips to withdraw into a snarl. He skulks around a set of boulders.

He growls. Laughs into the air. And the wind matches him, beating him instantly back with a gust of needle and leaf. Sethlan shields his eyes with his right arm, and wades into the sudden onslaught.

And then more. The elf stumbles, nearly toppling like a top-heavy tree felled in late winter. Ahead, his feet find the edge of a stream. Cold water and colder thoughts dash themselves against rocks not far from where he stands.

A flat stone sticks. Sethlan tilts his head, looking upon the mud scraped against its side. Near his feet, a clump of weeds is pressed in a remnant of snow, quick-frozen to the ice, as if a fast wind had hit and merged.

The snow smells of drycraft and fairies. *Niena and Titania.* The land still remembers their tread, for it has not been but a couple of days since. A smile curls on his lips. *We are not far behind.*

Chapter 25

Niena saw. And Niena didn't see. She reached out into the darkness and found emptiness. She kicked and struggled until the breath grew hot in her throat. There was nothing to hold on to. No wall or floor to push off against. Niena, last child of fairy-kind, was enveloped by the void.

At last, she screamed, and that was when they came.

Tendrils of mist weave their way past the embers of Niena's campfire, unperturbed by the girl kicking and screaming. Morning has come, but little of the dawn can be seen.

"Oberon," she yells, panting. Niena rubs her dry, sore throat. The feeling of dread, of a ceaseless hate, has not left her, but another need takes priority. Reaching into her bodice, she pulls out a waterskin and drinks greedily.

"Titania," she whispers between gasps. "Grandmother?"

But she is on her own.

Broken mosaics crunch under pole and shoe as Niena's leaves the campfire behind and strives further into the city. An hour passes, with little change in the weather. This second day in the ruins is barely distinguishable from the first evening. A thick fog slipped in during the night, setting up a dry overcast. She remains cautious while picking through this town, keeping to the shadows where possible.

The outskirts end in a short retainer wall. Outside, the road continues, weaving its way through columns that might have once been grand but seem pale and worn to the girl's eye. Here the land slightly rises on the left. To the right, the edge falls off sharply, and though eroded, signs of what once was a lake become evident. Only now, where reeds and rocks must have caught the silt from a river's run, there is mostly the dreadful soot-stained clay. A few weeds and spots of gray grass hold on, testament to what was once a thriving, fertile land. Whatever calamity brought this city down also drained the lake and wiped the course of its feeding river from the face of Hearth.

An hour on this course takes her closer to a ring of patch, grass-covered hills that pockmark the eastern side. The smell of the sea is stronger here, and the level of the ground lower. The road curves to the left, following the old lake shore. At high point, a mostly intact way-building sits abandoned, and Niena uses it for rest.

"Near the northmost hill, I think that's what's left of a river," Niena says, taking a sip from her flask. The weather has been warm, not hot. But the dust has made speaking difficult, so she does it now out of some silly fear that she might lose the ability. "Some wavy marks in the dirt. Probably was a marsh, once upon a time."

South along the road is the city.

"South," she whispers. "Maro Unsterbberiz." She now sees the blurred edges of a great wall. "Will Titania be there? But what of the north…"

For the past day, she has only taken small glances behind her. Both out of fear and of a desire to remain on the trail. Now Niena leans against the way-building's wall and shades her eyes to look that way.

"Chords…" The mist has taken the outskirts and runs against the ancient bank, flowing over it as some ghost of the water that once lapped at those shores. Niena takes another sip from her waterskin and shakes the road from her dress. Pole in hand, she sets out.

The hours while away, with nothing but the sound of shoes on the cobble as company. The last of the dust veil obscuring Maro Unsterbberiz pulls back further, revealing broken, ragged toppings where towers once were. Still, magnificent in death.

Niena stops at the main gate, awestruck by the enormous blocks of stones used to form the arch. Stones that still stand, blackened by some ancient fire and empty of their doors and fittings. Towers jut at either side, like broken sticks set in the mud by children.

"This city is dead," she mutters.

Her opinion changes little when she enters. The cyclopean walls dwarf her, blocking out the midday sun in the minutes it takes to traverse the threshold of the gate, and making the girl feel abysmally tiny. When she emerges, it is as if she has crawled out of some cave, the dull light blinding and painful. The few lopsided buildings that remain standing do so only to the first floor; the others have fallen into the street as if they were drunks tossed out from some tavern.

Still, the cold follows. The sun's rays trespass upon the city proper only to cast shadows, which they do often. Malaise tightens the girl's stomach. Humidity and stale air war with a sense of restlessness — an abomination for a place abandoned to nature. Though she considers the lack of plant life, realizing a city forgotten to nature may also be to nature forgotten.

I've made a mistake in coming here.

And nothing grows here. No gray-grass. Even the weeds that once cracked the stone at her feet, mainly old and witling back then, are gone. Tumbled walls spill brick and stone into the street. The western side seems to be spared most of the damage that befell the east, and this is the direction Niena takes.

Pole in hand, she continues, the road eventually widening to a large square. Here, for all the danger at her heels, she finds herself gripped by the sights. A gold-domed building remains largely intact, though its walls are burdened with soot. It stands on higher ground than the buildings at the edge of the plaza. Proud and dominating. Gray walls surround it, these in lesser condition. Leading to these fortifications is the open square, mostly cleared of debris, though large gouges wind around the middle pass. Over the archways of the main gatehouse, the sign for the customs can still be read.

So caught in this is Niena that she doesn't notice the mist flowing past her ankles until it has traveled several feet in front of her. Taken by surprise, she does the first thing that comes to mind: She runs.

Fifty yards sprawl from here to the domed building's entrance. Fifty yards, taken with the sound of her breathing over the wind. Niena races through the great archway, careening around a broken colonnade that has fallen near the entrance on the other side. She gains the courtyard moments before the mist and collapses to her knees, coughing. Still breathing heavily, she looks back.

Is it not following?

She boggles, wondering at what power holds it back. Wondering if she is yet walking into something worse. Niena stands. White stone foundations reign over the courtyard, dirtied by age, crossed by gold-hued veins that still catch light. These, alongside a massive staircase leading left, shout — not just hint — of grandeur. She swallows and climbs left, where another archway, this one in blue-hewn marble, awaits.

Who would abandon such a place? Niena trembles as she sets her first foot on the stairs. *Why wouldn't they come back?*

Through the archway there is the entrance to the main building. One great door remains on its hinges; the other has fallen further in. Stepping lightly, she risks a look into the cavernous opening. Inside is a huge room, the floor lost to dust and debris, while the walls are lightened by a few ragged hangings that look as if they would unwind at a touch. Save for these things, the place is empty.

"Forty years, and still nothing grows," says a weak voice. "Nor will it ever again, except for lichens and moss, other shade dwellers. You have chosen a strange path to walk, my granddaughter. Strange, and dangerous."

Niena spins to the side, catching herself on the door's threshold. Out in the courtyard, sitting on a broken column softly lit by the midday sun, is a hunched figure.

"Oberon," she mouths, forgetting all that has passed between them. A raised hand forestalls her from rushing forward. "Where have you been? For so long, I thought you might be..."

"Dead?" Oberon laughs. "I didn't think I smelled—" He lurches over, violently coughing. Niena can see the edges of the fairy lord blurring.

"Grandfather?"

Finally, the coughing fit ends and he speaks again. "I weaken, and I am close to the end." He looks into her eyes. "This is a place where dreams go to die."

"Why would Titania want me to come here?"

He breathes in deeply, his struggle echoing in the chamber halls. "Because she made a bargain with the Teamor. She will bring you back. To unmake everything that was and will be. Then they will betray her."

"I also would have used you." He raises his hand to forestall Niena's objection. "I wanted to take you to a time when my children still lived. Together we would have inspired men to new dreams, and we—It doesn't matter, I have lost."

Marny, my real grandfather, how I wish you were here... *Deliah, my sweet grandmother.* Niena swallows, choking back a sob. "What happens now?" Her quivering voice betrays her. *Who can I trust?* She stares at Oberon.

The fairy's features change. The last of the twinkle in his eye has died. Replacing it is … *fear. And weariness.* When he makes to speak again, she interrupts him.

"If what you say is true, then I am surrounded on all sides by enemies," she says. "Rein, the elf, you. What should I do when so much is against me?"

Oberon nods as Niena lowers her chin, ready to spit forth another question. But the fairy answers first. "You have your wits. You have the power of creation at your fingertips — and, behold, you are at the gates of Cuiven Lee!"

And the fairy lord rises from the stump of a column, appearing as he never has before: angry and wrathful. "Turn their desires upon them. Use them. Use me."

A cloud passes before the sun, and she blinks.

"That's not who I am."

"Then I can do nothing for you, if you will not stand for yourself."

Niena straightens. "But I will, and I will stand for others who can't."

"You are your father's child," Oberon says. The fairy's eyes flash, and in that moment, his face twists in pain. "I truly wish I could have spent more time with you."

"You can still," she sputters. "I can take care of you."

"I gave up that right," Oberon says sadly. "I am not here." An unfettered gale strikes from the south. Scouring dust rips through the ruinous inner hall.

"I never truly was. Niena."

Fragments of buildings and old wooden debris clatter on cobblestone. Niena throws her arms up to protect her head and steps back. Oberon's squeaky voice rises above the timbre of the storm.

"Beware the sorcerer the most. There is—"

The fairy lord is seized by the wind tearing through the mist beyond the walls, as if snatched by a dragon, then scattered. The departure leaves Niena without words, only the desire to sit and wait, and to stare at the column. The wind, however, does not relent; if anything, it intensifies, forcing the girl away from the domed building and dispersing the mist at the gates. A terrible clamor follows her into the open street, as dirt finds the cracks in the buildings, creating a noise reminiscent of howling, hungry creatures.

The fog is gone, scattering into the oncoming weather.

"What am I to do?" This road rejoins after the custom house, and many streets spike off from it. Niena looks at these, uncertainty pulling at her strings. Finally, she steels herself up and takes the straightest path around the inner wall.

"East," she announces.

And east she travels, not knowing what she seeks. Past stores, and avenues. Into a terraced ground that could have been a garden, or more, as it was once raised over the cobble. Now it is ruinous, like everything else. Whatever enthusiasm she had is gone as she climbs over broken fountains and around ancient monuments with little more than a glance around. At the entrance to a clustered group of broken shanties, thunder rolls in the distance, and Niena raises her hand to the sky.

"Vile," she says, rubbing the greasy droplet between her fingers. Her eyes travel, pockmark to pockmark, down a great obelisk in a square fallen to squalor long before the rest met its destruction. Then her gaze takes a plunge into the basin at its base. As she thinks on it, imagining the whole of Maidenhill lounging in the waters, a familiar feeling finds her.

Niena skulks, expecting to catch the culprit. There is no one. "East..." She presses up against a wall. She looks left, then right, staring past the obelisk. Peering into the depths of the streets as the rain finds her between patches of light and dark.

The back of her neck prickles, and Niena knows it is not only her imagination, or the effect of a hard night of sleep. She spins around, then waits. The sound of the rain on tile and stone drowns out her own heartbeat. Watching eyes seem to be everywhere.

"There's no going back," she whispers.

Chapter 26

Storm clouds overtake Niena, and she is driven further into the city, and further without her usual caution. The stops become less frequent as she spares only enough energy to squint nervously into a dark alley, or at a ruined cupola that might offer protection.

Little rain comes, and what does is filthy, stinging her eyes. Niena slinks around to avoid its touch and hides under a dripping monument — a gargoyle, its stone etched by past downpours. Now she presses against a leaning wall. Out of every alley, tendrils of mist worm, their forms holding firm against the wind. Seeing these resurrects the dread, the exhaustible hatred of last night's dream. In quiet moments, she remembers the night Titania found her, and the touch of the horrors as they dragged her.

"In and out. I meet Titania, get some answers," she tells herself, fingering the edge of the lyre for comfort. "Figure the rest out once I am safe." Evening threatens.

Niena squeezes into a space choked with wreckage. Foundations are all that remain above man height in situ, the rest seemingly tossed and torn violently. She ducks her head. Runoff endangers the jagged passage, pooling in a V-shaped crevice below the refuse. Her dress sloshes against marble as she drags rock and more behind her.

Midway through, she pauses and clutches her hem as if caught by a sudden chill. Slender lines of mist poke from holes left and right.

"No" she says, jerking her leg out of reach. Niena backpedals. Between one step and the next, she sees the outline of a figure far behind, dark against the light. Her hand flicks to a knife, but instead she ducks and runs forward.

You will not take me. Nails dig into brickwork. Crawling. Stumbling, then spilling out onto a cellar floor. The moon peeks from behind its curtain, and she waves her knife threateningly at the figure.

"Chords!" From one side, a tentacle erupts out of an inky mass, striking the wall closest to Niena with a crack. From another a beak, bulbous and jagged, breaks out of the same form, but this is met by her dagger.

Niena narrows her eyes. *No time for the lyre.* "*I cry, cry, my mother's song.*" The denied Udur wails, punctuating its rancor with staccato shrieks. "*The blood of the forgotten, driven mad.*"

Mad is accentuated by the rush of the second demon, gnashing, clawing. She answers, back, back, slashing and stabbing in her charge.

"*I sing, sing to the mortal life. A sail's full breath tossed in deadly waters.*"

The mess crashes right, spoiling the air with dust and leaving a gash where it passed. Niena drops her song and throws herself flat against the ground. Yet the workings of her spell were already done, and the tip of her dagger sparks blue, then ignites, casting terrible visions wide and illuminating the space in a way that only magic can.

Niena looks back to see a spiral of light bearing down. There is a flash. She shudders and ducks into her own arms just as the bolt's power carries over into another of the advancing Udur. Screams, hers, mix with the terrible cries of the void spawn.

Lifting her head in that moment, she sees the blurred outline of the figure trying to climb the wall towards her. But with the words of Oberon still light in her head, Niena decides against meeting this stranger, and tucks her knife against her arm, then barrels ahead towards the Udur that bars an archway leading out.

"Wait!" a voice commands.

Niena does not, screaming her way through and breaking the mist like a horse charging into water. The blade flashes blue, impaling flesh. But the creature is not done, lumbering a meaty arm towards her chest. This is met by blue fire, and new screams join her own. She raises the knife and bears down, hacking and cutting.

"Niena!"

But the girl's panic takes her through the arch, and beyond, and she joins either a new corridor or the open room of a gutted building — she knows not. The chant of the Udur seethes in the mist around her feet. *Out, there must be a way out.*

A three-pronged gouge has torn the floor lengthwise in the way she wants to go, ending in a pile of rubble at the far end. This she makes for, stopping only briefly to avoid stumbling over the rend. Dragon is on her lips. She swallows and leaps into a waiting alley, biting her lip against a panic.

This was done long ago, she comforts herself. Black stumps of what she thinks are first trees march in regular rows, spanning a space of perhaps thirty meters.

Mosaics crunch underfoot, and Niena's shoulder bumps into one of the trees. *Not trees, this is a hall.* She looks back to see the mist following, then ahead as she hastens. Low walls provide no obstacle for her. Nor does a toppled column, marking what must have been one of the side entrances long ago. Water pools underneath its rim and the incline of a proper alley. Niena catches a reflection of herself in the water.

Around the fairy-kind's shoulders, the night shimmers, as if shedding stardust. She places her head against a nearby wall, listening. Splashing footsteps echo her way left from a further split passage where buildings stand straight, their open third floors making them appear headless. Niena turns right.

Down; at such a speed, she cannot watch her surroundings. Water kicks up with every step, burning her ankles and announcing her run through the dark pathways. The damage here is catastrophic. She leaps over a wall and spills into another maze of destroyed arrangements or fortifications that could as easily have been the promenade leading up to a temple as much as a barracks.

A grinding cacophony from behind halts her. That way, little can be seen. But there is a presence, or so she feels. Niena bites her lip, and a thought passes through her like a blush in winter: all those years of wanting adventure... Her arm jerks backwards in an instant, fingers reaching for the Evercharm, then pull back. She could laugh, and it would be fittingly mad.

Wet hair drifts down her brow. The knife replaces the Evercharm at her fingertips, and the darkness comes alive as she draws its length. Witch-light travels the air, creating blue arcs as Niena navigates the ruins. She squints. There are few roofs left, and these are far enough to blur into the night. Yet the Udur stand out clearly upon these, their bulbous bodies thumping against walls, threatening to bring the last of them down.

Do they see me? She ducks under a wall held up by another. *No.* She shakes her head at the string of decisions that brought her here. After, Niena finds a wider corridor heading east —or west. At this point, she can't tell. More markings from the destruction give her pause along the way, especially a deep imprint that again shouts the word *dragon*. At this junction, Niena is forced to close her eyes to scurry past.

Cold hits her like a wall at the threshold of a squat house. Wrapping memory and current events around her like a blanket, she shivers. Niena takes a deep breath and finds herself slipping along a wall.

Oberon. Titania. She sucks in a gulp of air and coughs. Water dripping down a nearby roof catches her attention. *I need to be rid of them all.* Though the thought hurts, they would have to understand. If she is to do anything for anyone else, she needs to first be safe. She climbs over a horse trough.

Her footsteps splash upon landing, and the moon reveals the spiked end of a fence post, towards which Niena inches. There is an open expanse before her. It is here she sees the first skeletons, the white poking out of broken lean-tos or the shards of the bones scattered on the ground. More of the second floors are visible here. *Looks like the dragon must have landed and thrown a fit.*

A glint of light from the east reveals something falling along the length of a wall. The moon is high and full, without a veil, and pools of rainwater gleam.

Niena secrets the knife away once more. Instead, she reaches for the lyre, the Evercharm forgotten in all the rain. Her trembling fingers peel back the leather wrapping Titania made for it. Silver flashes against black lacquer and pantomime faces. She shakes her head as she cradles the instrument in her arms.

"Oh, this is not going to end well," she says.

Chapter 27

In another part of the ruined city, Titania seeks the ghosts of an earlier time. Memories walk with her through worn colonnades.

Children. Old men and women, and yes, warriors too, crowd around pillars or shiver next to a fire pit before the chieftain's throne. There is an instant when all turn their heads to Titania. And in this moment, with the fairy queen's form seeming to swallow the threshold, there is a strangled cry.

Titania raises her arms and hops on her tiptoes, stretching to reach the rim of an ornate column. For her effort, she is rewarded with dust fouling the sleeve of her green silken dress. Sparks from a makeshift torch clash at the line where her pale skin ends. Night rules here in the Skehfelthuz.

"Whatever happened to the Vale Watchers?" Titania says. The fairy queen crosses her arms and tilts her head in thought. "Does nothing of men endure?"

In the corner near a ratty tapestry, a boy, shaggy and awkward, tries to skirt behind a crowd of bigger and shaggier men. Titania can't help but watch, and then cringe as a stack of weapons crashes to the floor in front of him.

Where the boy was thousands of years earlier, nothing remains. Not the walls, or even the foundations. Most were robbed to build the fortifications, which in turn would be taken for a king's manor. Only the distinct depression in the ground where they should have been hints at the sides of the great temple.

But there is an even older story.

Titania's fingers once more grace the column. Snatches of memory from countless ages spark like dying fireflies in her head, until only one remains. In this remembrance, the column stands alone, nestled inside a cove. Cuiven's Lee. These ruins were set in a lush inland cove of sparkling gems, sapphire and green, where freshwater from the lake and surrounding waters drained before leading to the sea. This was the lay of the land before the breaking of the one world and the birth of the three.

"The Teamor will have to travel back, back to the beginning," she whispers. They will need Titania. They always did. She lifts her head.

Unlike men or elves, fairies are unbound to time. They can traverse the realms and timelines anywhere between the spaces of where their life existed, sending their own memories backwards in the case of personal travel. Which, for their people, was a finite, specific melody in the music of creation. Oberon wished to change this. Or perhaps just ferry Niena off to some other era, to alter the course of history.

Titania's eyelashes flutter; she is unable to decide if she is impressed by his desire or concerned. *I know little of Oberon's entire plan, only his desire to bring back his children, but he must have considered the consequences...*Altering the threads of the future. It was a foolhardy and dangerous desire, one which threatened everything — if it worked — and was a pointless waste of time if it didn't. *Impressed.* For their song was meant to dwindle and fade before the powerful chords of mankind, until there were only two still playing.

"I intend to be one of those."

Every fairy has an end; Titania knows, feeling the air fill her lungs. They may delay, but never escape this doom. It will come, yet she was not ready to die. This last knowledge was the linking commonality between their kind and men, and the first tidbit a young fairy learned on their journey to join the mortals that birthed and sustained them.

As if summoned by these thoughts, a melody finds her. Braided hair falls from the fairy woman's shoulders as her head sways this way and that, searching. Movement catches her eye: a flicker of scenery, a flash of day in the depths of night.

At the place where a sepulcher once stood, an old, bent-backed crone rocks on her heels — her phantasmal body shifting in and out of time.

"The Huldfolc are not welcome in these halls. The Huldfolc are not welcome among the children of Ljod." The crone twists her hand. A single stone appears, cupped between bony fingers. "Go, go back to your holes, or we will put the mountain upon you."

The stone flies through Titania and clatters into a nonexistent wall behind her, at once real and a memory. The fairy queen spins, from wall to debris and back again. Realization dawns quickly. *The Evercharm. The Evercharm! The girl is playing the lyre.*

"Such power," she stammers, proud. "That song will make the gods quake before her." And then Titania's face draws blank. "And call all to her."

The ghostly crone raises her head while the cloak of flesh fades around Titania as if made heavy. She lowers her hand, touching upon the threads of the past — then grasping, clinging to them. Through these lines, the fairy queen pulls herself to where past and present mingle in memory and the phantom and physical are one.

Ice covers the straw on the ground. Then doesn't. Icicles threaten, dangling precariously from a sooty ceiling. Then, more open to the sky, the air seems to stutter. Titania seeks the source of the music, of Niena, like she knows all others must be doing as well. She holds to hope, however, to reach the girl first.

The flames. As the image of a brazier is remembered in this reality, Titania takes a commanding stride through a mansion. She shades her eyes, while the ghostly folk closest to the door withdraw by a half step, and the air of each timeline hangs without a stirring of their breath. Somewhere nearby, a crow cries, and the fairy queen gives the faintest of nods. In an instant, all the torches, the fires, and almost every light, real or magical, in the city crashes. All lights save one.

Whispers turn to murmurs, murmurs to shouts as room after room, ruin after ruin the fairy queen passes sinks into almost complete darkness — almost, for she yet shines. Titania turns her palms out, and there is arrest of everything — of breath, movement. Chatter. Until a moment passes, and the fairy queen again lowers her hands. "Attend me, spirits."

A whisper follows a slight shift in the unstable scape. Titania sighs and continues towards the source of the music, towards Niena.

Through the city. Into the high quarters, where the militia stabled. The music flows through brick and stone, touching all times, all souls and their erected memories. Here in the present, Titania finds Niena.

"Granddaughter," she whispers, but when her fingers reach for the girl, Niena's outline ripples.

Titania frowns. *This is more than just a different memory; the present is not complete.* She drags her fingers through the girl's fading image, and in doing so, reveals the past.

Back, passing the blackened posts of a great hall. Back, into a cellar, where the girl's knife slides out of an Udur again and again, finally retreating with her, and the monster is made whole.

"Niena!"

The voice, Titania's and yet not hers, echoes. The fairy tugs at reality. There is a blinding flash, the wail of the demons. Then, at the entrance of the high quarter, where the dragon Forwurmaz did its worst, her own face looks back at her.

"I see," Titania says. "Time itself is strained here, and a branch has been revealed. Can I...interfere?"

Hand by hand, leg by leg, the fairy queen places herself over her own image until both appear as one, and closes her eyes. Phantoms of the past and phantoms in truth writhe around. The air crackles with energy, shifting and shredding as Titania's mind is sent to this moment, this version of her past. Upon opening her eyes, she sees Niena running ahead.

Shuddering into corporality, Titania struggles after her. The water burns her feet, the air her lungs. At a crest of debris, she gains the wall not long after Niena, looking down in time to see the girl about to be overtaken by seven Udur.

"Sol an lochhrein aleanta," Titania screams. A piece of her own essence peels from the fairy before pressing into a quivering ball of light, mimicking the Artisan spell. She shudders from the loss and reaches for more power. *"Saighead cridhe!"*

The non-spell spirals towards the cellar floor as if shot from her arms, striking near the girl. Udur wails in agony as the darkness shreds itself in an explosion of light. And Titania dizzily grasps the edge of the wall to steady herself, then climbs.

No, child, don't— She throws her leg over the wall. "Wait!"

Niena does not. Wielding a spell-worked blade, she dives into the remaining Udur.

"Niena!"

The chant of the Udur seethes. Niena staggers through the archway and out into the world beyond, ignorant of Titania's plea.

No. The fairy blinks. *I have crossed the Rubicon.* Her stomach sinks and she tries to follow. Stumbling. *The Teamor won't understand this; they will come for me. They will come for the girl with terror and violence.* Crawling, until her flesh leaves once more, and she can move through the layers of rubbish unobstructed.

Around the fairy, a chant is taken up. Along the edges of her sight, long-dead men utter "doom." She spins. At the lip of the cellar wall, the spirits of children too young to even understand repeat it. Their faces glimmer as they speak, like a winter star seen through the sheen of an icicle.

Titania hugs herself, staring blankly at the arisen. "Let them. They will not take my granddaughter." Doom echoes in the dead city.

Chapter 28

Higgins's hands brush a tuft of wet grass. "Tell me again why we're just marching down the road and not trying to find another way around?"

The elf's scouting, the apprentice's science, and Rogard's optimism have brought them to the edge of Maro Unsterbberiz. All three have shown signs of faltering in the dusty wastelands.

"Because a child will want to keep to what is familiar," Sethlan says.

"I don't think we can call her that. We could be walking right towards the enemy's main gate," Higgins says. "We know Titania is ahead of us, and we can guess that whoever is controlling the Teamor might be there as well."

"It is not a great plan," Rogard says. "At least the rain has stopped."

Sehtlan motions for the others to join them on the high ground, a small way-building near a great dried lake. "We do not have the time," he says wearily. "Look."

Shapes seethe out of the ruins they just left. At first, they are little more than crude imitations of deer, and other wildlife foreign to this place. Higgins's eyes narrow, and dart all around one such creature's head. This beast twists in the midday sun and wails in pain. Beaks then erupt from the ill-formed abdomen, tearing through the false flesh in twitching, jerky movements.

The apprentice raises an eyebrow, then takes a tentative step to the side. *Lousy, stommert pannerkoek.* Higgins swats away his inner voice, scraping his palm against a shattered post in the process. *I think that means pancake, anyway.*

"Should we avoid the straight path?" Sethlan looks down upon Higgins. "Should we navigate around the lake?"

The pained cry subsides, and a tumble of fog envelops the outer edge of the ruins. A cloud comes before the sun, and the party members quail as if sensing the oncoming rush.

"Into the city," Rogard yells.

From here onwards, the party's journey towards the Maro Unsterbberiz was spent between looking forward and looking back. Forward, to the imposing blackened gates and the dangers they will face. Behind, to the journey they have made thus far, and the tide of Udur that floods the lakebed.

When Sethlan stops them, it is to check a track or a mark. Each is faint to the human eye, and each pause means an increased effort after. At one point, just before the gatehouse, a sign causes such a reaction in the elf that he immediately draws his knife. The wreckage of the main gate becomes his perch, distancing him from both men.

"What is it?" Higgins asks. "What do you see?"

"Many sets of tracks in the mud," Sethlan says, his body angling for a sprint. "The Udur have already come here." He faces the apprentice. "Both within and without."

"Then we cannot rush ahead," Higgins cautions as Rogard inserts himself between then, his own attention square on the battlements and other fortifications.

"Those walls are hale. We could make a stand in the gatehouse," Rogard says. "I stayed in the eastern tower once. It is a safe spot, if any could be called safe."

The Isfall man then waves Sethlan ahead. The elf's cloak whirls in an eastern breeze, on the pinnacle of a bronze strut, then disappears over the side.

"Hold on," Higgins yells after. "Not without us!"

It is the apprentice who leads Rogard now. Through the great threshold, then right, following the elf as best he may. Over fallen columns, through corridors flooded by an earlier rain. Higgins's instincts pull at him, dragging him through many twists and turns. Because of this, he manages to keep sight of the elf.

However, in the lee of an inner fortification that surrounds a monumental building capped in bronze, the chant of the Udur returns. His attention becomes divided between keeping track of the elf's cloak and searching the crevices and corners for malice.

"Blasted pebbles," Higgins snorts, upending his worn riders — a bad choice of foot apparel, in a sea of other mistakes. "There can be one damn stone in the whole road, and sure enough, it'll find its way inside."

"The sun will be tucking its head in the rabbit hole soon," Rogard says.

"I beg your pardon?"

Rogard smiles. "Haven't you ever heard of the rabbit in the moon?"

"I'm far more concerned with our own long-eared friend."

"Well, I wouldn't call them long."

Here he risks looking back, and immediately regrets it. A tide of darkness flows along the paths they once trekked. He hurriedly re-dons the boots, struggling to shift them as Rogard keeps talking.

"We will need to find cover," Rogard whispers. "We shouldn't be out." He blanks then, turning to where the elf disappeared.

"Spilled milk," Higgins says.

"We could still turn back."

The apprentice barks a short laugh. "I have a feeling that is no longer an option. But you know this place, more than the rest of us. If we are challenged, it will fall to you to delay the Udur until either Sethlan or I can react."

"I will do more than that," Rogard says, beaming. "I will win!"

Nothing moves ahead. To the east, down what might have been a wide gate road, are heaps of rubble hills. There are no trees, and brickwork fallen from the walls of buildings lies about in the street.

They turn right at a crossroad, then onward into a wider passage. Rogard stops them here, and gestures toward the top of a set of stairs, where the elf is waiting.

"A temple," Higgins says.

The two men approach Sethlan, who is standing like a statue among the promenades. Higgins does so cautiously, as if afraid of the elf they have come to know. Rogard, with more energy, thrusts himself ahead of the apprentice.

Sethlan perches on a tumbled statue. "Here they will not come." His eyes follow the apprentice as the latter climbs. Black blood drips from the elf's knife.

"What do you see?" Higgins says.

The flow of the Udur ebbs just outside of a smaller gatehouse, not daring to pass the threshold. Indeed, the temple's columns, stairs and courtyard are an island against it. An unease settles on Higgins's right shoulder. As if a ring is closing in on them and the hunters lie just at the periphery. Sethlan kneels on the column, leveling his gaze with Higgins's.

"Niena is close," he whispers. "I can hear her song."

"Then we should talk," Higgins says, raising his hand against the elf's protest. "I will know now what you plan to do with the girl?"

Sethlan's attention is sudden, and piercing. "One voice cannot out sing the many."

"That's the sort of talk men make before they do something awful," Higgins says, shaking his finger at the elf. He leans closer. "The Curators never gave your people a choice, and you would do the same to this girl?"

Whether it is this gesture or comparing of the elf to men that earns Sethlan's anger, the result is the same. They remain like this, until Rogard lumbers through the temple door.

"We can't stay here," he says. "This is the former temple of the moon. A sacred place, a place for worshipping…"

He looks at the elf as if to rush forward and grab him by the shoulder, then his eyes drop off. "Fairy kind." Rogard raises his hands. "It has been many years since I have been here, and the memory of this place has faded. But I have seen my markings. All of Maro Unsterbberiz is a tomb, and the very air you breathe the stuff of graves. And we have strolled right into the center."

"He is right," Sethlan says. "The dead are here. But I also fear no man, living or dead."

"This is not about bravado," Higgins says. "Nor about luck, good or bad. There is a young woman that could use our help."

Higgin turns to Rogard and makes the sign of the cross. "If you have been here before, then you must know a back way out."

"Cuiven's Lee is here," Sethlan says. "Titania will take here there…" He touches his finger to his lips. "And then."

Beyond the chatter, beyond the site of the ruined city and Rogard's lazy eye, the elf's comment reverberates in Higgins's mind like the last few notes of a lone harper. At his word, the door of memories is reopened. He blinks, feeling an invading chill next to the ancient frescoes — night and cold that had been forgotten in their hunt — and steels himself, knowing, as only he could, the minds of those departed.

Higgins looks at Sethlan, then at Rogard, the latter taking it as a command to move. At this, the apprentice raises his hand. "If the Teamor have the girl, then we should all be dead. Unless—"

Sethlan beams. "They do not have what they want yet." The glow doesn't rest upon his face, but finds a way to lift the corners of his mouth into a smile. He looks at Rogard. "When we find Niena, we will give her other options. We will make sure the Teamor cannot threaten reality." Then, suddenly, he peers at Higgins and settles here. "Thank you, Mannelig."

"Th…Thank you," Higgins stutters. "Whatever for?"

"For reminding me of who I am."

"It is nothing," Higgins stammers. "This is what friends are for."

Sethlan cocks his head and his eyes flutter quizzically. "Friends?"

"Yes," Higgins says. "Friends."

Sethlan's lips twitch. "I fear we must cut this rest short." His eyes also seem to glimmer as he looks up through the broken ruin and into the starless night. "Do you now hear it, Mannelig?"

"Music," Higgins says. "Someone is singing."

The elf saunters around a fallen door. "It is Niena with the Evercharm."

Higgins shakes his head. "What does it mean?"

"I tell you what it means: It means the greatest trio of heroes ever to walk Hearth must get to their heroine," Rogard rumbles. Without another word, he steps inside the temple. At the threshold, he looks back. "Are you coming?"

♫

The moon and stars overtake the world left by the retreating day. It is a clear night, and if it weren't for a natural fog mixed with the unnatural, even Higgins could lead.

"Are you coming, elf?

The mist hides both Rogard's arm and much of the ruin it rests upon. But Sethlan can see the danger beyond.

"The song is stronger," he tells Rogard. "Though I believe we should head east from here."

"East is no good," Rogard says. "Well, no good if you are of the breathing type. We'll get there, elf. We'll get there. Now let's go."

It is not the last thing he says. As the Isfall man disappears into the fog, he mumbles, "Elf. My da would say I'm crazy if he heard me now."

Sethlan smirks. Higgins's labored breathing announces the man's approach. The elf ducks his head under a low-hanging beam and follows.

More than once they are forced to backtrack, either finding a place impassable or because of Higgins's insight into the Udur. The latter is troubling to the elf. And more than once he finds himself watching the apprentice. *Look at how he stares into every corner.*

"Hi—" but he stops himself. *How many times has that man died? It is unnatural, what the Curators have done to him.* Sethlan shakes his head. *Maybe, in a sense, Higgins too has been betrayed.*

A loud splash interrupts his thoughts. The street the Isfall man chose is narrow, with the decayed remains of houses leaning over like nosy neighbors. Sethlan's eyes dart from rooftop to rooftop, watching for more projectiles.

"I do not think we should be going this way," he says.

Rogard looks back and sniffs. "Too late for us to backtrack again, and if we were to have taken the right fork, it would have been bad. I fear the dead less than other men, but I am not stupid. Not on a night like this. Where we are is bad enough."

"I fear being brained by a piece of tile," Sethlan whispers. Drain water drips in time with his steps. He shakes his head, again looking over the Isfall man's shoulders.

"We are in the old city," Rogard interrupts. "Which is mostly a tomb. This place we are passing on the right has the look of it..." He stops before a corner to glance behind him. "Unless you want to do some cracking, we best move on."

Sethlan stops. "Cracking?"

Higgins coughs, shuffling at his side. "Grave robbing."

"Aye, grave robbing," Rogard laughs. "The best kind: Folks don't fight back." He blinks, then frowns. "Or didn't until recently. It was a joke anyways."

Sethlan's cloak swirls around him as he surges past. Budding questions are silenced with a gesture, allowing him to listen at a corner. "Udur," he mouths when Higgins presses close.

Empty windows blur to the right. Stairs to the left. Sethlan's eyes widen at the clump that lumbers through the street. "*Lim,*" he curses. He turns to the men, and whispers, "We are close to the Evercharm. Unfortunately, so is the enemy."

Higgins's face appears at this side. "How many are there?"

"Eleven, maybe," the elf says, returning to the street ahead. "Legions more are coming. There is also a man with him, I believe. It seems that an enormous mausoleum is their goal."

"A man..." Higgins's voice trails off. "Wait, I see him." The apprentice freezes, then makes to run. Sethlan's quick hands, with the grace and speed only one of his lineage possesses, stops him.

"Do not be the chevalier. Hoping to run in, rescue the girl, and everything else will fall into place." Here, Sethlan leans forward, his back stiff and his cloak snapping in the breeze. "We cannot hope to defeat them by strength of arms yet."

"But with Rein, we would stand a chance." Higgins shakes his palms at the elf. "He needs our help, can't you see?"

"That is not what I see," Sethlan says. "This needs a better look. Come." His eyes find the stairs. "Let us spy upon them safely."

Neither ruin nor wall hinder the three as the elf guides them from one to another, and in twelve breaths they gain the rooftop of what was once a temple's outbuilding. More Udur wobble in their solemn march, following the rest — following the man Sethlan sighted.

Rogard looks at the roofs and raises his hands. "Something is —"

A stone gargoyle crashes to the street, hurling Rogard onto his back and Sethlan stumbling to the side. The elf turns in time to see Higgins rushing from a doorway as shapes plummet from further rooftops.

"Four," Higgins says at his side, his whisper rising with the count. "Eight. Eleven!" He glances at his hand, at the undried blood, then towards the blotches of Udur that slither together on the road.

"Do not panic! Their desire is deep, deep into that building. This is no mere mausoleum. This is something greater. This must be Cuiven Lee's," Sethlan says. "I do not think they notice us."

Higgins sighs in relief, until one of the creatures separates from the rest.

"Hold here." Sethlan braces himself on the shattered remains of a roof and leans over. While he looks upon the void spawn, something that passes as a maw forms out of a sleek body. The creature rears back on all fours; more beaks, snouts, and other indescribable things erupt and absorb the sleek lines as it sways back and forth.

"It does not see us," Sethlan whispers. A second such monster joins the first. "They are listening for something." He looks back at the two men huddling in the shadows and presses a finger to his lips. "Keep the big one quiet until I return," he tells Higgins.

A second such monster joins the first. The elf leaves them and circles around the top of the building and onto another building's second floor, then slides along a broken rail to land on the ground without so much as a sound. Dead grass over the front door moves stiffly in a breeze. The road beyond appears deserted.

With a sigh, he flows through, the Udur's staccato shrieks echoing behind him. The front of dormitories that line the left side of the way darken as if clouds have passed over the moon. A fast noise follows, like a cat makes as it moves from the table to the floor. He flows forward, then right, with the sounds of the hunting creatures not far.

"Closed," he says, running to a dead end. The elf leaps at the wall, kicks off, twists, then strikes at the other, where he is then able to grasp a bit of crumbling brick and master the building's roof, disappearing over, over, and into a following street.

Bracing himself on a stack of faggots, he listens.

"The nightingale cries, but we are silent; where is my spring?"

The voice is familiar to him. He follows it until spring, and then at a crossroads, he stops. Before him, a bridge crosses a narrow cut; whatever water once flowed underneath has long since disappeared, but there is a rushing sound.

"When will I become like the swallow so that I may fly away?"

He tilts his head. *Niena.* Her voice resonates on the old stones here, but she moves. Flitting away like the bird she sings of. The elf waits, listening.

"The wind wants to carry my name. The sun needs to know me."

He looks behind him and sees nothing. Ahead, there is an arch where the bridge and the road meet, and uncertainty beyond.

"Let wind fill my wings. Let the snow melt and let me sing, if I can sing of spring."

For a fleeting moment, Sethlan believes he sees a phantom climb from the riverbed and pass through the arch as a winter's ghost in autumn — leaving the bridge behind as a train of her dress cuts the fog.

"A frigid wind at the roof of the world will go unnoticed," he groans. "And a chill upon its feet only deserves a muttered complaint. I am getting too old for this." The ancient elf sighs. He shakes his head, wishing for the first time in many weeks that his brother was here. "The end comes; the pieces are in place. I must get the others."

Chapter 29

"Stay here," Higgins says to Rogard. "I will only be a moment."

Rogard starts. "Are you mad? You aren't exactly the quiet type."

"Yes." Higgins smiles. He bends quickly, grabbing a piece of broken timber and dust from the floor. As Rogard tries to balance his weight on the rafters, the apprentice crushes the wood and dust together, and sprinkles it over his head, saying, "*Na leig le cemsam bith tuteam.*"

A prickling wind, high and humid, announces the spell's completion. Higgins then strikes the ceiling. Dust from the roof falls between him and Rogard, separating them in a flurry of motion. Like gray sheets tossed from a high bed. When it clears, Rogard's searching eyes tell the apprentice everything he needs to know.

Unlike the elf, Higgins is no acrobat. He instead backtracks down the stairs and into the street below their perch. Here he looks around, expecting more of the monsters, but for the moment they appear to have all run after the elf. The way seems quiet, and clear.

Higgins hesitates on the stairs, then reaches into a cut in his coat and withdraws a piece of the child's femur from the dungeons he and Rogard were trapped in. "Sorry for the disrespect, little one." He crumbles the bone and says, *"Folaic miona marha."*

It may not work, he knows, since the Udur are not technically dead. "God, I would love to end this nonsense," in a whisper. "Travel back to the healthy, smoky pits of London, manmade and god-fearing, and leave this dreary devil's nightmare behind." He shifts his hands to his hips. "Where to go, ol' Higgins?"

The lower floor of the opposite building offers an unobstructed view of the street forward. *Chasing after your master's heels, as always, old boy.*

So, he does. The street Rein passed is empty of Udur but filled with garbage. It is a slow walk, but even Higgins can see the path taken. Dormitories lean on his left, unbroken in a line to a bridge and a far archway. On the right, it is not so, and many passages spread off. Higgins hopes the elf took one of these, and maybe the rest of the Udur with him.

Moonlight creeps like a shy dog, with a whimper of wind. Higgins takes measured steps forward, listening to his own breath as neither footfall nor handgrip, thanks to his previous spell, marks his passing. It is an awkward rhythm, and one he keeps up for the half hour it takes to reach the end of the way. A queer light hovers just beyond the bridge's first span. Higgins shades his eyes, uncertain of what he is looking at.

Sometimes dreams trickle into the waking world. Half-realized wispy things of both want and regret, they huddle in the corners of our vision. Tickle our ears. And when finally departing, leave behind little to remember.

"Are you a phantom?" Higgins says to the creature hovering there. "Or something more?"

Amber locks sway in and out of reality as a woman turns to meet his gaze. She smiles coyly, her green eyes shining in the dark. And he freezes, realizing the spell from before must have failed, until another recognition dawns.

"Sofie," Higgins says, struck as he always was by her beauty. "What in the Lord's name are you doing here?"

"Contemplating my choices so far," she says, then lifts her chin. "A lot has passed between us, some that you may not know. Now that you are here, I think I will dispel one thing. I am afraid I have misguided you, dear Higgins. My name is not Sofie, or at least, it is not only." She raises her hands and her images shimmers, mimicking the starlight above.

"I don't...wait. You are no phantom, but fairy. Titania," Higgins whispers. "Could it be, are you the ghost we have been fighting against all this time?"

Her face draws blank, uncertainty tinting those green eyes. "Yes, I suppose I am," she says. Then the fairy queen flows slowly to Higgins like a budding thundercloud held back by the mountains, and with almost as much violence. "And what of you, apprentice, what would you demand of my granddaughter?"

Sometimes nightmares tear away the sheets of reality and expose you to monsters. These, you never forget. Higgins starts, averting his eyes from the sudden terror. He gestures towards the river, risking a look over his hands. "She has a right to her freedom." He straightens then, slowly puffing himself up to stare daggers at the fairy. "I shall not let my master, or the elf, or you challenge that."

"I see." Titania's visage settles back into the beauty, as on their first encounter. She looks away and appears to float past. "Then you may go."

Higgins brushes a lock of his curly hair away from his mouth. Turning slightly to follow, he says, "Have you seen my master? What is it I should expect ahead?"

"I have not," she says. "I was following the trail of plucked chords after I lost her, but this is not a way I can cross. The bridge is out, and I am not fated to go here." Once more, she shows her face, and it is pained. "If that was your master who passed earlier, then he may need your help. Many of those creatures were around him."

"Thank you, milady," Higgins says. "I am afraid danger awaits both of us now."

"One might find an evening stroll in winter pleasant, while his neighbor frets that nightfall may come without a star," she says.

"So, they can," he says, watching her pass. "When did you ever become so philosophical?"

The last word punches the air, unheeded. And like a thunder-crack on a sunny day, Titania breaks away, disappearing with a moonbeam. Higgins goggles, despite his years of service to Rein.

"Lord," he says, brushing back his hair. Only a few clouds mar the night sky. Somewhere, birds cry, but not the sort he is used to hearing in the forest and dales. Only disappearing patches, where the moon cannot penetrate, show where the fairy might have been.

"Blast this whole place."

The bridge's missing span appears clearly. *At least this much she said rings true.* Four timbers zigzag, nearly reaching the other side, moored in a wreckage that defines the word "unstable." It is a delicate mire, one which he does not relish crossing, given his girth. Even so, Higgins supposes that if Rein has passed over it, he should be able to as well. He tests the timbers' fitness.

"I am no acrobat," he thinks, recalling the words he told Rogard before. "But here goes."

Wood complains at every step, and when Higgins strikes the other side, wood also gives way. The apprentice clamors up the snapping timber, and grasps desperately at a stone buttress, feet dangling, dangling. Then touching water.

"Are you…" He growls, then drops, splashing into the shallow stream. The bridge fords twenty feet of what once was a strong current, but is now just the trickle that graces his ankles. Higgins curses, then scrambles up the opposite side, climbing the stones sealing the canal.

"Looks a bit like London," he says to the skeleton of the buildings that encroach. "No, Venice. The ghetto." Closeted, segregated. "Old Bonie did right there. I suppose even a broken—"

"Curas."

The wall nearest Higgins shudders with ruptures of red and green. Splinters pepper his coat. He squints at the approaching figure. *Master?*

Rein emerges from behind a stack of crates. *"Togasan talam."*

A barrel rises, and with a wave of the Inspector's hand, flies at Higgins, only to soar over the apprentice's head and crash harmlessly on the bridge behind.

"I never was great with that one," Rein says. "I am also terrible at cricket, I must say."

Higgins, shaken by the attack, cringes at the sight of his master, casually strolling before him. "What in the world are you doing?"

Rein spreads his hands. "Trying to kill you?"

"Curas!"

"Giath," Rein intones, tossing something in an arc. Higgins's spell strikes the verge, then dissolves, falling in red sprinkles with the dust.

"You are getting aggressive," Rein says. "I like that in you, Mister Higgins."

Higgins blinks. "Why are you doing this?"

"Because you are an annoying little git," Rein says with a smile. From an inner pocket he draws a small wooden stick, a wand, and then: *"Leig an talam tuteam do chean."*

The spell is long, drawn, and mesmerizing. Shifts in color climb along Rein's arms as the man twirls. At the middle incantation, and as Higgins readies a counter curse, the ground starts to rumble.

"Lawks," Higgins draws blank, narrowly avoiding being brained by a piece of the building. More debris clatters around him as the spell finishes, until the entire right side has spilled into the streets.

Higgins runs his hand over the back of his neck. *Blood.* His master — *no, not my master* — leaps upon the fallen debris and raises the wand once more.

"Curas," Higgins yells, pointing just below Rein's feet. Bricks shatter, dusting the air, and the master tumbles down the pile to meet his apprentice.

"Mallach abais," Rein screams as Higgins grabs his arms, diverting the spell. Rein uses his height to bully down. The wand dips lower, lower. Almost to the point of touching Higgins's head, who reacts by shoving a hand into Rein's pockets.

"Mallach—"

A wave of dust flies from Rein's pockets and the apprentice's hands, filling the air between them as Higgins yells, *"Giath,"* while Rein's own spell is finished with: *"Abais!"*

But Rein grabs him by the neck, and once again presses down, bringing Higgins to his knees with a terrible, unholy strength. *"Mallach abais,"* striking the ground nearby. *"Mallach abais."* And the walls behind.

Higgins paws at Rein's coat with his bloodstained hand. "*Teine.*"

Rein screams as the wool of his coat lights up in flames. He throws Higgins away from him, and quickly doffs his coat.

"Master," Higgins begs. "I don't know what has gotten into you, what is…please stop this, stop this!"

Rein seethes as his clothing simmers. "Your master is dead. Just like his dear wife Anna. Just as you will be soon enough."

"Chancy," Higgins says, standing. "No, it can't be."

"In the flesh," Rein/Chancy says. "In *his* flesh, that is. Do you think it suits me?"

"No…" Higgins clenches his fists. "Not while I have anything to say of it." He ducks low, scooping up a brick into the air. With a cry of "*Basna beata,*" Higgins's bloodied hand cracks it and sends a stream of force, silver-streaked and deadly, towards his former master, who answers with a counter spell.

The air shudders, and the ground heaves up when their magicks meet. Both apprentice and master are stricken by the edges of each other's craft, but it is Rein who collapses.

"This is over," Higgins says. "I don't know how you came to inhabit my friend's body, but I will draw you out."

"Well done, lackey," Rein says, raising his hands to the oncoming Brit. "Well done, I am defeated. You did forget one thing, however."

A hiss shudders out of the building behind Higgins. He swallows, jerking back in time to meet the attacking Udur that flows over the debris, maws and hooks forming along the slithering mass as it seeks to sink into him and shred him. Realizing it is too late to escape the monster, he does the only thing he can: Higgins charges.

"*Solna nea, Oran cruchaid, an beath!*"

271

The balefire sweeps over the Udur as if spreading from the wound itself, joining his own shrieks with the crackle of demonic flesh.

"Solna nea, Oran cruchaid, an beath," Higgins repeats, striking another would-be attacker. Bricks crack like thunder from the heat, and flames erupt out of the once still ruins.

"Solna nea, Oran cruchaid—"

Higgins stumbles, knees shaking. Then falls face-first into the ground. "God..." He blinks, vision blurring. Further words are cut off as an oily tentacle wraps around his arm, lifting him up, and up. More Udur surround him, nipping at the fringes.

Rein leaves the glut of the baying demons and regards them, slowly turning his head this way and that. Then tips his hat. The void spawn gripping Higgins twists, raises him even higher to face Rein. The ring of Udur shift in the mist around him. "Master," Higgins cries.

"Well, that was inelegant," Rein/Chancy says, weighing the now bloody brick in his hand. For a moment, he considers the brick, and the apprentice's head, then signals to the creatures milling around. "Take him. I think I may have a use for this one yet."

Chapter 30

Niena's fingers inch along what should be the bark of an elder tree, long out of bloom. Dew clings to the folds of her dress, and it snags on a low branch.

"Dead, like this city," she says, bending to hike up her dress. In reply, her body trembles.

The branch of the elder tree breaks, and Niena's eyes snap open. The Evercharm she displays boldly forward, as a shield against the encroaching darkness. Protecting. Enchanting —the latter working more against her, for Niena's feet move almost of their own accord. From the edges of the grounds to the barren courtyard devoid of ruins and life alike. To a lonely altar, half buried in mud.

Temple stones shine on the far periphery, catching the moon's hue and burning away the fog. Even so, there are horrors between her and this outer wall. Unnamable lurch in the dark, carrying the faces of men.

Chords bless... She strums a few bars on the lyre, and the glow of the Evercharm blossoms once more. Driving back those faces. All of them, save one.

Droplets of water fall through Titania's form as it might pass through a sieve as she moves from real to a form as sheer as her muslin, and back. Yet, through all the transformations,

Niena imagines the Teamor's presence bubbling around her feet like a spilt cauldron.

"Stay away from me" lies unspoken on Niena's tongue. So does "traitor." Instead, she forces a smile, pushing those thoughts down, down, to use in another moment. "Took you long enough to get here."

But the coldness of the reply is not lost on Titania. "I came when I could," she says through a thin smile.

The girl follows Titania without so much as making eye contact once. At the entrance to the next area, the closed grounds give way to wide-open spaces. *A garden, a living garden... here?* Wonder appears to wipe the furious set of Niena's mouth. Somewhere, the sound of footsteps disturbs the awkward quiet.

"I know you are angry," Titania's says at her side. "Trust that I didn't want to leave you alone."

Niena's jaw stiffens as she moves away with Titania. Here the monuments have not fallen and remain readable. She passes a column, one out of three that flank what appear to be enormous roots. These are the only plants here that do not thrive, having apparently dwindled long in the past, until nothing of the tree except this remains above ground.

"It is Cuiven's Lee, or at least what is left of it," Titania says to the girl's back, answering the unspoken question. "Not even a dragon could foul the sanctity of this place. Those columns remember the beginning of things, and there the roots of Irminsul still twine."

The wonder is gone. Niena flushes and directs her attention south, where a vibrant smattering of reds, blues, and yellows overflows. She moves away from her grandmother, eyes and fingers gracing the petals of tulips.

"The lyre has brought you here, as I thought it might." Again, Titania rushes to keep up, but a blur of action at the edge of vision arrests both women. She takes a quick breath, then runs to Niena, swiveling around and stopping the girl just as she is about to bend over. "There is not much time, I am sorry child, but—"

Niena interrupts her. "I want to know everything." And Titania is only able to open her mouth before the girl adds, "I want to know the truth. Did you make a bargain with the Teamor? Did you sell me to them?"

As if frightened by their name, the stars retreat behind a veil of clouds.

Titania draws her lower lip between her teeth, then presses her lips together. For a moment, she looks into Niena's glistening eyes. "What did Oberon tell you?"

"Plenty," she says. "But I want to hear it from you."

Now it is Titania's turn to flush an angry scarlet, and the effect carries over into the air surrounding them. Further noises punctuate the rapidly deteriorating scenario, and she makes a move for Niena's hand, but the girl will have none of it. She remains resolute, chin up, and defiant.

"It is true," Titania croaks.

Truth. Niena swallows. Truth is a coarse thing, for a throat not used to speaking it —almost as painful as the ringing in the ears of one who isn't used to hearing it. And upon looking at Titania's face, part of Niena instantly regrets asking for it.

"I was dying, I thought had little choice," Titania says. She again reaches for Niena, and again the girl rebuffs her. "I was wrong. I don't know why, I don't know…Everything has changed," in a whisper. "I care about you, Niena. I don't want to see you get hurt."

"So did Oberon," Niena answers quietly. She grits her teeth, then pushes Titania out of the way. "That apparently doesn't stop either of you from lying to me, from using me."

"We can still mend this," Titania begs. "We can still—"she looks away, biting her lip. "I did not lie about the spell of unbinding I taught you. Without the connection, the Teamor 's hounds would be scattered between the worlds and times. Their agent would be stuck here, and they would have to raise another on Earth to direct and find you, giving us a way to escape and undo…"

Titania tentatively steps in front of Niena, her face screwed in determination. But at the last step, the girl turns away. Whatever persuasions were upon Titania's lips slip. The fairy queen, for the first time since meeting, appears uncertain.

"It was a hope." Titania's hands drop to her side.

"Dawn is coming," Niena says.

"Yes," Titania gasps.

Starlight interrupts the conversation, blasting through a sheet of clouds and illuminating the tattered remains of banners on the walls like black dots against the bleached grain — like blots of ink on an otherwise blank page.

From east and west, the mist approaches. The women regard the sweeping tide in silence, until Titania steps away. She takes one long look at an altar in the shade of the columns, then, rising to stand in contrast to the ruins — not pale, but bright, her light piercing through night and fog alike — she glides to meet the darkness.

They come. Over ruin, and column. Trespassing upon sacred grass and flower alike. Niena gestures to these shapes silently. As they look on, more and more of the creatures fill the ranks. Titania straightens, standing imperiously among the hortensias, keeping the columns to her right. She looks back to meet Niena's eyes once, and never again.

The rush of the Udur slows. Then halts yards away from the women.

Between two of the void spawn something else emerges. Thin, wispy, framed by the passing light of the moon, is a man. The fog clings to the figure like a trailing cloak, and the Udur flank both his sides. He approaches now, in long strides, every step measured by a long stick. Titania sees him, and freezes.

Walking forward with purpose, the man stops within arm's reach of the fairy and takes off his hat. Titania's own light falters.

"Rein," she whispers.

"What a lovely little gathering we have tonight," he says, pausing to replace his hat.

Niena raises her hand, shading her eyes against her grandmother's light. The man's frock coat has been torn in places and recently mended. His top hat needs more attention, and there is a weariness to his movements. Yet Rein's face, while much leaner than before, still has the hints of the merry, odd rescuer she met only weeks prior.

It is Titania's movements that give the first hint something is off. The fairy hesitates, then crosses her arms. For Niena, a presence here does not fit with her memory. This confirms in her mind that there is something different about her former savior.

"We meet at last, officially," Rein bows. "Though I have seen you in passing before. You are, as Rein always described you, lovely and clever. Indeed, the clothes do not make the man. You, my dear, may call me Chancy."

"Where is his little fart catcher and where is the elf?" Titania hisses.

"Ah, there is the Sofie I've heard stories about. I am sure they are around somewhere." He laughs, then juts his chin in a quick gesture, and at the same time a high-pitched yelp forces Titania to squint. She sees an Udur with many arms wrapped around a stout little man.

"You heard the lady. Where is your friend?" Chancy asks, looking behind him. "Where is the oath breaker, the elf?"

Higgins gags on black slime as the Udur envelops his face, and Chancy takes a step towards the women. Now Niena can see what her grandmother saw. There is a terrible aura around the man. Terrible, familiar, and yet unknowable. He pivots to his side, and smiles while the fairy queen steps back.

"I have done everything asked of me," Titania stutters.

"You lie," Chancy interrupts. "Which is as my masters expected." And now his features twist, turning angry, feral. "Gunpowder, treason and plot!" Then he matter-of-factly adds, "Or that is what the British would say."

"You cannot open the way back yourself," she says, voice straining. "You still need me."

"Quite right on that, milady." Chancy's appearance softens, and he shrugs. "The bargain for now holds. Think of us as an escort," he adds. "Jolly good company for the long road ahead. So long as you stick to the road, milady. And you will both want to do that because there is more to the wild than trees and darkness."

"I am not going anywhere with you."

"Shush, child," Chancy tells Niena. Higgins's cries of pain add urgency to the exchange as he is dragged forward to face both fairy and man. "Shall we go, my dear?"

Titania's shoulders slump. "And what about Rein?"

Chancy/Rein shakes his head slowly.

"Traitor," Niena screams behind her. "I knew I couldn't trust you. I knew—"

Titania walks past Chancy, past the captured Higgins, and stands in front of the columns, facing them and the roots. At the yard, and in a bed of daffodils, she raises her hand and sings.

"And the skies flow gray — as the sea, and the night till morn."

The spell echoes in the night, and the stones vibrate, as if they too were joining in song. Titania closes her eyes. *"Light carries the days — like leaves, lost in the wind."*

Rain, cold and slick, returns in a drizzle. *"Fairway, come again."* Thunder rolls in the background, and Titania opens her eyes to see the gateway to the past ripple. She presses upon the portal her will, roving towards the memories of the time before the worlds, with a shining path leading deep into that time.

"And the waves crash — against shores, heaven bred."

A vortex crackles open in time with a lightning strike. Smoke and shadow flow into it, as if being swallowed by a gaping maw. Titania's voice rises into a fever pitch: *"Where time is born — and remains a rare guest."*

At first, the change is barely noticeable. Time does not affect the garden like other places. But as the decades cross a key threshold, there is a sudden flip.

"Fairway, come again."

The brown roots thicken. The columns disappear, replaced by stone monuments. Green ivy spreads over them and the ground alike. Here Titania pivots. Here the song changes from the spell to open the Fairhome back into its ancient roots.

"The tide shall turn — and tread upon celestial paths," forcing through her teeth.

Niena clutches the Evercharm close as an Udur rises, then stumbles forward, struck by something unseen.

Chancy drifts towards the portal and looks back, beaming. "Come closer, girl. This is, after all, your moment. Come, don't be shy."

Even if Niena wanted to run, the Udur prevent it. And Chancy's piercing eyes also deter her fingers from finding the Evercharm's strings. Dejected, and defeated, Niena strides forward as beckoned.

"Good, child, good." Chancy snatches Niena's elbow.

Titania falters, struggling. Then something in her demeanor changes. *"Until the night renews day— and the old ways are forgotten."*

Chancy's guiding hand stops before he and Niena can cross Titania on the left. His face tenses, watching Niena continue, then in one quick burst he throws himself forward and up. The shock of magical energy crackles around his hands as the agent of the Teamor finds a barrier.

"Niena," Titania gasps, spinning to face Rein. "I can't hold it against him forever." The fairy wavers, struggling against the will of Chancy.

The crack-crack of her barrier is followed by the quick expulsion of light. Niena hesitates and moves as if to call out to Titania. A thunderous crash of magick ends this.

Chancy's hands press into the shield, and he yells, "We shall not be denied."

A shockwave strikes the girl's hand, and she reels back in pain. Titania cries out, "Hurry, through the portal," and Niena turns towards the shimmering gate. Beyond its threshold, the façade of the ancient monuments appear. Ivy falls away, revealing an empty field. An impression shows where the roots should be.

At her back, the Teamor's creatures start a terrible howl, and the shrill commands of their master follow.

"Kill Titania," Chancy yells. "Take the girl!"

Niena glances back to see the queen throw herself low, narrowly avoiding an Udur's lunge, then raise her hands palms outward to clash with Chancy.

"Fairway, come again," Titania sings.

♫

"Why did you not stop him?" To the elf's eyes, the Mannelig seems to disappear into his coat, a tattered thing taken from an equally tattered villager. Rogard shifts, turning towards Sethlan in a flourish as if to say, "How could a mere mortal hold down a wizard?"

Sethlan rubs a piece of birchwood between his fingers, flakes of bark falling off as he does. "I should not have left the child."

"If you didn't leave Niena, then—"

"I was referring to the apprentice. He went running after his master alone." Sethlan sighs. On the white marble where he perches, there are deep gouges. Scars in the stone, and freshly made by the Udur that came at their magician's call. The elf jerks his head in the direction of a distortion — a blurry, quivering field of air — and the two combatants near it.

"You must make it to that portal," he says, facing the Isfall man.

"You are out of your elven mind," Rogard says. "How am I supposed to get past, all…all of that?" Shaking his hand at the press of Udur that surrounds their master. "Maybe I should just walk up to him and ask both Titania and that other to scoot over a little so that I can get by?"

And there are at least a hundred feet south to Titania, which the young man is quick to point out, but Sethlan merely shakes his head and says, "I will guard the way. And if you cannot fly, fear not, for I shall be as a bird!"

The elf hops over, then pivots to catch the edge of the roof. From this, he swings right and strikes a piece of jutting wall timber. The wood snaps off in Sethlan's hands, and both tumble.

"Elf!"

At the last moment, Sethlan again twists in the air and uses the wood to catch the remains of a balcony. Elf, timber, and half of a wall disappear inside the first floor, and into darkness.

Dust clogs his lungs as takes a deep breath, shaking. *That was foolish.* A brick crashes to the paved courtyard somewhere behind him, then another, and another. Sethlan winces after each one. *What did I say to the Mannelig?*

"Run," he hears Titania scream.

The elf clambers over a hedgerow, avoiding more of the falling debris. If he were to look up, he might see Rogard descending cautiously. Instead, he just hears his curses. Ahead, the magical combat continues. Sethlan sucks in more dusty air, finally acknowledging the identity of the magician. Titania has met Rein, their wills clashing again and again with a thunder that shakes more loose stones from the floor above the elf.

"This is not good," Sethlan says, still looking ahead.

The ground heaves, and the elf narrowly avoids an early burial. Sethlan leaps over a hole, and spares only a brief look towards Rogard, as all the cursing and coughing already spoke enough to his condition.

"…I should use your ears to wipe my—"

"No time," Sethlan says. "I shall take out the wizard."

"Take him out," Rogard says quietly. "Take him out with what? Going to cut him some flowers too?"

A wave of energy flushes the edge of the portal, and it shudders. "I have my means," Sethlan says, stalking towards Rein.

But the way forward is not clear. The battle raging between Titania and Rein and the power of the portal, now a vortex, is beginning to break reality. All around the elf, the scenery shifts as the timeline doesn't seem to want to settle on anything. Walls that moments ago just erected themselves, once more fly away. Trees erupt and fall around them; the ground heaves up and down.

He skulks forward, and Rogard follows. The Udur, that once quailed before the assault, now draw to their master, swarming along his back and blotting out the horizon so that the world is divided between light and dark.

The elf launches into a sprint. *If my aim is true…* The fairy queen's screams rise in sync with the heaving and shifting of the earth. He stumble-slides into a lunge, a roll — and then throws the dart at Rein.

Lightning strikes the missile, and it falls to the dirt, far from both apprentice and fairy queen. Titania's power, bright and heaped in chaos as if pulled straight from Fairhome, continues to vie against Rein's, whose own power swells as a dark, loathsome thing with him as the head of a bloated tick.

If Culsan were here… The thought is dashed away by another blast of magical lightning. The elf takes a step forward, then another, trying to resurrect a lost idea. He shakes his head. "My brother alone of us had the skill, if—"

The flash of Rein's teeth is all the warning Sethlan gets. He tries stutter-steps as a blue-bolt of magic flies towards him. Unlike his own, this missile does not miss, but glances his right side, burning the cloth there and shattering his rib on impact.

"Elf!"

A second bolt flies towards Rogard, but this time Sethlan's reaction is faster, and he throws his arm before the blast. The crack of another bone echoes on the battlefield, and the elf collapses before the Isfall man.

"Rogard…the portal," Sethlan gasps.

Titania presses the advantage and pushes Rein back several feet. Sethlan blinks away the pain. Gray muddies the zone between light and dark, each area broken only by the occasional swirl of arcane power. And it is in one of these flashes that he sees Higgins going slack against an Udur.

"I do not need to be carried," Sethlan snaps at Rogard, thrusting the Mannelig behind him. Man and elf rise together to stagger within a rock's throw from the battle.

"Your kind have no place in the world we are creating," Rein hisses to Titania. He looks to the two approaching him, menace in his eyes. "Interlopers!" But this time his outstretched hand is met by the fairy's own, and his attack goes wild, hitting the dirt behind them.

"Create? Oh, sure they'll create, like geese in the kitchen," Titania yells back.

The timeline shifts. Chancy's reply arcs over Sethlan's head, thumping the ground just shy of a pack of Udur. The elf shoves Rogard forward, then yanks him back as a great pine materializes before him. The air is suddenly full of winter.

"Stay behind the fairy," Sethlan says. A bush waylays them after, but the flipside appears stable, cut off from the rest by a translucent shell. *A barrier.*

The season shifts to spring. Rogard crashes through the brush and the magical shell with a shout. And Sethlan, suddenly afraid, rushes forward. But no attacks come. Their destination, previously only seen through the haze of battle and the pain of a doomed world, ripples before them.

Five meters tall and five wide, the vortex swirls with menacing energy. Beyond its threshold, they can see shapes, perhaps people, distorted as if they were peering through a glass of water. Yet one holds something glowing with a power that is vivid and clear even through the rest of the blur.

"You will get no more argument from me here on." Rogard grabs the elf's uninjured shoulder. "What are you waiting for, elf? This whole damnable world is diving headfirst into madness around us."

Autumn shows through that tunnel. At this, Sethlan frowns, turning away from Rogard's hand as a small creature flutters from the portal. The little bird's red breast fluffs out, and it trills a greeting, then disappears as if it were never there.

But at the edge of the barrier, Higgins fights a desperate battle with the Udur. His legs and arms are now completely engulfed, and his face threatens to be next.

"What a welcome reunion this is," Rein growls. "Look, even the elf has shown up." His head tilts to the side, and his gaze slices across Sethlan's. "The Teamor shall be quite pleased to hear your account."

"Go on ahead," Sethlan says to Rogard. "I must retrieve our apprentice." He faces the Isfall man. "I shall be right behind."

Rogard hesitates, then nods. "You're a good man." Clapping the elf once again on the shoulder.

Sethlan does not watch the man go. Nor does he rush to face Rein. Instead, he shades his eyes. The magical battle between the fairy and the Inspector has reached the sky now. The stress on this world, the revolting timelines, will crack it. But this doesn't matter. Nearby, Titania takes a step backwards, and the ground heaves again. Wails that could be cheers, if not coming from inhuman Udur throats, strike Sethlan every which way.

"Did we not have a deal, elf?" Rein sputters.

"*Lim,*" the elf's whispers, nursing his right arm. *Another fool promise made by me.* But his eyes find Higgins's. *Culsan, you were right.* Anger replaces confusion. *How dare the E'tah, how...*He sighs, then straightens.

"You never completed your end of the bargain," Sethlan shouts at Rein. "Not all of the Artisans are dead."

Rein snarls, stepping forward as Titania buckles. "What say we make a new deal, right here, right now? You kill this blasted fairy, and I won't peel the skin from your face?" The imposter shakes his head and smiles perversely at his Udur. "*Par les chemins creux de la lande, les noirs lutins, les loups-garous. La nuit venue en sarabande...*" He snaps to Sethlan. "*Se poursuiv-ent comme des fous.*"

Sethlan shifts his feet, ever so slightly. "Why have a new bargain, when the old is so close to being fulfilled? Here, let me help."

Higgins's lips rise above the squirming Udur's hold; he gasps, then screams, "Get out of here, elf, save Niena!"

Reaching within his coat, Sethlan draws another poisoned dart and leaps towards the imposter, tossing the projectile and landing in a long slide at the end. This time the missile strikes Rein in the shoulder and sends him to his knees.

The elf turns to Higgins, seeing the Udur's darkness leech into the man's exposed face. "Let me tell you that story," he says, then springs again.

He collides with both, dragging them against Titania's barri-er. The mild pain from striking it before is nothing compared to what racks him now, as the Udur's presence lights up the entire length. The oily black mass engulfing the apprentice smokes on contact.

"This is the tale of the snake charmer's wife, and how her son got his bread." He continues the spell, wrapping his good arm around the Udur. "Their family was poor. Once they had been magicians, healers of the Medinet Temple, but now, wh–"

The shield of protection held by Titania flounders, even as she sets upon Rein. The Udur surge forward. Her raging laugh echoes through the ages.

"Rogard is here!" Thumping into Higgins and Sethlan. The trio jostles before the combined weight brings the Udur through as the greater barrier shatters into a million shards, shredding all caught in the wake. But the creature, not being done, grabs hold of the new assailant and bites down on his leg.

"Their family was little more than beggars now," Sethlan re-peats weakly. "One day, like all other days, the snake charmer's son was hungry, but he could not find any bread. He looked high…"

"Get 'em off me, get 'em off me!"

"…And he looked low. For he knew that mother kept bread hidden, away from the day's heat," the elf continues over Rogard. "Until he came upon one basket, nearest the door."

The Udur writhes, thumping its mass, and all three attackers, against the ground over and over. In a fit of madness, the monster rampages, even striking a shield that has re-formed around Titania and Rein. The reek of burning flesh makes Sethlan gag.

"Oh, chords," Rogard whines. "He's shaking, he's shaking like a damn dog."

Sethlan grips Higgins's head with both hands, splaying his fingers so that they touch his mouth and nose. "This is where they found each other. He and the snake."

The portal roars, drowning both the hiss of the Udur sliding up the stairs and Rogard's complaint that "this is not story time, you dumb goat's ass."

A clash shatters the roar of the vortex as if it were glass. Behind, Titania and Rein wrestle. Sethlan, wincing, continues, "When his hand dipped into the darkness, it struck. And his screams…" On cue, Rogard's gasps.

"His screams brought his mother, for she too was as sorcerer. And I will say unto you, as she did. I shall draw your evil into me, as poison from a wound."

Blinding light strikes all as fairy and Teamor spew words of power at one another. The ground turns in time with the portal. The Udur holding Higgins trembles, then shudders against the spell. Cracks appear all along its body.

Smoke pours from the rent flesh of the beast holding Higgins, thrown into the wind as the creature dissolves, then sucked back. Back and seeming to encompass Sethlan's good arm in a blue-black miasma. Higgins chokes against the slime, helped to his feet by Rogard.

"You are here," Sethlan gasps, and collapses. "It worked." He grimaces, looking out towards Rein and Titania.

"You came back for me?"

And at this, Sethlan smiles up. "And leave a friend behind?"

Pain shoots through his arm then. Man and elf, sorcerer and hunter look at the wound, and the pulsing black tinge on the edges. "Leave it," Sethlan says to the men. "Leave me, I am done."

"Not a chance of that," Higgins says, as he and Rogard lift him.

Another wave of magical energy rips its way through all. Portions of the ground begin to break and heave into the air as if buoyant. Light cascades around the edges of the field, and several seasons break upon them at once. It rains. It snows. And the desert's heat blasts them in the face.

Rein's snarl turns feral, his attention returned to Titania. "You think you have won?"

A tree crashes silently to the elf's right. A boulder crumbles to his left. His knees buckle, and only due to Rogard's dogged stamina can they master their way back to the threshold of the vortex.

Titania's body winks, flickering as Rein becomes dominant. "I may not have won, but you've lost. You will never have the girl now."

The agent of the Teamor chuckles darkly, drool falling upon her dress. "Did you really think we wanted you to get her to sing the song? No, we just needed you to open the door."

Blood wells in half circles on Sethlan's hand from the tightness of his clenched fist. A cloud meanders as the scene plays out, shielding his eyes from all forms of light.

"Time to go," Rogard says. "Gently now. This next bit has a real kick to it, more than soured milk."

Every step beyond bears a weight that clings to the ankles. And time here is stable, if that is a proper word — but stable in the layer. A great fanciful garden dissolves into a groomed forest, and in turn flutters away through an age of overgrown weeds. In another, effigies surrounding a great stone burn away in a clouded night, and fade to embers.

The last layer spills them out into an open circle. Finally done, finally on solid ground, Sethlan looks up to see double: two lights. Two lyres, glowing against a backdrop of trees, held by the same woman. And standing before a group of three thrones. One of gold. One of silver.

And one of bone. He blinks. *And is that Niena?*

Sethlan rubs his eyes. As he focuses, Niena's twins separate. The one, clear, stands before him. The other, off to the side. The elf shades his eyes to the Evercharm's light, then averts them, choosing instead to focus on the thrones and their occupants.

"Ah," Oberon says, walking past Niena. "You have come back; we were worried you'd never get here."

Chapter 31

Spirits swarm around the two, Titania and Rein. The same phantoms the fairy summoned from earlier. They whisper into her ear. Giving her strength. Power. But mostly, they remind Titania of what is coming.

Doom.

"The Teamor will kill everyone, everyone. Can't you understand?" Titania says as this man, Chancy, entwines Rein's fingers around hers.

An Udur taps at Titania's last barrier, but she ignores it. She risks a glance at her attacker, and gazes at the sky before returning to his blue eyes. But she can find no trace of her former lover there. *Bastard.* A sudden surge of strength startles the imposter, and Titania twists with his movements. They roll, roll. Until their former position is flipped, with the fairy now dominant. Now Chancy pushes desperately up against Titania, and loses.

The fairy snarls and twists his right hand, harder as Chancy tries to look away. *Rein. Where is Rein?* This thief has stolen his face — his life. A man who was never a great man, or even a wholly good one. Only, once upon a time, hers. She raids his thoughts. Relentless, even when his groans become screams. Hoping to find something familiar. Something of Rein.

Fragments surface. A still picture of their first dance in Stockholm. The sound of his sobs, as news came of his wife. Joy mixed with sadness. The leftovers are riddled with holes. Tattered. Despair becomes anger. Titania rages and turns her anger upon Chancy's own mind.

Ghent was Chancy's first home, and he was the rat in the walls. Saint-Étienne wasn't any better. Lyon in his early teens. Just another hole — and another prison for his drunk father to throw him into. The black city would witness the last of his boyhood fancies depart the world then, swinging from the gallows. Then, last, he came back to Amsterdam. Still a boy in form, but no longer in heart.

"Where is he?" Titania cries. "Where is he?"

"Oblivion." Chancy's laugh turns into a wheeze. "The same place that awaits us all."

"I will send you to hell first," Titania chokes. "For Rein, for me."

Chancy laughs again, his voice full of suffering. Weak, and growing fainter. "Yes, kill me, kill Rein," he hisses. "But then, I was never meant to live, only to be a conduit."

Titania tilts her head and widens her eyes in shock. Chancy surges, bending back her hands and forcing the fairy queen off.

"Rein's hatred let me in," Chancy spits, his face both pale and flush. "My hatred for you, for all of this...has allowed the Teamor into this world."

It is Chancy's turn to rage now, towering over Titania. Red spittle flecks his lips, and there is a zealot's smile on his face. "And. You. Opened. The door," he screams.

The vortex shudders in reaction and the edges fold inwards, ripping at the seams. Chancy opens his mouth as if to scream, but instead a black mass flows out towards the closing portal like smoke from a thousand fires.

"No," Titania shouts. The fire leaves Chancy's eyes, dropping them back into Rein's blue. "No," she whimpers, holding Rein's face in her hands — a man Titania realizes she loves.

Rein smiles. Then collapses in her arms.

♫

Holland. Vaguely Holland, by the lack of any hill over ten meters. Chancy closes the book he was reading. "Gibberish," he says, sneering at the windmill on the horizon. "Ah yes, I am in a dream, aren't I?"

Movement across from a campfire catches his eye. A man rests there on a log, his face obliterated by the fire's sheen. Chancy rubs his knees, then leans forward. Just like the book's text before, the rest is blurry. As he stands to get a closer look, a familiar voice greets him.

"Could be a dream," Rein says.

The aging buffoon of an Inspector sits opposite, poking at their campfire with the end of his umbrella.

"I bound you…"

The season changes then as if on a sliding bar, leaving him at a loss. Trees sporting specks of red and yellow parade around like a pack of Parisian women, then bend and shudder under the weight of snow. Chancy waits, expecting this to end with the melting and the return of songbirds —and this does come. However, autumn quickly follows, and the whole cycle repeats again.

"Pining for oblivion is both ignorant and very Byron of you," Rein says, opening his hands.

As the glow from the fire dwindles to a tiny wisp of light, the two men stare at one another. Chancy crosses his arms. Weather flashes chaotically around, morphing from a bright and sunny day to storms to snow in the blink of an eye. He looks at a nearby branch and watches the snow slip between the pine needles, crashing to the ground.

"I fear I will never understand you," Rein says. "Someone with your history, and you join up with *them*. What, were you not beaten enough as a child?"

"To your question, I am not surprised," Chancy says. "No. I am not surprised that you don't...." He taps his lips, considering, while the wind picks at the leaves of a scraggily tree above. "Or that you do."

When Rein's face twists in confusion, Chancy continues, "You are ruled by your fear. Fear of failure, of the unknown. Now, I understand that this is just your way, while still not understanding it altogether."

"That is a very interesting choice of a topic, for a man standing before a crossroads, and conversing with a figment of his own imagination."

"Whatever do you mean?"

Rein shrugs. "Do you remember what just happened? I say just, but time is relative here, though not relative-relative per se. Your uncle has nothing to do with this."

Looking down his nose, Chancy catches Rein's fidgeting. The Inspector moves with a strange, rigid energy — like a fist that is constantly being clenched and unclenched. A contrast to his own loose and graceful motions. And Chancy, mimicking Rein's energy, puffs himself up and raises his finger in mock importance. Then deflates. A shadow crosses his eyes, and suddenly the Speaker of the Teamor is only sure of one thing.

"I died," he says.

"Maybe we died," Rein says. "I a bit before you, I'd say." He motions to the horizon with the stem of his pipe. "I wonder what awaits you beyond. You aren't going to the Curatorium's Netherworld, you know."

"You are such a child…" Chancy says. "What do you expect to find out there, *dear sir?* The Teamor—"

"Are not the only powers in the world," Rein says, then corrects himself. "Worlds, and certainly not there — there, beyond, where all men fear to tread." He leans forward then. "Do you really want oblivion, my friend? You seem to be too much in love with yourself elsewise."

Chancy's clenches his hands into a fist. "Friend…" He relents, his posture fast resolving into the stiff elegance of a country gentleman. "You lost my leave to call me that, after Anna."

"You do not deserve to say her name!"

"Neither do you."

A gust threatens Chancy's hat, and he clamps it down with both hands. On the horizon, the windmill he noticed before creaks on, spinning, spinning. The scene, though, appears off somehow. Faded, even after squinting. He tut-tuts, removes his hat, and lets the wind rumple his hair.

Rein then looks at the floor, as if suddenly very interested in his shoes. "It is rather strange how you start to forget. First, it's their face. Then the way they felt in your arms." His voice drops into a whisper. "It's not her I've been thinking of the most, though, but I do often wonder how she died?"

"Who knows…This world will be remade," Chancy whispers. "Nothing that has passed between us will matter then."

"Even before this — this…whatever this is. The fall of the Curatorium resurrected old thoughts in me." He narrows his eyes, staring intently at nothing, and chuckles. "Yes. What I have done is wrong. Serving the Curators is wrong. But your choice is worse," he continues. "Can you really sit there and tell me your Teamor would be better, men so ruled by spite? If we can even call them human now."

Chancy shakes his head. "Faith is not only for the righteous."

Rein tosses his pipe aside. "So, here we are finally: your vanity concealing zealotry?" He throws back his head and laughs. "Do you really dare to believe I would swallow the lie that Jacob Chancy Jansen has faith in anyone other than himself?"

"You can believe what you will."

"You are no fool," Rein snaps. "You know full well your masters will create nothing. They've already discarded you! Perhaps that is better."

"You said it yourself," Chancy argues. "They can only touch these worlds of the living, so why do I worry about what happens to the material? There will never be truly nothing if there is always something they cannot touch."

"But you do worry."

The Inspector withdraws, hands pulling into his sleeves, almost like a tortoise. Behind him, a summer lark raises a trio of hatchlings. One by one, the birds leave the nest, flying off to who knows where. Chancy watches this, just as winter comes and covers their nest. Then he looks down upon Rein, his former friend. He blinks.

"One can hope for the best outcome," Chancy says. "Yet remain cognizant of reality."

Rein grumbles and sets his jaw. Around them, the dreamscape flickers briefly. Trees that had stretched into summer now shiver again in winter. Spring comes then, and the sound of the birds and chittering squirrels awakens. Chancy finds this all maddening, and in a fit of sudden energy, he spins on his heels and throws up his hands. He walks away from the fire and looks out over the dreamscape of Holland. To breathe deep once more, taking in the cool yet lively air.

"I murdered her, Rein," Chancy says then. "I murdered Anna." The admission racks him, and suddenly, he is filled with nervous energy — just like the moments after he first started to poison Rein's wife. "You would be surprised what illnesses resemble arsenic poisoning, if it's doled out in little doses. And how little money it takes to convince the doctor."

The dreamworld reacts. It heaves as if being tugged at both ends of a rope by two warring giants.

"She wouldn't listen to reason," Chancy says, wringing his hands. The jitters leave him, and all he can feel in this moment is a deep weariness. "She loved you." He clenches his fist.

Chancy blinks in confusion — gone are the trees, the underbrush, and the dirt. White merges into black as the snow on Rein's top hat melts. Chancy investigates the Inspector's face then, expecting something. Anything. What he finds instead makes him take a step back.

Blank? The flames of the campfire flare as if consuming Chancy's gaze. The man stumbles, then braces himself against a bench. "What new sort of devilry…"

The snow, like summer before it, is now gone — but not alone. First, the colors begin to drain from the very world. White is no more white than black. A gray pall coats everything he sees. The foliage and fauna surrounding them retreats, and the fire dwindles, losing the last of its warmth.

"Rein?" he says, reaching out. The old sorcerer makes no move, and in truth appears no more than a caricature — cut out from old newspapers but held up by some unknowable force against a background that is deeper and more real than it.

Chancy yelps and backs further away. He careens to the fire first, but finds that the last color has drained, and the merry crackle has fallen silent. "This is just a dream."

Holland is gone. The world is gray now, and a fast darkness is promised upon the horizon. "Dream?" Words become difficult. Thoughts, irregular. Chancy whimpers, trying to hold on to the thread of an idea, turns and lunges towards his former friend. But then, Rein, too, disappears.

"Don't…" The last light in this world dwindles, and there he manages to finally eke out: "Don't leave me alone."

Chapter 32

Three thrones. One of gold, one of silver and one of bone. We are here, but who are those sitting on them?

Niena looks up to see the living roots of a massive tree. Yet there is a double image that hurts her head, as if she had too much to drink. She closes her eyes.

I don't drink, not since father— A hand falls on her shoulder, and another turns her face. Niena opens her eyes. "Grandfather?" She steps back and blinks away a sudden onslaught of tears.

"Not yet," Oberon says. "Though I will be soon, and always. It is a peculiarity when we fairies travel back or forward, we can only send our memories." The fairy looks past her then. "Ah, gentlemen...You are just in time to escort my granddaughter to Earth."

The fairy turns Niena to face the new arrivals: Higgins, Sethlan and another she does not recognize. She returns to Oberon, confusion replaced by irritation. "I am not going anywhere with that elf."

"You won't," Oberon says over her shoulder. "He shall be going with you."

The fairy always looked eternally ancient, yet at this moment he seems to emanate strength and youthfulness.

"Where am I? Why Earth?" Niena pulls herself away. "I don't understand what is going on."

At first, everything past Oberon appears like a double image. Then she realizes it is something else entirely. Her eyes skip to the silver throne. There sits a tall man, dressed in furs and resting. Then to the one of bone, where a flame-haired woman waits imperiously. *She is elven. Wait, who is that?*

Before all of them stands a woman that could be Niena's twin, holding the same lyre. Man, elf, and mystery move as if seen through a waxed screen, and oblivious to one another. She squints and lifts her hands as if about to ask a question.

"You are here and back there, but also not," Oberon says, stealing back her attention. "When you stepped through the portal, I took you to the side, so to say. You exist next to the original timeline. Linked, yet separate. Preserving who you are, even while you hold the threat to everything that comes after."

He strokes his chin and gently turns Niena aside to look at the others. "It is not the unbinding that might bring about the uncreation the Teamor desire, but the paradox of the action."

"Fairy meddling," Sethlan hisses.

"It is indeed," Oberon muses. "Fantastically so, by myself and Titania." Someone snorts and the fairy lord's face lights up as he spins back to his granddaughter. "She no doubt told you that with the song of unbinding, you could also find a way to escape. Perhaps not only elsewhere, but else when?"

Voices cry out around them, and beyond. Some rising in question, others in terror. The sky, which was brilliant moments before, darkens. Clouds sully from a normal gray, then to a dirtier ash-laden soot, as if a thousand hands were reaching for the sun to cast it down. If she wasn't before, Niena is now acutely aware of other presences. Elves. Men. *Fairies?*

"She said something like that," Niena says, shaken to attention by Oberon's grip.

"She was right," he says. "The unbinding, of course, will prevent the Teamor from locating you across time and space through the new branch you create. Leaderless, they may never even be able to do so. Normally, this would also strand you; however, she knew this place offers a narrow chance at escape, through the roots of the old world. But there will undoubtedly be unforeseen consequences. Would it be like taking a cutting from a tree, to grow on its own?" Oberon beams, looking distant. "Or will it destroy us all?"

The man on the silver throne leaps up in challenge, but as the elvish queen tilts her head, he vanishes, leaving behind an oily stain where his body was. Chaos erupts among the men. Challenges. Threats.

"*Lim,*" Sethlan curses.

"Now, wait just one moment, what do you mean unbinding?" Higgins pushes his way to Oberon. "We just need to use the same spell Rein did to get us here. Then we could go back and consult with our betters — maybe the Curators?" He turns to Sethlan. "Or the elven Matriach?"

"Your Curators are likely dead," Sethlan says.

The old fairy raises his hands, and the clamor between them dies. "The chords must be cut, the strings connecting the worlds severed. Titania knew this, else the Teamor will find their way."

The air turns hot. The sky inks over. And now there is a chant, something which she has not heard before. The hunters, Sethlan and a new face, join their voices to the rest in confusion. But Higgins cowers, wincing with every uttered word that falls to them from the sky. Oberon lifts his hands and a barrier not unlike Titania's forms.

"I am afraid the Teamor have already found this place," he says.

A terrible wail precedes the not-thunder. Men panic on the other side, people try to flee, but there is nowhere to run. They watch as a dome of shadow envelops Cuiven's Lee on three sides, and fast closes on the last.

Oberon moves towards the other timeline. "You must go. Sing the song Titania taught you," he says. "Find your answers. Find your truths." He pauses, then pushes Niena into the arms of Sethlan.

Elves gather in front of the throne of bone in the second timeline, and Valfreyja, their queen, without a further word, raises her hand. The air bends like a letter being folded, and in the next breath both the queen and her folk are gone.

"Lords preserve us," Rogard mutters. "It's like all the old stories have burst forth from my da's head and decided to have a picnic." He then squints, looking towards the throne. "Is that silver? I'd be a rich man with just that arm."

Higgins stands, slowly drawing up to his full height, then wanders. His movement unintentionally blocks Rogard. "Are the Curators really dead?" Unsteadily, head in the clouds. "Bloody Rein. My poor master, has it been all for naught?"

"The song of unbinding," the elf says to Niena. "Do you know it?"

"Yes. It begins with the same chords as the spell we use to enter the Fairhome."

"Then lead us, my lady, and I shall follow," says Sethlan with a bow.

The shadow of the Teamor is complete now, surrounding them on all sides. Against this darkness, she has the Evercharm. Her fingers flow over the strings, touching upon the old melody. New chords join as the tune lifts. Then more, through the middle, and into the depths. Finally, the three merge into something different, yet familiar. Here, Niena sings:

"In Cuivananlee, the fairy bud,
The spring may bring the rain,
The tits may twitter, the waters flood,
The flowers bloom again,
Cloudless nights may shew the jewel,
Crowning the travelers' stars,
That lyre of old, the heavenly tool,
That strummed creation's bars
To lands where old men lie,
To the hollows of elven dance,
Where in barrows buried deep,
The roots of life do chance,
Above all fair is home,
And clear like fairy bells,
Where dreams true children dare to roam,
Until they bid farewell."

The last light blinks out. The Udur, or the Teamor shudder above them. Snow, cold and harrowing, falls in this ancient springtime.

"The unbinding...it is done," the fairy says. "Hurry to the passage; the thread frays, soon it will be no more." Oberon slowly falls back on his own throne. The air around him vibrates as he passes from this timeline to the other. Upon seeing their lord, fairies too gather to him, but instead of fleeing like the men and elves, they merely sit upon the ground as if to wait the coming storm.

"Wait! What am I to do, I don't..." Niena chokes, then clears her throat. "Will I see you again, Grandfather?"

And Oberon smiles weakly. Through the muddle of time, Niena hears: "Perhaps in a dream."

Niena shrugs off Sethlan's hand. "Don't," she cries. The image of the fairy blurs into the rest, until he is barely distinguishable from the others who gather to him. Niena, who has been reaching for him until this time, drops her hand. At her side is again the elf, desperately trying to peel her attention away.

"Look at the tree," the Sethlan says.

Massive and foreboding. Behind the roots, it shivers as if shy of attention. From root to bough and back again, she tries to pierce its secrets with her eyes. *Wait, those roots.* Panting, suddenly at a loss for breath. *Those are just like the roots back in the library at Sunford.*

"Botany is not my specialty," Higgins says at her side. "However, I don't need to be one to know there is something strange going on with that."

"It is the worlds' tree," Sethlan says at her other side. "The roots connect the Fairhome, Hearth, and Earth together." His piercing gaze alights on Niena. "They are also allow—"

"Ways to travel between," she says. "I know."

Higgins steps forward. "You mean I can go home?"

"Yes. I have traveled by this way once, long ago, and in friendlier times," Sethlan says. "Though not from here. Some say there is a tunnel underneath each throne. If you hold firm to your memories, you may pass. We must merely choose the right throne, the one who Earth belongs to, or—"

"Then that would be the silver throne," Higgins interrupts. "The one the man was sitting on."

The ground heaves. The tree quivers. "No, it would be the throne of bone," Niena says. "Earth was meant for the elves."

"Niena," Sethlan says. "You must lead. Only one of the fairies, or those of their blood, may do so." His eyes narrow, and she can't help but to look his way. "You must focus not only on the where, but on the when. Else we will be lost to time."

A curse comes to her mind then, but Niena wipes it away along with her tears. She looks at the hunters, Sethlan, Higgins, and this other man.

"Let's get this nonsense moving," Rogard growls. The man himself looks transfixed, staring ahead and through the sheen to the other reality — to the people fleeing in chaos.

"Hurry," Higgins says. "I do not know what is keeping the Teamor at bay, but it can't last." His temple furrows. "Nor the ways into the worlds."

Sethlan jerks around. "Aie! Look at its withering bowl! Even now, the tree dies. It will not survive the shadows upon its roots."

The elf takes them to the throne of bone, and behind it. The living roots are even larger when standing before them, monstrous and thick as ancient trunks of trees themselves. At first, Niena is unsure of where they are going, but as the shadows above move, a little light finds its way. Buried near the feet of each throne is a tunnel. The apprentice summons his own light, further revealing worn stairs that travel deep beyond.

"Higgins," Niena says, motioning for him. "Everyone, lock hands.".

"At least there won't be much work needed for our graves," Higgins grumbles.

"Shut up, wizard."

Niena looks at Rogard, then Higgins. Sethlan, though, is to the side. Niena narrows her eyes, concerned at the way he moves his arms. "Are you all right, master elf?"

His smile is as weak as the light that plays upon his face. He nods, and Niena makes a curt gesture towards the hole. "Just like back…" She hesitates, then bites her lip, forcing herself to face the steps. *Home.*

"Come on," she says finally.

Stone stairs. Earthen walls. Eventually, these give way to hard-packed dirt, and little seems to hold up the tunnel they follow except the root itself. Spring is shed, as is whatever vestige of light there once was. Behind them, the terrible roar of the Teamor comes closer, closer, infiltrating both realities.

"Pick up the pace," Niena says, holding her lyre aloft like a torch. The wood of the root that was once a nut brown slowly fades to a familiar gray with each step, as if by preparing to travel through this world, through one age to another, it seeks to lose all remnants of color.

Age. *Time.* Niena starts and reaches for Higgins. "Tell me of your home, Higgins."

Higgins hangs his head in thought. "London, I know. If India is the jewel of the empire, then London is the monster under your bed." He pauses, almost stopping the group. "That's not a great metaphor. But...like a monster, it sprawls. Grimy, noisy. All eyes are upon it."

Niena sighs. "Anything specific, maybe a place there?"

"Fleet Street. I've had to rescue Rein there many a time... many a time..." His voice trails off until he shakes away the memory. "Paint yourself an image of a tottering road filled with taverns, inns, and you name it. Think of the King's Head Tavern. A leaning four-story affair of wattle and daub, with bay windows on the face up until the third. Paint your—"

"That will do," Niena says. "I am not sure if it will help, but I will try to focus on that."

The familiar flecks of silver in the wood glimmer ahead. Hereafter, she sees that the root breaks from the floor and climbs to the wall. Thinning in girth. But the smell of earth — of ages bygone — thickens in its place, and there is a feel to the walls of sodden cold. *Like a grave,* as if she knew what one felt like.

Long is their travel from this point, with an unending, monotonous continuation of the before. Minutes give way to hours, and hours pass into what should be the night. Limbs and minds become weary. Even the constant flashes that seem to announce curves, or declines, dull in their thoughts until these appear long before the light from the lyre touches them. At one corner, they stop. Niena lays her hand upon a spot of twisted wood. Dirt, brittle and hard-packed, it comes off in her fingers, which she rubs against her dress.

"Have we crossed?" Sethlan asks.

"I'm not sure..." Her whisper quickly dies. "Oh chords, this again."

The wall is wet, and the air chilly, rushing to them and carrying distant clamor and voices. Veins of silver glow, retreat, and return as she jerks back, seeing once more faces in the knots in the wood. Faces that twist. Smiling. Grimacing. Even their eyes seem to mock the twinkle of the living, winking at her when she moves.

"Don't stare too long," Niena says, quoting Oberon. "These roots were here when the three worlds were one. There's no telling what secrets this tree has drunk."

"That sounds like gunfire," Higgins says. "No, I'm wrong. Cannon fire?"

"Your reality is changing, my friend," Sethlan says, drawing all three to see him there, clutching his broken arm. "There is no guessing what we face ahead."

Niena pulls the Evercharm back to her, and in the dimness she can see something dark wiggling along the elf's other arm. She tilts her head. "Sethlan?"

"We must know what waits for us," he says, pushing ahead and ignoring Higgins's hand. "Who better than this ancient hunter?"

Higgins follows the elf, but stops as he reaches Niena and bows. "My dear young lady, I wanted to apologize for—" He looks down and removes his hat. "I wanted to know that no one here is going to force you to do anything."

"Thanks," Niena says. "I think…" She straightens and repeats more firmly, "Thank you."

"What are you all sitting there gabbing on about," Rogard growls behind them. He slaps the apprentice on the back, which sends the top hat tumbling into the tunnel ahead. "We've got a lot of adventuring to do!"

They walk on through the tunnel, and the sound that Higgins has described becomes clearer, and louder. His pace seems to quicken until he is not far behind the elf. Earthwork is eventually replaced by stone, and now at the back of the party, Niena grumbles back, "To adventure."

But what sort of an adventure? What choices are before us?

Shadows flee when she tilts this way and that, and for a mere second, the profile of a familiar old fairy appears at the corner of her eye. But when Niena wipes her eyes and looks again, it is only another twist in the root. She sighs and hastens to join her new comrades.

Chapter 33

There are worse things than your own death. "Like the death of someone you…" Titania opens her eyes. But this is not the Fairhome. Rein's head still lies cradled in her arms. His face is contorted, somewhere between Chancy's manic zeal and peace. Sweat mats his hair.

The rest of the former Inspector's body lies broken before the fairy, racked by the power released. She is no medic. But the blood speckling his lips with every cough cannot be a good sign.

"I love you," she whispers.

What have I done, she thinks, avoiding his eyes. What would she see there, Chancy or Rein? "I should have never helped him crossover to Hearth. I should have never accepted that bargain with the Teamor."

The land quakes. The unbinding takes badly to the world of Hearth. Fissures break the ground, and the sky reddens.

"None of it matters anymore." Titania looks away.

"Sofie?"

Rein! But there was nothing left? There— the face. The set of his jaw, and the way he lifts his upper lip. She swallows. "It's me. I am here, I am here. Everything will be… Rein?"

"I love you too."

He spasms, and his hand grips hers. Somewhere, one of those foul Udur cries, its death wail sounding like a cross between a banshee's and a cat's. Here, only the pale of Rein's face matters. His breathing slackens.

Titania panics. The strength — her strength — for the spell of healing trickles up from the fairy's heart. "Do you remember the story of the two dancers?"

Folds of Titania's dress ripple in the wind, and she brushes a stray lock aside. "They were the only two on the floor. Him, tall, dark…and gangly. With cuffs not long enough for a man of his stature, and breeches that were at least three years out of fashion."

"And her," Rein croaks. "Wearing a *robe à la française* with a cut that brought me low."

Titania smiles gently. "More than their steps were mirrored in that dance. He, a Dutch gentleman with a heart of lace. And her, the out-of-her-place queen of the fairies. Gangly and awkward."

"Queen?" Rein blinks, then lifts his head. "Do you mean?"

At Titania's nod, the Inspector pales — but the confusion on his face earns him a laugh.

"I seem to remember it differently," Rein grumbles. "You were the epitome of grace, spiraling towards me like a celestial inevitability. Your dress writhed like midnight on a heavenly stage. Dark, flighty…"

Titania smiles, shrugging away a sudden dizziness. "You would make a terrible writer."

Rein's face puckers, and Titania wants to laugh again. Only, she cannot. The last time she felt this way was—*Oh.*

The cries of the abandoned Udur ring, but distantly. They are separating. By time, distance, and much more.

Rein lifts his eyebrows. "Dangerous. I, on the other hand, was blessed that the dance didn't allow me to get close enough to trod your feet, Mrs. Sofie Van Coeverden."

But as Rein seeks to fall back into her arms, he instead finds himself on the grass, drifting through Titania as if she were a trick of the light. It is his turn to panic now, and the Inspector reaches out as if to catch the sun.

Titania looks sadly at Rein. Thunder plays upon a now cloudless day, and the earth below her revolts against gravity, drifting up through fey and air alike. Yet she does not notice. Instead, she reaches out towards her lover and says: "Till the next dance."

About the Author

S.D. Reeves was born in 1980 in Huntsville, Alabama. He currently resides in Switzerland with an undetermined number of cats greater than zero, and a propensity for nonsense. On those cold nights where the wind steams off snowbanks, he is known to write award-winning fantasy novels. And curse his wife's cold feet.

If you feel generous and have a couple of minutes, please leave a review. Thank you in advance.

Visit his website at https://sdreeves.com/

You can also follow S.D. Reeves on social media:

Instagram: https://www.instagram.com/evercharm_stories/
X: https://twitter.com/SD_Reeves
FaceBook: https://www.facebook.com/SDReeves.Author

About the Publisher

Sulis International Press publishes select fiction and nonfiction in a variety of genres under four imprints: Riversong Books, Sulis Academic Press, Sulis Press, and Keledei Publications.

For more, visit the website at
https://sulisinternational.com

Subscribe to the newsletter at
https://sulisinternational.com/subscribe/

Follow on social media
https://www.facebook.com/SulisInternational
https://twitter.com/Sulis_Intl
https://www.pinterest.com/Sulis_Intl/
https://www.instagram.com/sulis_international/